Shining Like the Sun

Patricia Connor Williams

Published by

MELROSE BOOKS

An Imprint of Melrose Press Limited
St Thomas Place, Ely
Cambridgeshire
CB7 4GG, UK
www.melrosebooks.co.uk

FIRST EDITION

Cover designed by Jeremy Kay

ISBN 978-1-908645-04-3

Printed and bound in Great Britain by:
Mimeo Ltd, Huntingdon, Cambridgeshire

FSC
www.fsc.org
MIX
From responsible sources
FSC® C019549

Contents

Introduction

The Young Space Navigator

Space has been called the final frontier. Far out in space, many light years' distance from Earth, is Sirius the Dog Star – found in the constellation Canis Major. Probes and radio signals have been sent for some time from Earth, searching space for signs of life, but so far none has been found, nor wished to be found.

Unknown to man, the Dog Star hides secrets. Out of the reach of Earth's searchers, it conceals the existence of two planets. The larger Usaurius, just smaller than Earth, was to nearly the end of the twentieth century the home of a superior race, similar to man but extremely gifted: tall, peaceful people, gentle and not given to war, their only enemy being the Voraks, a race of people of small stature, who were envious of the Usaurians' height and especially their medical knowledge.

The Voraks have many times visited Earth, terrorising all who unfortunately come into contact with them. They were delighted when the planet Usaurius was destroyed by a series of cataclysmic events: first volcanic eruptions, then crop failures, followed closely by a shower of meteorites, and an asteroid which hit the planet like an atomic bomb.

The Usaurians decided to move to somewhere else. But where? The only possible reachable place they knew of was the inhospitable other planet. Everything they considered essential was loaded into three large spaceships. Disaster seemed to follow them. Two of the spaceships collided and many lives were lost, along with all their medical, technical and scientific knowledge and their history. Only one spaceship managed to reach what became known as the Two Islands planet – their future home. It was a shock to all of them but they were resilient and made the best of what they found on landing. The one exception was young Benon. He couldn't settle.

Fortunately for the survivors, some useful things were saved. Livestock, including horses, had already been transported to the new planet. The Usaurians had a crack team of flyers known as Space Riders, and they had gone ahead and laid out a runway for themselves.

The crash of the spaceships was seen with horror by a youth not more than sixteen years of age. Tears ran down his face, as he had now lost all his close family – his parents and a younger brother. He was alone, apart from his uncle, Prince A'Bron D-A'Huartan. On the prince's shoulders fell the task of uniting the remaining Usaurians on the new planet.

They numbered about twelve thousand. Two thousand were members of the elite known as the 'Old People'. Everyone else was referred to contemptuously as the 'Others'. Accepting it as their right, the Old People chose the smaller of the two islands, leaving the larger island, which was mostly desert, to the Others to make of it what they could.

Benon, although only sixteen, was an accomplished flyer and asked his uncle if he could search space for somewhere else more hospitable to live. His uncle agreed. On his uncle's orders, Benon took a companion with him. This companion was careless, and a stupid accident caused his death. Benon decided to go on alone as he had an ambition, not disclosed to his uncle. He wanted to reach Earth. His grandfather Guson, now dead, had visited Earth many years before, and the boy wished to also.

The boy was mature for his age, and steeled himself to search the ashes of the crashed space ships for some signs of his family. He saw something glistening among the ashes and, to his joy, found the diamond that had been part of his mother's betrothal ring. Nearby, still intact, was the ring his grandfather had worn and passed on to his father. It was thought it had been a gift from his paternal grandmother to her beloved Gus. Benon slipped it onto the small finger of his left hand. It fitted, and he was determined never to part with it.

Benon's uncle, trying to deter his nephew from embarking on such a hazardous journey, offered him a plot of land on the larger of the two islands. The offer was accepted with alacrity. Benon knew his uncle was trying to stop him making the journey, and that the gift of land was a bribe to persuade him to remain in comparative safety. Years before, he had visited the new planet with his grandfather, and the old man had noticed the area was rich in minerals and possibly valuable gems. He was correct in his assumption, and a clever Benon discovered material which contained a good quantity of diamonds.

His grandparent had fired the boy's imagination with tales of life on planet Earth. He had explained how money was required to pay for everything. He told him how gems were sold for huge sums of money and were in great demand by the rich and famous. Despite his uncle's misgivings Benon was determined to try and reach Earth. He decided to use the name his grandfather had used, shorten his first name, and call himself Ben Haraldsson.

He took with him documents his grandfather had given him years before, when he was still a small boy. "You are the only one I can trust with them," said his grandfather.

His grandson was proud of this request and had honoured it faithfully. The papers were all now concealed in a pocket of his flying kit. Bidding everyone goodbye, he kissed his uncle and made to leave.

The companion chosen by his uncle to accompany the youth on his journey was a little older than Benon. Soltan was a little cocky, and felt he should have charge of the vessel. This did not suit Benon (soon to be known as Ben). After all, the ship was his, and he knew how everything worked. Fate played into Ben's hands. There was an unwritten rule regarding safety, which was second nature to him. It soon became clear his companion was inclined to ignore any rules Ben proposed they should both follow. The result was Soltan received a dose of radiation, which led to his untimely death. In the process Ben received a lesser dose, which was to affect him for the rest of his life.

Fortunately Ben's ship was not completely out of range of the planet and as he was being accompanied by other flyers who were escorting him for part of the way, these flyers were able to pick up Soltan's body for return to the Two Islands planet. Ben didn't wait to receive commands from his uncle to return himself for much-needed medical checks, but pressed on alone. He had made a bet with his friend Pagan Anion that he would get to planet Earth first. His friend was also alone and had taken off without any orders. Prince Bron would have preferred the two to fly together as he knew his nephew was rather a daredevil, who from a child had always got himself into scrapes. However, Ben was a first-class flyer and Pag, as Ben addressed his friend, was too far out in space to consider returning home. The journey was long and lonely, and it was some relief to Ben when he sighted Earth's moon. Soon the oceans of Earth were visible, and he marvelled at their blueness. He looked forward to exploring them. Food was a serious problem as his stores had also been contaminated by radiation, and he longed to eat solid food. He was anxious to make his landing unobserved if possible. He came down in the sea near land, clearly visible. He feared someone was bound to see him.

PART ONE

CHINA

CHAPTER ONE

Doctor Chang Lin Weng

The small Chinese gentleman, Doctor Chang Lin Weng, a Doctor of Philosophy with a teaching post in Shanghai, who also taught Chinese past culture including the Ming Dynasty was, on a certain cold morning, sitting on a harbour wall near a bay just south of the city, waiting for sunrise.

This had been his custom at Chinese New Year for more years than he cared to remember. As he waited he heard a rumbling sound over the bay, and saw a flash of something silver, cigar shaped, thirty feet long, appearing out of the mist. He was frightened and fell back in surprise, knocking his foot. It was a heavy fall and he called out in pain. He became aware of a tall figure watching him from the craft, which was now close by. A gentle voice apologised for frightening him and asked if there was any way he could assist.

The stranger, only a boy, was able to speak the Mandarin language slowly but well. He knelt and examined the injured foot, saying it was not broken but a bad strain. "Can you walk?"

When realising this was impossible, the boy hoisted the slight figure into his arms and calmly asked where he could take him.

Dawn was not far off and the good doctor would have preferred to witness the sunrise, but common sense prevailed and he directed his rescuer to a largish house on the outskirts of the nearby village.

They made an odd couple – the boy scantily clad, and the other wearing the ceremonial robes of a mandarin. The doctor dressed this way every New Year. It was how he honoured his ancestors.

The house was known locally as 'the house with the red pagodas', as there were three red pagodas painted on its wall. Ben was intrigued by the sound of wind chimes that pealed as they entered, and he thought how they suited the house, which he found out later was furnished in an old-fashioned manner.

Two servants rushed out to meet them, and Ben gently laid the injured man down on a low couch. They introduced themselves to each other and Ben asked if there was any ice available, as he thought the injured foot would benefit from a cold compress. He skilfully bound the foot, and the doctor asked with a twinkle in his eye whether Ben would care to share a meal with him.

"Oh yes please; I am very hungry," Ben replied, "but l would like to wash first." He glanced at his rather dirty clothes and pulled a face at the mess. He was led to a washroom and offered the gardener's overalls. They were clean and he was told he could keep them. This was a tactful way of saying what he had had on was fit only for throwing out.

Ben was very taken with the style of life as lived by Dr Weng. It was simple but he found himself relaxing in its calm atmosphere. He was to discover it was part of the charm of China, and he would always enjoy returning there. He was to find some things he didn't like but accepted that perfection is hard to come by. Chopsticks amused him, but he mastered their use after only a few attempts. He was told the food, which he found a little strange, was from the area where he now found himself, but that every region of China had its own cuisine, and Chinese restaurants were famous all over the world. The food, as well as being nice to eat, was also very healthy. Without appearing too inquisitive, Ben asked questions about China as he was eager to learn all he could about the country and its culture. He was, however, very guarded about himself. He told the doctor, "My home is very far away. Please accept just that." He was very interested in what the doctor told him of his own profession.

Chapter Two

A Favour

Like his home, Doctor Weng was a little old-fashioned. Had he been a communist he might well have handed Ben over to the police, but he took a distinct liking to the tall stranger. "Tell me, Ben; are your papers in order?"

Ben was bewildered. The kind man went on to explain how the Red Guard or the police could ask to see them at any time and that strangers were always likely to be challenged and, if suspected of even a trivial crime, could be imprisoned without trial.

The doctor said he could give Ben the name and address of someone in Hong Kong able to provide a set of the necessary documents. He was a forger known to the underworld, and was incidentally a member of the doctor's tong. "He doesn't do this type of work often but will, I am sure, out of respect for me, undertake to get what you require." He then asked Ben if he had anything negotiable, and was amazed when Ben took a small pouch out of a bag he had with him. Into his hand Ben poured a small fortune in diamonds. He warned Ben not to display them all at once and, if selling any, to be very careful. The last thing he wanted was the boy to be robbed or cheated in any way.

"Before you go, come and see my collection of jade." The doctor led the way into another room. Ben was delighted to see displayed a beautifully made collection of figurines and animals. He fell in love with a prancing horse, and the kind doctor pressed it into Ben's hands. With tears in his eyes Ben thanked him, and said he would treasure it always.

Dawn had arrived and there was concern as to how Ben could reach his ship undetected. The doctor's male servant offered to lead Ben to the harbour by a back route. As he made to leave, Ben brushed against a small table and a magazine fell to the floor. On the cover was a picture of a beautiful Ming vase. The doctor sighed. "Only the very rich can afford to own one of those. They occasionally come up for auction, but few people have the money for such a luxury."

Apologising for knocking the table, and with profuse thanks for all the hospitality and kindness he had received, Ben left. He reached the harbour undetected. He was still wearing the overalls he had been given and, although a little tight, the gardener's shoes helped with his disguise.

A few weeks later the doctor was delighted to receive a gift from Ben. He found, contained in a crate, a beautiful two-feet-tall Ming vase. The note with it read '*Pour vous, mon ami. Merci.* Ben H.' There came also a parcel and the note read 'For your very kind helpers. I hope they like this material.'

The doctor's servants did like it, and an animated discussion took place between them as to how it should be made up. Over the years Ben kept in touch with Dr Weng. To Ben the older man was in fact his saviour, and they never lost contact with each other.

Chapter Three

To England

Anxious to acquire the papers he understood were necessary, Ben made for Hong Kong with all speed. He had told Doctor Weng of the name he wished to use, and was told he could possibly pass for an Icelander, Norwegian, or a member of any other Scandinavian country. "They all tend to have fair hair like you."

The Chinese New Year was still being celebrated, and the police were too busy controlling the revellers to bother with Ben. He easily found Jen Kwok, the tattooist recommended by Dr Weng, and the man was only too pleased to undertake the making of the necessary papers. He was well known in the underworld but still remained faithful to those of his tong who required assistance. He used his talent only on rare occasions. He was pleased to recommend Ben to a bespoke tailor, who he said would make Ben clothes "fit for a king". Ben was sceptical but Mr Teddy, as the Chinese tailor was known, was a master craftsman and, true to his word, Mr Teddy had a superb well-tailored suit ready for Ben within twenty-four hours. Mr Teddy suggested Ben would look good in *boots*, and produced a pair he said had never been collected. He offered them to Ben at a special price. They were a little tight but after a short spell on a stretching machine they were ready. When Ben looked at himself in a full length mirror he couldn't believe the transformation. He looked quite the elegant man about town. Mr Teddy was enraptured. Ben had shown the tattooist one of his diamonds, and Jen Kwok was pleased to loan the money to pay the tailor. Mr Teddy, on Ben's enquiry, gave him a note for a very good jeweller close by. The jeweller was instantly keen to do business with such a fine young gentleman, feeling further business would follow. Ben's papers were soon ready and were very good indeed, and it would have taken an expert to realise they were false. Ben chose to be an Icelander from a far-from-well-known locality.

Ben journeyed to both Amsterdam and London to sell his diamonds. He had been warned by the dealer in Hong Kong to beware of various cartels, especially those of southern Africa, who told him it wasn't wise to flood the market. Ben heeded this advice, selling carefully and not too often.

Whilst in England he visited the south coast to look for his grandmother's house. He had only the sketchiest outline, and had no luck in finding it.

Chapter Four

Miranda and Madam Fanny Su

Ben was still in his teens and not very streetwise when it came to girls. He was unprepared for a girl like Miranda. She was about the same age as he, and what was known as 'a bit of a goer'. Her father was a historian of some repute, and tended to be strict. He was a widower and felt his responsibility towards his rather wild daughter, who badly needed a mother's influence. Miranda fell for Ben and hoped she could get him to marry her. At their third meeting she proposed sex. How could he refuse? Later, feeling far from satisfied, he was dismayed when she snatched the ring off the small finger of his left hand. "Just a keepsake," she said. The ring was precious to him. Since finding it in the ashes after the two spaceships crashed, it had never left his finger. He felt it was a talisman and a link with his grandmother. On his return three months later, it was to find Miranda had left to marry a French student she had met at the art college they had both been attending. The marriage had been rather a surprise to the owners of the village store, and they wondered what her father the professor thought of it. They knew she was considered a bit on the wild side. Ben never saw her again. He wasn't to know her influence would be far reaching in his future life.

The one place in the world that Ben was always happy to visit was Hong Kong, English being spoken and payment accepted in euros or the English pound. Ben made sure he had Chinese currency as well as Australian dollars, and never had a problem. There were still bars where one could easily get a

Harvey Wallbanger or Buck's fizz

The evening had been sultry, and he was glad to seek the air-conditioned refuge of Mr Fu's Bar in the 'English' quarter, or what was once considered as such. He was about to take a seat when a husky female voice spoke almost in his ear, "Won't you buy a lady a drink?"

He turned, to see the beautiful Madam Fanny Su. Once she had been pointed out to him as a famous brothel keeper. He remembered she was famous for seeing 'clients' in bars. Well, it seemed now it was his turn. Asking what she would like, in his faultless Mandarin, he turned, but the bartender was already pouring her favourite Bloody Mary. When they were seated in a corner hidden by a pillar, they looked closely at one another. He soon found she was no one's fool. She was, he knew, of mixed race. No one had any idea who her parents were. It was thought her father had been European, her mother Chinese.

On her part, she had never known anyone who was not a resident of Hong Kong able to speak Mandarin so fluently. "You appear to be an accomplished linguist," was her first comment.

"You, Madam, are very beautiful," was his reply.

The next hour sped by too quickly. She was extremely cultured, and wittily brought him up to date with sketches of the characters of several personages, whose ears must have been burning. When he said this she laughingly agreed. The bar was filling up. It was time to go. The apartment was, as Ben anticipated, in a good quarter – not entirely European, yet not Chinese. At the main entrance a doorman let them in, saying "Good evening" politely, obviously used to Madam Fanny bringing guests in late in the evening, although by Hong Kong standards it was not so late – the place never seemed to close down for long. The streets were still busy at midnight.

Fanny explained her maid had gone home, and she hoped he liked the way she made coffee. She did this quite expertly. They talked for a few minutes, and when the conversation started to get a little stilted Fanny took Ben's hand and led him into her bedroom. It was tastefully and expensively furnished. Fanny undressed first herself, then Ben. It was clear what she expected.

The next hour was a revelation to Ben. He thought he had a few tricks up his sleeve. She had more. She obviously liked his figure and looked hard at a certain part of him. Ben grinned. "I assure you, Madam, it hasn't let me down yet." At this she gave a delighted chuckle.

Inspecting her, he saw that her body, slim and tall, was almost that of a European, and clearly different from smaller Chinese women, not that he knew much about them. Her bone structure was completely different. She demonstrated her profession expertly, and they spent an enjoyable time together. Suddenly she surprised him. "I will show you how to make love to a woman – a special woman whom you have yet to meet. That is in the future." It was so very erotic and very sexy. "Now you see why I have shaved that part of my body." She showed him where and how to kiss her. She was very gentle and there was nothing he could say. He just felt stunned, surprised and not a little ashamed, but she saw this and said gently, "Save it for a very special person. You will know who she is and when the time is right."

When Ben returned from using Madam Fanny Su's very smart feminine bathroom, which was lined with mirrors, he found more coffee waiting and Madam Fanny was laying a pack of tarot cards out on the coffee table. "Let me read these for you. I am quite good at it." Barely waiting for his assent, she began, "I see you are a very complex person with several sides to your nature. Extremely gifted in many ways. You are an accomplished sportsman. I see you are the leader of a people now sadly depleted, who look to you for guidance in their lives. I cannot see where they are – this is hidden. One day you will meet the girl of your dreams, but not yet. She is very beautiful and will bring you much joy and, sadly, some sorrow. One day in the future you will acquire the house you desire. As I have already mentioned, you are an accomplished linguist." She paused for breath and an angry Ben swept the cards off the table. "Don't be afraid of the truth. I see also you have good business acumen. You are used to playing the markets, and precious stones are also involved. You will acquire immense wealth." Fanny wasn't put out by his display of temper. He took out his wallet, but it was now her turn to be angry. "No. Put that away. Are we not friends?" There was nothing more to be said, and he left almost immediately.

Feeling quite shaken by the reading of Fanny's tarot cards, Ben nevertheless felt he must give her payment of some sort. Calling on a jeweller who in the past had proved honest and trustworthy, he asked his advice. The man's eyes twinkled. "So you want a special piece of jewellery, eh? What do you think of this? I am sure any young lady would love it." Ben agreed. The piece in question was a simple gold bracelet embossed with rubies. "It is 24-carat gold, I assure you."

Ben bought it, even though it was very expensive. He sent it by special courier to Madam Fanny with a note in French saying: '*Merci Madam. Votre ami Ben*'. It would be many years before they would meet again, on the other side of the world, under very different circumstances.

Chapter Five

Travels

Ben started to travel a lot. He was asked to give lectures on global warming and its effect on the oceans and fishing, and the changing climate. He made no charge for these lectures, merely asking for travelling expenses. He was very popular, especially with the ladies. They tended to lionise him, much to his amusement. He was careful to steer clear of emotional entanglements.

He was asked to lecture in New York, at the United Nations, and in Washington. France, however, was still his base.

One morning in Paris, feeling at a loss for something to do, he bumped into an acquaintance, who was talking to a young man younger than Ben. He was an up-and-coming broker, having a reputation for not taking risks. They were introduced, and Ben and Lucien Gervaise became firm friends. Lucien put together a portfolio of shares for Ben, and Ben in return offered his own expertise, which was considerable. They both made money.

Life on Earth was very much to Ben's liking. He acquired a taste for fine wines, Havana cigars, and of course good quality clothes and boots. He was in no hurry to return to his own people. He promised himself he would one day return to England and continue the search for information about his paternal grandmother.

He liked the south of France, and kept his craft in a small harbour not far from Nice. His mail was sent to a local hotel 'The Merlin', where he also had a suite of rooms for use when life on his ship got too restrictive.

He was never short of money. He had couriers who brought him supplies of precious stones and gold from his mine. These provided him with all the money he needed, and he soon acquired the knowledge of how to manage money. He found it truly made the world go around.

He did indeed become the underwater diver which was the occupation declared on his passport. He decided it was prudent to apply for French citizenship, and was duly accepted. Gradually, without fanfare, he acquired a reputation as an underwater expert. He was following in the footsteps of the late lamented Jacques Cousteau, whom he graciously acknowledged as his master. He loved all aspects of underwater life. He found, to his delight, that he could communicate with dolphins. He felt safe when they were around. He wisely kept his talks with the dolphins a secret. He did not want to be thought eccentric. He might have been thought so if it was known he took with him on dives the jade horse – carefully wrapped so it was not damaged – that Dr Weng had given him on his first arrival. The two men kept in touch, and Ben was later in life able to further the kind doctor's career by recommending him for a post at the United Nations.

The years seemed to fly by, and Ben realised his youth was gone and he still hadn't found a woman he could see himself spending the rest of his life with. He had managed to visit his own people a couple of times, where he found things had not changed. The Council, composed of ten members of the Old People, were very set in their ways and not given to new ideas.

He was pleased and not a little relieved to return to Earth, usually accompanied by Pag Anion. His friend was happily married to a charming Italian lady by the name of Dorita Maria. Pag worked for Air Italia on an ad hoc basis, usually in the holiday season. At other times Ben had his services as his chief courier. When Pag was away helping Ben, Dorita Maria, and later the couple's two sons, would spend time with Dorita

Maria's relatives. It was an arrangement that suited everybody, and Pag's two sons were fluent in Italian and English and loved their Italian family.

Whilst still a boy, Ben had been betrothed to Mu-Ani, whom he had never liked. She was forever badgering him to set the day when she could formally become his wife. He asked Uncle Bron to release him and when he pointed out he and Mu-Ani had both been too young to know their own minds, it was agreed. Much to his chagrin he had to part with some of his mother's jewellery, but he got Mu-Ani off his back and celebrated with Pag, getting a little drunk in the process. Pag was more like a brother to Ben, as they had known each other since childhood. They both enjoyed life on Earth, and were always pleased to return.

Time went by pleasantly enough but it was a solitary life for Ben. He was teased by Pag, who told him he was turning into a crusty old bachelor. Ben ignored this, saying, "I'll find her one day; just you wait and see. I'm not going to be pushed by you or Uncle Bron."

Meanwhile, they were careful how they returned to Earth, and always watchful.

The letter was from Uncle Bron. Ben looked at it suspiciously. "Yes, it is a telling off. The old prince thinks you have been leading what we here would call the life of a playboy."

Ben snorted. "He is wrong, and well you know it. I work extremely hard."

Pag was sympathetic, knowing what the letter contained. It requested Ben to return home and take a wife, as his bloodline must continue. "If you won't accept one of your own people, perhaps you may wish to look at a woman from where you are, as your grandfather did all those years ago."

Ben was very angry. "Why won't the old devil leave well alone and not interfere. It's my life, and I won't be dictated to."

Pag sympathised. He was extremely happy with his Dorita Maria and their two sons, and wouldn't want to change his way of life either. He loved his wife but knew her heart was firmly fixed in the Tuscan countryside. She would never consent to life on the Two Islands planet. Their sons loved their Italian relatives, and were learning French as a surprise for Ben.

Ben was dismayed to discover his people were now in urgent need of food supplies. He had tried, unsuccessfully it seemed, to show them how to conserve stocks, but they ignored his advice and went their own wasteful ways. He decided to have one last look at the area in England where he knew his grandmother had lived. If not successful this time, he would regretfully return to his own people. Meanwhile he arranged for emergency supplies to be sent to his people via his couriers immediately. He always impressed on the couriers the need of making sure their craft got into space undetected. It was a tricky operation, as satellites were on the increase. So far they had been lucky, and had used a smokescreen to confuse any radar or other device that could have tracked them.

PART TWO

DÉJA VU

Chapter One

The Meeting

It was mid-morning on a cool spring day in March, and Ben was engaged in surveying what is known as the Jurassic Coast, in Dorset. He knew it was the area his grandmother had hailed from. He was hoping to see a girl – one he had felt a certain interest in. At last, after an hour's wait, he saw her running along the beach. She usually had Pookey, her dog, with her. This time the dog was nowhere to be seen.

He put his instruments away, and his notes about soil erosion were almost complete. Perhaps this time he would get to speak to her. He was surprised to see the girl was in some distress. She had a tear-streaked face, and her hands and clothes were dirty. When she reached him she challenged him. "Haven't I seen you here before? Are you stalking me?"

Ben raised his hands in mock horror, saying with a smile, "My dear young lady, I wouldn't dare, not that you are not worth stalking, or would be if cleaned up a bit."

At this remark she stamped her foot in anger and the heel snapped off. Ben said "Temper, temper" and sat her down firmly on the rock he had just vacated. With a swift stroke of his hand the heel was soon in place again. He handed the shoe back with a slight bow, still smiling. She wasn't exactly grateful. Fate decided to intervene and her hat and hair ribbon blew away. An agile Ben caught both, and she burst into tears. Not displeased with the turn of events, he took her in his arms, ignoring the dirty clothes and the slight farmyard smell wafting off them. A few gentle promptings from him, and the whole story came out. She was spending her vacation with her grandfather and attending an agricultural course, now almost complete. The boys on the course told her that as she was the youngest, by tradition she should be thrown in a slurry pit. She had other ideas, and fought the boys as they tried to grab her, and escaped to the beach, where she hoped to find someone to help her. A smiling Ben said, "Well you have, Sweetheart. Will I do?"

When he wished to be, Ben was a good listener. The girl seemed not anxious to leave. There was a cool breeze blowing, and she was shivering. The coat she was wearing was not a warm one, and she started to hiccup. Ben, a kind, thoughtful person, then removed his merino wool scarf and wound it about the girl's neck. She was embarrassed. "Oh, no! I can't accept it."

Ben smiled down at her. "Please take it as a gift from me." Turning, he unscrewed the top off a flask of coffee, saying, "Drink this," and without a murmur she did as ordered, and thanked him. He was glad to see the colour return to her face. "When did you last eat?" was his next remark. He guessed she had skipped breakfast.

Her guilty look confirmed this. She said shyly, "You are the first person to be so kind to me in a very long time."

He was appalled, and could hardly believe her. Poor little girl – she had told him more of herself in those few words than she realised. It must be quite lonely living in the house of an autocratic old man and a housekeeper who resented any extra work. The girl looked at her watch and gasped, "Oh no! I will be late for lunch, and grandfather is such a stickler for mealtimes being at a set time, and I am expected to obey him in all things."

Getting to her feet, she blew him a kiss and dashed off down the beach before he had time to ask any more questions or find out her name.

On the way back to his ship Ben thought about the girl. He realised she was young – not much more than a schoolgirl – and certainly not what he had heard called streetwise. He felt she was a ripe peach ready for picking. Was he the one to even consider this? She attracted him in a way he hadn't thought possible, having maintained a rather cynical attitude to the females he had come across, always holding them at arm's length. He had never had a moment's hesitation when it came to making use of them when his sexual urges got too pressing. He had the feeling this one was different. Her French accent was more pronounced when she was upset or angry. He had a strange feeling that she might be Miranda's daughter.

He intended to find out. He thought the village store might be able to help, and as the larder on his ship needed several items, he made his way there. How to start his enquiries? He was pondering this when a bunch of louts entered the shop, laughing over the way they had taught that "stuck-up French girl" a lesson. Ben decided this was not the right time to mention her. Picking up his groceries, he bade the shopkeeper good morning and left. He couldn't get her out of his mind. Still, he told himself "Tomorrow's another day," and he would wait and see what it brought.

Ben felt he must first of all find out the girl's name. She had departed so quickly the previous day that introductions were still to be made. He waited some time the next day but she didn't appear. Had he teased too much? He had the feeling she was going to be more than a casual acquaintance. Great was his relief when she did turn up the next day, looking decidedly tidier. He greeted her with "Hi! Nice to see you. By the way, my name is Ben Haraldsson."

He waited, and in a low voice, slightly embarrassed, she replied, "You may find my name a little odd. It's Ariadne, and not really French. My family lived near Annecy."

He smiled. "I know the area well. I often ski near there, where I have the use of a ski lodge. Do you ski?"

She confirmed she did. Neither of them were novices, and it was a start to find they had something in common. The girl then calmly told him that she was an orphan as both her parents and her father's father had all died when the car her mother was driving had plunged into a ravine. She was only five years old at the time. Her English grandfather had paid for her education and she had lived ever since with Grand-mere in the family home known as the Chateau le Papillon. Their garden was famous for butterflies, which people came to see. There was even a butterfly carved in the stone portico over the main entrance. Grand-mere didn't mind visitors as she was trying to run a small vineyard, and visitors often bought some wine.

Ben took a deep breath. "You are visiting your English grandfather now?"

The girl's smile was a little rueful. "I don't suppose you have heard of him. He is Professor Harvey Dawson. Oh, my family name is Villiers du Pre."

Ben went cold. So she was Miranda's daughter, as he had suspected. Should he keep the girl ignorant of his former liaison with her mother? He felt discretion was the better part of valour, and decided to keep it secret. He didn't want to spoil their growing friendship.

The next time they met, Ben decided to ask the girl's help with his so-far fruitless search for information regarding his grandmother. She arrived, accompanied by her small dog, which thought Ben's boots were a likely meal and tried to chew one. Picking up the small animal, a grinning Ben said, "Now look here, Pookey; my boots are very expensive, and not a meal for a small dog."

Pookey decided she liked this big man, especially when a tasty biscuit appeared. Ariadne and Ben both laughed. Ben thought her laughter was delightful, and felt deliriously happy.

On Ben giving her the information he had, Ariadne thought she could help. Perhaps the local library or newspaper archives might have something buried away. "We must try the local churchyard," she said

They went there first. On seeing the sexton digging a grave, Ben, jingling some coins in his pocket, queried if there was a grave for Lady Clarissa D'Vane.

"Sure, but she ain't in the family tomb. It was believed she committed suicide and she was not allowed to be buried with the rest of the family. She was the last of them, I think."

The man pointed to a neglected grave covered with brambles. Ben thanked him and tossed some money, which was grabbed with only a grunt by way of thanks. The sexton had mentioned the vicar would be available at vespers, which Ariadne explained was at sunset. Ben met up with Mr Childs the vicar, who was only too pleased to agree to his request that Lady D'Vane's grave was cared for. The vicar was appreciative of the large donation Ben made to church repairs, and promised to see to the matter personally.

Having started their search, Ben was anxious to find out as much as he could about Clarissa D'Vane. The local library had a book – not much requested – but the librarian was happy to assist them. She was much taken by the tall handsome man, and when she heard he was the grandson of the subject of the book they requested, went out of her way to be helpful. The library computer held a copy of the book, she told them, and Ben easily obtained all he wanted from it. Ariadne was amazed how quickly he was able to scan the screen. On leaving the library he bowed to the librarian, thanking her, and she blushed when he gallantly kissed her hand in the French manner.

They went to the local newspaper office next, and found sheets of newspaper in large files. These had yet to be put on computer, they were told, but this was in hand. It took a while to find the years they wanted but there was even more information, including an obituary which Ben found very moving. Ariadne saw how easily he was reduced to tears, and thought he had a soft centre, which he hid too successfully at times. He was, she knew, quite sophisticated and cultured – something which, she sadly admitted to herself, she was not. "I think there has been a lot of trauma in your life, Ben. Am I not right?"

He sighed. "Darling, you are very observant. I have had my share. If seeing a midair collision, knowing both my parents and younger brother were on board is trauma, well, yes, I have known some. Apart from an uncle, there is no one left of my family. He is the head, and I am the next in line."

He was lost in thought, and the girl wondered at the expression "next in line" as if he was a nobleman. She, however, held her peace. If he wished her to know, he would tell her; of that she was sure.

Being well pleased with their various searches, Ben now had a good idea of how life had been led by his grandmother. She had been among the select few women who had ferried planes from factories to airfields during the Second World War. After the war she went to Europe, where she met Ben's grandfather. They both worked for the same organisation, whose task was settling the thousands of war-displaced people. Unfortunately, with no papers to prove who he was or where he came from, the lovely Clarissa knew her family would never accept this man as her partner. They married in secret, and Ben's father was born in the south of Germany. The child was named Carlin Frederick Haraldsson. Gus told his wife he wished to take the child to see his own parents. He got his way and took all their papers, including wedding lines and the child's registration documents. She never saw either of them again. Ben knew his grandfather had been very bitter about the separation. He was not allowed to return, and often wondered what had happened to the girl he had left behind.

Ben discovered how his grandmother had died. Her plane had flown into the sea off the south coast of England. No one believed her when she said she had a husband and a child. The strange thing was: a physical examination to prove or disprove her assertion she had given birth was not considered. It was thought she'd had a nervous breakdown. The estate was inherited by cash-strapped distant cousins, who could not afford to spend what was required to return the small gem back to its original pristine state. It was very much in decline. Ben, accompanied by Ariadne, had looked over a wall at the estate, only to be told by a rough-looking gamekeeper to "clear off or I'll set the dogs on yer". There and then Ben decided that when the time was right he would acquire Swanbrook Hall and, if still around, he would get rid of the loathsome gamekeeper who had ordered them off so roughly.

How to thank the girl for her invaluable help? Knowing how difficult it was for her to get away from her grandfather's set meals routine, Ben suggested a plan. She could say her group at the agricultural college were going on a farewell visit to a farm, which would mean she would be unavailable for lunch on that day. As schemes went it was ideal, but not so easy to put into practice. Ariadne was not a good liar but did her best and, wearing her stoutest shoes, as if there was loads of walking expected, met up with Ben at their usual spot on the beach. She was not at all sure her grandfather had believed her, but didn't wait to find out.

Breathing a sigh of relief, Ben took her in his arms. "How about a picnic?"

Ariadne's eyes sparkled. "Oh, goody! I love picnics."

It was a feast, with a bottle of champagne, and strawberries and cream – everything he thought a young girl would like. Ben discovered something on the picnic. He was madly in love. He felt he just couldn't live without her. Would she want to marry him? He knew it was the only way he would be allowed to have her. He tried to make love but with only limited success. When he undid some of the buttons on her blouse she did them up again. She was wearing slacks – not very helpful to him. Was she a virgin? He was sure she was. There was something almost childlike about her. He decided to play it coolly. No sense in rushing his fences. He tried kissing her but she appeared frightened by his ardour, which was growing. He had never raped a woman in his life, but his love for this girl was becoming almost an obsession. He shakily packed the picnic away. "Time to go, Sweetheart."

She shyly whispered, "Thank you for a lovely day." For her

maybe, for him it was almost torture.

How had it happened? He had not intended it to go so far, but Ben knew he was in love. He spent a wretched night and hardly slept, rising at his usual time of 4.00 a.m. He recalled asking Pag how he would know if he was in love, and Pag's answer: "You will know. You are in heaven one minute and hell the next." He admitted to himself she was very young. Too young for him. Would she laugh in his face and give him what he had heard called a 'brush off'? He made his way to the beach and waited impatiently for her to appear. She didn't come. He was so deep in misery he was at first unaware of the small dog licking his fingers. He heard, as if from miles away, her voice calling him. "Ben, you look cold. How long have you been waiting for me? I am sorry to be so late but I've been running an errand for grandfather."

At first he couldn't speak, and it was her turn to take him in her arms.

"Darling girl," he said, "I thought you had had enough of my company and decided not to come."

She gave a little laugh. "Silly thing! You know I would miss you if you were not here."

He kissed her, murmuring into her neck, "I had visions of going to ask your grandfather how to find the Chateau le Papillon."

She gave a delighted gurgle. "I can just see his face if you did. He would send you away with a flea in your ear."

He was holding her close and, for the first time, she smelt the aftershave he used. It was a very expensive French one, and it suited him. It made her feel quite dizzy. He had added something of his own to it and it was quite the most sexy, alluring part of him she had yet discovered. She drew away, not sure of the strange effect being so near him was having on her. "I must go; duty calls."

He groaned. "Must you, Sweetheart?"

She gave him a hasty kiss, and was gone.

Once his mind was made up, Ben pressed ahead. There was no way he would be thwarted in his desire. He wanted Ariadne but knew the only way he could possess her was by marriage. He made numerous plans, only to discard them all. Fortunately for him Ariadne's grandfather was invited to a conference in London. He was reluctant to leave his granddaughter alone but had already promised his housekeeper a holiday. She was going to visit her sister in Yorkshire, so Ariadne would be entirely alone for several days. Ariadne assured her grandfather she could look after herself and he was not to worry.

With relief she waved her elderly relative goodbye, delighted that for a short time she and Ben could see as much of each other as they wished. Ben took her to the only French restaurant in the district, where they had a delightful meal. Much to their amusement the only French employee was the sommelier, and he spoke to them in rapid French. Ariadne guessed he was from the Champagne area of France. He confirmed this was so, and recommended a very select vintage, which Ben was delighted to accept. The girl knew it was very expensive but also was aware Ben didn't like discussing money. It was quite late when Ben stopped the car he had hired specially for the occasion. He took Ariadne in his arms and asked her to marry him. She knew she liked him. In truth, she was quite taken with this tall, elegant, amusing companion. He kissed her but she neither responded nor refused his embrace. Taking her silence for consent he grew bolder, and gave her what is known as a French kiss. She was affronted, and slapped his face hard. "Ouch! That hurt. You sure know how to pack a punch. Have you never had that kind of kiss before?"

The answer was clear. She was, as he had thought, a total innocent. "Darling, please say you will marry me. You are driving me crazy."

Her reply was calm. "I am not yet eighteen. It won't be allowed. Neither of my grandparents will permit it."

Ben could be very persuasive, and he used all his charm

to cajole the girl into seeing his point of view. "Darling girl, you know that if you return to France, Grand-mere will expect you to work both in the chateau and in the vineyard." Ariadne agreed he was correct in his assumption. He could see she was wavering. "When are you eighteen?" was his next question.

"I'm eighteen next week."

He was delighted, and, taking her left hand, kissed it before slipping on the most beautiful ring she had ever seen. It appeared as if by magic from a small box he held in his other hand. It was exquisite – an engagement ring she had never seen the like of before in any shop window. It was made up from a large white diamond surrounded by sapphires. "I will get a special licence, and we can be married just when you say the word. Shall we say on your eighteenth birthday?"

Ariadne felt she was being swept along by him far too fast. Her feelings were very mixed. There was the excitement of his presence. She was so happy to be with him, but asked herself, was it love.

He was so sure, saying, "When you are eighteen you don't need to ask anyone's permission." He kissed her more gently, asking, "Have we a deal?"

She felt she needed more time, and said so. He drove her home, feeling he had made some progress, and he felt fairly certain of the outcome. Afterwards neither of them could remember what they had eaten at L'Escargot, but could remember the champagne. Before she went to sleep Ariadne searched for a hiding place for the ring. No way was she going to let it be seen by anyone. Wrapping it in the merino wool scarf he had given her, she put it in a loose corner of her wardrobe and pushed the wedge of wood back. It would require a knife to prise it open. She fell asleep dreaming of Ben.

Chapter Two

The Wedding

Ben gave Ariadne enough money to buy a suitable wedding outfit. Her taste was good but never in the past had she had enough money to indulge herself. She noticed a new boutique in the mall in the nearest town, where she occasionally shopped for her grandfather. Rowlands was a little pricey, and she wondered if it was possible to find anything at the price she could afford as she would also need shoes, a handbag and a hat. Gloves – she could do without. Bracing herself, she entered. The owner of the shop came to assist her, thinking, 'What a beautiful girl, but so tall!' When a blushing Ariadne explained she wanted an outfit for her wedding, she got a welcome surprise. Smiling, the saleswoman told the girl, "I have an outfit that was made for a model as tall as you. It has been marked down because I could think of no one slim or tall enough for it. I am sure it will fit you. Would you like to see it?"

When it was brought out Ariadne gasped with delight, and she fell in love with it. It fitted her perfectly and required no alteration, and the price was unbelievable. It was made of a non-crushable material, and was soft and silky. She was told it was most likely shantung. It was in a soft creamy colour, with a beautiful embroidered collar. The saleswoman clapped her hands. "Oh, it is just you!"

There was enough money left to also include a simple plain straw hat in a coffee shade, and shoes and clutch handbag to match. Feeling as if she was walking on air, the girl left the shop; and watching her go, the saleswoman wondered who the lucky man was. She had noticed the magnificent engagement ring the girl was wearing. Her clothes didn't do much for her but she guessed that would change, and hoped for her future custom.

Arriving a little late – as usual with brides – Ariadne was presented with a posy of orchids by her prospective husband. The registrar was trying to remember why the bridegroom's name seemed familiar. When she remembered she rang her contact at the local newspaper, and a reporter was sent along to cover the wedding. He had a camera as well, carefully hidden. It wasn't often that such a distinguished Frenchman gave him the chance of a scoop, and he intended to take full advantage of the situation.

Ben had noticed a young couple gazing into the window of an estate agent, and asked them if they had the time to witness the wedding ceremony. He handed over, as a sweetener, a large sum of money, which they were delighted to accept, and agreed to skip their lunch for the occasion.

Ben was his usual elegant self. Ariadne had never seen the pale grey suit he was wearing, and shyly told him he looked marvellous. For a change he was wearing a pair of simple black loafers in place of his usual boots. "You look so distinguished and debonair."

He smiled down at her. "You, my darling, look good enough to eat."

The ceremony didn't take long, and Ben thanked the young couple and wished them well. He noticed the registrar was looking at her watch and, always sensitive to anything unusual, hurried Ariadne out. He saw the reporter taking a photograph. "How much do you want for your film?" He quickly did a deal and slipped the film into his pocket. If he had the time, he would develop it himself at a later date. He soon had Ariadne in his hired car, and sped away before the reporter could get too inquisitive.

He had arranged with caterers to prepare a wedding breakfast, and was anxious not to leave it in the open air too long.

It was under an awning, but inquisitive seagulls might start investigating. Ariadne was dismayed to find Ben lived on a ship.

The wedding breakfast was all that Ben had requested, and more. Ariadne looked at it with some dismay, and realised she just couldn't do it justice and was not the least bit hungry. She knew Ben had gone to a lot of trouble, and she felt guilty. He offered her a glass of champagne, which she drank too quickly. It was clear she was very nervous and she asked herself, "I must have been mad to agree to marry Ben. What was I thinking of?" What did she really know about him? Very little. Her lips felt dry, her stomach was turning over, and tears were not far away.

Ben commented, "Looks as if the seagulls are in for a feast." After throwing the food into the harbour he swept Ariadne up into his arms and carried her into the cabin. He hoped she was in the mood for lovemaking. He was impatient, and surprised Ariadne with an odd request: "Please, Darling, use this razor and remove all the hair on your body except that on your head, and when I say all, I mean all."

When he returned he frowned as it was clear she had not finished. Taking the small razor, he ordered her to lie back, and he completed the task himself. Scarlet with mortification, Ariadne clutched at the sheets, which she dimly realised were a lovely shade of blue silk. He whipped her nightdress off, commenting, "Let's get rid of this." When he had reached the more intimate area of her body she tried to stop him. His terse comment was, "There is no need for this display of modesty, Darling. You know we will soon be united and be husband and wife. Remember our wedding vows, girl."

Ben looked down on Ariadne, and he frankly felt frustrated. She lay on the bed, more like a frightened child than a bride. After fifteen minutes of coaxing and explaining things to her, she was still like a cold block of ice. He rose and went out on deck. He lit a cigar and watched the seagulls feasting on the remains of what should have been their wedding breakfast. Ariadne could smell the aroma of the expensive cigar as the smoke drifted back into the cabin. Ben returned, determined to have one more try. He cleaned his teeth and, taking the champagne, returned. He offered a glassful to Ariadne, which she ignored. Feeling increasingly angry, Ben threw off his robe. He was naked so she saw a full- frontal view of his body. He wanted to shock her and he certainly did. Oh yes, he was well worth looking at. The girl had seen the statue of David in Florence on a school visit, but had never thought to see such perfection in the flesh. A slow blush suffused her whole body, and she felt hot all over. Mockingly, Ben said, "As you can see, my dear, I am well endowed in a certain area. I don't want to rape you but I have needs. I am well within my rights to insist you co-operate."

She suddenly surprised him by reaching up and, drawing his face down, kissed him, and it was no ordinary kiss. Days before, he had tried to give her a very personal kiss, and now she was returning the same kiss. Hardly believing it was happening, he made love to her, gently at first, then growing bolder and using the knowledge he had gleaned from Madam Fanny, he succeeded in making her his wife in the fullest sense. "Do you love me a little then?"

She didn't answer but started to kiss him in such a way his doubts were swept away. He loved her breasts. To him they were just wonderful – not overlarge, but firm and high. They drove him mad. He was a very amorous lover and, not content with having her once, made love several times in the night. At last she fell asleep in his arms. He stroked her hair. For him it would always be "shining like the sun", and he had never felt happier.

After the civil ceremony there was still the prospect of having to tell Grand-mere. The newlyweds travelled to France, delaying a honeymoon, to meet the one Ben had dubbed "the old witch". The old lady was astonished at the couple's news, and insisted the *Abbe* officiate at a religious ceremony. Ben would have been content to leave things as they were as he felt already married, but fell in with her wishes for the sake of peace and quiet. The brief ceremony was soon over. During the prayers Ben couldn't but help notice the old woman was grinning widely, as if enjoying a private joke. Ben paid for a lavish reception, which was attended not only by the vineyard workers but, it seemed, by everyone else in the district connected with the chateau. It was hugely enjoyed, and there must have been a number of hangovers the next day. Ben offered to install a manager for the vineyard and arrange for him to be paid. This was accepted by the old lady as she would greatly miss the assistance she had expected to receive from Ariadne.

On their return to their 'home' harbour Ben was dismayed to see a letter waiting. It was marked 'Urgent and Confidential'. It was from the office of the French president, inviting him to join the elite Legion d'Honneur in two days' time. The investiture would take place in the President's private suite; and the honour was being bestowed in recognition of Ben's work on oceanic research and global warming and its effect on the seas and fishing. His work had brought not only prestige to Ben himself but to France also. Ben was delighted as, even though being a French citizen, he had no idea he could receive such an award. He thought he would require to have been born in France. It presented Ben with a problem. There was no way Ariadne could be permitted to accompany him to the investiture. Time was short and she, like all women, would want a new outfit etc, and he couldn't risk exposing her to the scrutiny of the paparazzi. What a field day they would have, linking one so young to a sophisticate like himself.

What could he do? Ben asked himself the question, and the answer was simple. He contacted his Paris agent, for that is how he considered Lucien Gervaise. He found him in his office and lost no time in coming to the point. "Lucien old boy, how busy are you tomorrow? Quiet, I trust, as I have a big favour to ask of you. Can you spare me the whole day? You will be surprised to hear I have recently married." There was a long silence and Ben chuckled. "My wife is very young, very beautiful with beautiful green eyes, and legs that go on for ever. She is badly in need of some clothes, and I would like you to escort her to some of the fashion houses that cater for the young." Lucien was still silent, and an amused Ben said, "Well, are you going to congratulate me, or have you lost your tongue?"

Lucien dryly remarked, "Well, it certainly is a surprise." He, however, graciously congratulated Ben and said he would be delighted to escort Madame, and made a list of several rather exclusive fashion houses that Ben reeled off to him. Ben said money was not to be spared, and the list of his requirements was breathtaking. Lucien was eager to meet the girl who had won the heart of one whom he had always considered a confirmed bachelor. He cancelled several appointments, and after several Emails etc, felt he could leave his office for a day with a clear conscience.

Lucien knew there were rumours going around that Ben was to receive an honour, and wondered just how young Ben's bride actually was. Arrangements were made to put Ariadne on the shuttle leaving Nice for Paris at about 10.00 a.m. the following day. Lucien wondered at her unusual name, which was not really French. He asked Ben why he wasn't free to take the girl himself. He asked outright: was it the day of his investiture. Ben grimaced and coolly said it was. Lucien thought he would learn more on the morrow. It was none of his business, and he could only shake his head, asking himself what sort of marriage it was when confidences were not shared.

Arriving at the airport on time, Lucien sought a vantage point from where he could view the travellers arriving from Nice. Ariadne came through the channel reserved for domestic flights, bubbling with excitement. From the way her husband had described her, she was easy to pick out. She saw Lucien at the same instant, and moved towards him. "How did you know it was me?" he wanted to know.

Laughing she said, "Well, you look like a man of affairs. I mean a broker or banker, whatever you are; I am not sure. Oh, and your moustache. Ben described it to me."

Not sure if he was having his leg pulled, Lucien decided a plan of action should be worked out between them. She excused herself, saying she needed to visit the ladies' room. This gave Lucien the chance to contact Yvette, his girlfriend, who owned a hairdressing salon in one of the most exclusive areas of Paris. It was much patronised by the wealthier members of society and had an excellent reputation. He was dismayed to find she was having a day off work. She had been partying the night before, and had a slight headache. He rang her at home. She sounded fine, and he was relieved she was not confined to bed. "Yvette, you know you want to visit Majorca for a weekend? Well, you can, no expense spared. I have a favour to ask first." He went on to describe his problem, and she reluctantly agreed to do what she could to make Ariadne more presentable to the fashion houses she was to visit.

Upon meeting her Yvette took an immense liking to Ariadne, who was younger than herself. She washed, cut and set the girl's hair, gave her a manicure and pedicure, and then proceeded to make her up with all the skill she possessed. When finished, even Lucien couldn't believe the transformation. He said merely, "Wow!"

Yvette looked with pleasure at her handiwork. Ariadne was like a butterfly just emerged from its cocoon. She was ravishing. Lucien bought Ariadne some very elegant sandals that showed her legs and ankles off to great advantage. They were ready for the fray.

One needed to be very rich to afford purchasing Franco Borelli's creations. They were considered the very essence of haute couture. Ariadne had heard of the eccentric designer, who was very choosy as to both models and to whom he sold his creations. Fortunately for Ariadne he was away in New York so it was left to the head of sales standing in for him to attend to Lucien and Ariadne. They were received cordially enough and were unaware that enquiries had been made before their arrival, and it was known that M. Gervaise was a wealthy broker with a good reputation. Ariadne quickly made it clear she was not going to be patronised by anyone, and handed over a list of colours she preferred and sketches of styles. Staff were sent scurrying about, and the girl was soon trying on fabulous gowns the like of which she had never in her life dreamt of owning. As she was tall and slim, very little was required in the way of alteration. She chose three beautiful evening gowns – one, a black off-the-shoulder embroidered with jet and edged with lace. Her second choice was in midnight blue, and which was deceptively simple. It clung to her body and was very sexy. Even the young *vendeuse* assisting her dress was impressed. Her final choice was a gown in peacock blue, which fell about in layers. It was the most expensive, but when Lucien saw her arrayed in it he felt Ben would love it. Ariadne also bought something else, which she didn't show to Lucien. It was the most alluring outfit, but had to be worn for its full effect to be appreciated. It was a Chinese cheongsam in silver brocade, with a dragon embroidered on the front and petering out to a tail at the back. It had been made for the daughter of a Chinese diplomat but she hadn't liked it. The head of sales was glad to get rid of it as she felt it was unlucky. All would be sent by special delivery to The Merlin within the next twenty-four hours.

After a hasty lunch, Ariadne insisted she went on her own to purchase her lingerie. Ben had been very critical of her simple underwear, which was far from glamorous. She wanted to surprise him, and had brought enough cash to meet her needs. She had looked at several ladies' magazines on the flight from Nice, so had a good idea of what she required. She hoped she had enough money. No way was she going to let Lucien see what she was buying. That was for Ben's eyes only. She asked Lucien: could they visit the Louvre and Notre Dame cathedral. He phoned Ben, who was then on his way back from Paris. He was amused at her insistence that she bought her own lingerie. Yes, it was OK to stay an extra hour. Ben grinned as Lucien hesitated. "I trust you are not being rushed off your feet?"

Privately Ben chuckled when the visits to the Louvre and Notre Dame came up. He hoped they would get all that was needed. He didn't feel like traipsing around shops himself. Feeling very satisfied with her purchases from the Janet Reger boutique, Ariadne still had enough energy to look for accessories and shoes. By early evening the pair felt they had had enough. The afternoon had included visits to two other fashion houses. The girl turned to Lucien. "You must think me a brat. I've rushed you all over the place. Time for tea, I think."

Lucien was more a coffee man but was glad to sit in the quiet of a small café, and the tea, he found, was pleasant and relaxing. In the Louvre they queued to see the *Mona Lisa*. Ariadne was thoughtful, and asked if it was known why La Gioconda was smiling.

"Oh, there are all sorts of theories."

In the Notre Dame Ariadne knelt for a few minutes while Lucien looked at the splendid interior. They were both tired when they eventually made their way to the airport.

Arriving at the President's offices, Ben was dismayed to see the paparazzi already there. The grapevine, he supposed, and he was photographed as he entered. On showing his invitation he was directed to a long corridor, the walls of which were lined with beautiful pictures which Ben would have loved to have lingered over, but he told himself he wasn't there for pleasure. Remembering he had a tie in his pocket, he tried to knot it but without success. An amused voice made him turn, and an attractive lady about his own age, saying "May I help?" made him presentable and steered him to a door, where an aide was waiting to usher him in.

Ben towered above the President, who was not tall. He guessed the private investiture was because of this. He was directed to kneel on a stool, a citation was read out, and he was kissed on both cheeks by the President. Ben was now an officer of the Legion d'Honneur, and he was congratulated. Thinking it was all over, he rose to leave, but was stopped by the lady who had helped him in the corridor. She was pushing in a trolley and offered him a cup of coffee. He would have preferred something stronger. The President said, "Nicolle, *Cherie*, this is Ben Haraldsson – an adopted son of France. A noted expert on global warming and climate change."

Nicolle Chevalliere smiled and flicked at Ben's tie. He saw she was openly flirting with him under her husband's nose. Bowing low, Ben, highly diverted, said "*Enchante*, Madame" and he held her hand a little longer than etiquette prescribed. He was grilled by the President over his work until, on a whispered aside from an aide, the President, with a sigh, said "Duty calls" and left them. Madame offered to show Ben a discreet way out, which he accepted. At the door she leaned forward and kissed him full on the lips, before gently pushing him into the street.

Compared with the quietness of the place he had just left, the boulevard seemed incredibly noisy. The kiss bestowed on him by Madame, the First Lady of France, had been very sexy, and he realised she wasn't in love with her husband but with what he represented, namely power. He knew it had a strong attraction. He strolled towards the Seine and watched a *bateau mouche* ferrying tourists. He felt how lucky they were to have such simple, uncomplicated lives. Feeling in need of a reviving drink, Ben made his way along the river path and found a bistro he fancied. A clock at a nearby church struck the midday hour. A lot had happened that morning, and he felt suddenly light-headed. He ordered a dry Martini and sat back, feeling all he would really like to do was fall asleep. No such luck. His mobile rang and Lucien was on the line, requesting an extra hour. "Is she driving you crazy?" Ben asked.

"No. Indeed, she is a perfect darling."

As usual, Ariadne had worked her spell. "The little witch," Ben murmured, half aloud.

An English voice broke in on his reverie. "I beg your pardon, Sir. Were you addressing me?"

Ben turned and, half annoyed, said coldly, "No indeed. Do

you often listen to others' telephone conversations?"

The man looked at him keenly. "Forgive me for asking, but are you not Ben Haraldsson?"

Ben sighed, "Yes I am. Who wants to know?"

The other, not put off, said, "I'm Henry Forbes Berringer. We have met before – in Africa. I was in the Foreign Legion, and you saved my company from being wiped out. Those that survived that affray have never forgotten."

Ben asked casually what happened to Jan Van Den Hoof and his sergeant.

"Oh, Jan's now a colonel, working in Paris. No one knows what happened to Jean-Paul; he disappeared on discharge." Ben realised time was getting short and reluctantly bade the other goodbye, saying it was nice to have met him again. It seemed he would never know what happened to Jean-Paul. He still had to meet Ariadne's plane.

It did not take long to return to the ship, and Ben hastily changed into casual clothes and made his way to the airport to meet Ariadne. He was gratified to see Lucien was with her. On seeing Ben, she dropped all she was holding and rushed to meet him. Laughing, he lifted her off her feet. They kissed, and Lucien realised Ben certainly was smitten. Amused glances were directed at them as they continued their long kiss. They separated only when Lucien gave an extra-loud cough. Looking not at all put out Ben said, "I think it is time this young Madame got to bed."

He tossed his car keys to Lucien, asking him to drive them to The Merlin, where Ben had reserved a room for Lucien. The sleepy girl was carried in by her husband, and arrangements were made for a morning business meeting between Lucien and his superior. Ben knew Lucien would be anxious to get back to Paris so the meeting was more or less held over breakfast. Lucien was always amazed how little Ben ate, and wondered where he found the energy to do all he got through in a day. He knew he found time for active sport. One thing he did envy him was Ariadne. Ben realised that Lucien was also under the girl's spell. He told himself, "Sorry, old boy; I got there first. She is mine." He slyly asked Lucien how the day had gone in Paris, and was assured that Madame Ariadne knew her own mind and he hoped they had not spent too much. Ben spent a delightful morning as Ariadne paraded like a model in all the finery she had purchased. He told her he admired her good taste, and tried not to whistle at the cost. Lucien was aware Ben was getting at him, and turned the tables before he left by asking how the investiture had gone. Ben grinned and said, "Well, I almost fell in love with the President's wife. I think she fell for me."

Lucien shook his head. "*Mon ami, vous ete une homme impossible.*"

Ben agreed he was, but shook Lucien's hand and thanked him for looking after Ariadne.

A couple of days after her trip to Paris, Ariadne was in the fish market buying some of Ben's favourite bass, always fresh from the sea, when a Paris newspaper was thrust into her hands and she was surrounded with well-wishers asking her to pass on their congratulations to Ben for the honour he had received a few days earlier. She smiled and said yes she would. On the front page was a picture of Ben and a resume of his work. He was said to be one of the most 'eligible bachelors in France'. Returning to the ship, she slammed the paper down in front of Ben. "So this is why you were unable to accompany me to Paris, and made Lucien my escort."

Ben tried to explain. "Darling, what else could I do? The invitation arrived too late. You would have needed your hair done, a new outfit and goodness knows what else."

She wasn't satisfied, and went off in a sulky mood. It was their first quarrel. Ben wondered if the offer of a holiday would smooth things over, and it did. "After all, Darling, we haven't had a proper honeymoon."

They spent a delightful month visiting, in their ship, the Greek islands, the African coast, and finally Egypt. All too soon it was over, and they returned to the small harbour near Nice that Ben looked on as 'home'. He said he was expecting a friend he would like her to meet. When a tall man saluted Ben before realising she was there, he was reprimanded in a strange language the girl didn't recognise. "Let me introduce Captain Pagan Anion, known to all as Pag. He is a pilot with an Italian airline, married to a charming Italian lady, Dorita Maria, and has two little rascals – his boys: Giovanni, who likes to be called Georgio, and Sandro Francis, known as Sandy."

A smiling Pag kissed her hand and Ben told her, "We grew up together, and I look on him almost as a brother."

The two men continued speaking in their strange language, and the girl was left feeling puzzled and intrigued by the stranger.

Ariadne quite liked Pag, though with reservations. She felt there was something mysterious about him. She felt closer to Lucien, but he was too busy expanding his business to spare her much time on her frequent visits to Paris. Ben insisted her hair always looked immaculate, and she went to Yvette's salon, where manicures and pedicures were given on a regular basis. Ariadne told Ben this was a waste of his money, but he had his reasons. When Ben thought Ariadne was ready, he intended taking her to the casino at Monte Carlo.

Aware of her youth, the girl tried to be more mature. The only thing she and Ben clashed over was his insistence that she was more discreet in her mode of dress. She told him, "You are more like a Muslim husband. I am not Princess Yasmina. She has to obey her father."

Ben's eyebrows rose. "How is it you know the daughter of Sheikh Kassim Abdullah?" he wanted to know.

"Oh, we were at school together. I taught her French, and she was kind enough to teach me Arabic."

Although not a gambler, the Sheikh found it convenient to meet clients and cronies in the casino. Ben didn't tell the girl of the proposed meeting. He hadn't made up his mind how to introduce her – as wife or girlfriend. In any case he asked her not to wear her rings. He would decide her jewellery after she was dressed. Ben was unaware that the two girls were in constant contact. Yasmina told Ariadne, "You are so lucky. You are in love. It shines out of you. I may have to accept my father's choice of husband but I am not going to marry someone I don't love. I'll stay single if I have to."

The girl wasn't the only one puzzled. Pag was also. He couldn't explain it but felt the marriage of his friend to this lovely girl was somehow doomed, though they appeared to be very much in love. He wondered whether Ben had rushed into a hasty marriage to get the heir his uncle had urged him to think about. He, however, congratulated Ben, and hoped for their future happiness.

"Can you get a message to Uncle Bron?" Ben asked him.

"Sure. What do you wish him told?"

Ben laughed. "Just say I am now married and hope in the not-too-distant future to present my heir to him."

Pag's eyebrows rose. "Is she pregnant then?"

Ben roared with laughter. "We must wait and see."

With that enigmatic remark the matter was closed, and the two friends went on to discuss the next shipment required to be sent to the Two Islands planet. Ariadne on her part, after bidding the tall stranger goodbye, couldn't help wondering about him. For a start he and Ben were both physically alike. They had the same colour hair and spoke the strange language she couldn't place anywhere. When she tried to pump Ben he very gently shut her up, saying, "I know there are things about me and Pag you would like explained, but now is not the time."

Ariadne knew there was a lot she still had to discover about the charismatic man she had married, but knew she would have to be patient. She felt it would all come out in time.

Ariadne was excited at the prospect of visiting the casino. She decided to find out as much as she could about roulette, and asked innumerable questions. Ben was amused and thought, So, little one, you think you can pump me, eh? and decided to mislead her. When his teasing dawned on her she decided to do it her way. The day arrived at last. Ben told Ariadne several things. "You will wear your black gown. It makes you look older, and is glamorous enough for the casino." He took from his safe a jewel box. Ariadne gasped with delight at the contents. He said, "This jewellery belonged to my mother. I am sure she would wish you to have it. It has all been carefully cleaned, ready for you."

The girl asked, "Are you sure you want me to wear it?"

Ben was sure. "It is some of the few things I managed to save, as it wasn't included with my parents' luggage, so missed the crash."

Ben carefully dressed her hair. It was something he loved to do. It took some time but the result was wonderful. He had threaded pearls into her hair in a sort of Juliet cap. On her right wrist was a superb gold-and-diamond bracelet. Diamonds were also at her throat. They were, he knew, priceless, but he had no fear of theft. Each piece had a small microchip cleverly inserted that could easily be traced. He stood back to admire her. "Darling, you look just *magnifique*." And it was true. She was quite breathtaking, and totally unaware of her beauty.

Relenting a little on the way, Ben told her of the large sums of money that were often staked and sometimes lost. He gave her several thousand euros, and cheerfully expected her to lose the lot. "If you do play, remember what I've told you, and don't ask me for any more."

She assured him she would be sensible, but couldn't keep the excitement out of her voice. They found the casino crowded, as several boats with wealthy Americans had recently arrived in Monte Carlo's harbour. Ben took her mink wrap, tipping the attendant and asking if it could be put in an accessible spot.

Famous the world over, the casino at Monte Carlo was used to being patronised by beautiful women. At first, little notice was taken of Ben and Ariadne. He was well-known there, but Ariadne caused something of a sensation. A buzz went around, especially among the women. They wanted to know who she was. Remarks were made about her gown, her air of elegance, and her jewellery. The men admired her beauty, while some of the women were openly envious. It was just the effect a scheming Ben had hoped for.

Across the room Ben saw Sheikh Kassim threading his way towards them. "Ben, my friend, won't you introduce me to this charming young lady?"

Ben's smiled. "Of course, Kassim. Madame Ariadne, meet my friend Sheikh Kassim." He did not say "This is my wife" as he had asked the unsuspecting girl most specifically not to wear her rings. The Sheikh bowed and kissed her hand, which surprised her. When the men started talking horses Ariadne excused herself. She was anxious to try her hand at the roulette table. Call it beginner's luck, but she started to win. Ben watched her out of the corner of his eye. When he saw she had amassed quite a large pile of chips, she felt his hand on her shoulder. "I think, Darling, I'd better change those for you. Time to go, I think."

She was disappointed but amazed when forty thousand euros were placed by a smiling Ben into her hands. "Did I really win that much?" Saying she was going to the powder room, she went instead to the entrance hall, where boutiques were located. They hoped to lure winners into parting with some of their cash. In one was a beautiful Rolex watch she felt was just what Ben needed. He was hopeless at remembering times and dates. It was very expensive and had not attracted any attention. The shop owner reduced it, hoping for a quick sale. Ariadne bought it. It gave information on the movement of the planets, the stars and phases of the Moon, and details of tides on Earth. She hid it her evening bag.

It had turned chilly, so Ben wrapped the mink stole he had bought for Ariadne's nineteenth birthday carefully around her shoulders, and made to leave the casino. Ariadne was amazed and still could hardly believe she had won. Ben was pleased also.

He had fully expected her to lose. She gravely told him, "Here is your stake money."

With laughter in his eyes he replied, "No, Sweetheart, you keep it."

But she insisted. "You have already spoilt me enough. My nineteenth birthday isn't yet, but this stole must have cost you quite a packet."

The Sheikh stopped them on the way out. "Ben, my friend, will we see you at the races this year? Ascot, or perhaps Longchamps?"

Ben told him their plans were fluid and perhaps they might. Wickedly, Kassim added, "My daughter will be with me, and I know she is longing to meet up with Madame Ariadne again."

Ben smiled ruefully and sighed. He had been rumbled. "*Touche*, my friend. The joke is on me."

The other man's laugh was like that of a rumbling bear: deep and throaty. Once in the car Ben had hired for the evening, Ariadne laid a sleepy head on his shoulder. When they reached the harbour he stopped, saying, "It isn't wise to have so much money left around. Let me bank it for you."

Ariadne said shyly, "There is not much to bank, as I bought this for you", and she handed him the watch.

Ben looked at her gift. Speechless, he took her in his arms. "I will never part with it, Darling."

When she received her next bank statement, the girl saw there was more in it than she expected. She knew Ben had topped it up. When she challenged him he said casually, "Oh, I thought it was time you had a little more money to fall back on and not need to ask me every time you require funds." With this remark, she had to be content.

Chapter Three

After

The first twelve months they were together seemed to Ben like one long honeymoon. Ariadne, he found, needed a lot of educating. Her French was almost the same as that spoken by the peasants who came to work in Grand-mere's vineyard. Through example, and with a little coaching, she started to speak with a more refined accent, similar to that spoken in Parisian society. Ben taught her a lot without her being aware she was being taught. He rode well but her only knowledge of horses was the occasional ride on the old nags used about the vineyard to pull the carts containing the grape harvest. He enrolled her in a riding school, and she made excellent progress. He insisted she learnt to school horses, and the art of dressage. One day he knew she would thank him, as where he came from horses were a way of life.

He also insisted she learnt to drive a car while he was away on his lecture tours. She found the mechanics of this easy, but had poor road sense. She was humiliated when she failed her first driving test. Ben took her in hand, and she was anxious to please him. Her next test was a success, and she waved her pass in front of him, almost dancing with glee. He kissed her, almost as delighted as she. There was one accomplishment he left to no one but himself to teach her. He wanted her to learn to fly. He found she had a natural gift and loved nothing more than being at the controls of his Cessna. "Oh, it's wonderful! I feel so free."

Ben knew the feeling, and at the end of five months she was able to fly him to the various places he had interests in. He didn't neglect her in other ways. She was taught to read the sky at night. Very soon she could find Cassiopeia and Orion's Belt, as well as the more recognisable stars like the Pole Star and the planet Venus. One evening he made her use his very powerful telescope and find the Dog Star, Sirius. She wished to know why he was so interested in this particular star, but he merely smiled and put the telescope away.

The district surrounding the small harbour where Ben had moored his ship was increasingly popular with tourists, and accommodation was eagerly snapped up. Hotels were being built, and extra floors added to some properties where thought necessary. One such building site overlooked Ben's ship, and there were many wolf whistles when Ariadne sunbathed. This disturbed Ben, so a canopy was installed to give her some much-needed privacy. The builders were often immigrant workers and they didn't suspect their comments were understood by both Ben and Ariadne.

Ben was often away as his lectures were in great demand, especially in America. When away he insisted Ariadne moved into The Merlin. He felt easier in his mind, and an Arab boy he had recruited to clean the ship's galley was asked to sleep on board and keep an eye on things. "See, I have a knife and I am strong. Madame will be quite safe when I am around," the boy boasted to Ben.

When Ben returned, exhausted but pleased with the reception his lectures had received, he fell into Ariadne's arms, always eager to make love, and was never disappointed. They had been married seven months. Ben ordered a bottle of champagne, together with a superb dinner which included oysters. "Not that I need an aphrodisiac. You turn me on every time."

The following morning the girl couldn't face breakfast and was violently sick. "I feel terrible," she moaned to Ben.

He looked at her searchingly, took her pulse, and as she said her breasts were sore, asked when she had last had her feminine cycle.

"Oh dear! It's at least six weeks."

He smiled down at her. "I think, Darling, there is a possibility you are pregnant."

Ariadne was shocked but a testing kit from a chemist proved he was correct. Ben wasn't sure he was pleased or not. His plans would need to be put on hold for at least a year. He called Pag. "You had better get a message to the old man."

The girl missed Ben when he was away, as he often was – in America. His lectures on global warming and its effects on the oceans and climate were in great demand there. She missed his lovemaking, although at times it was extremely arduous – more than she really liked. When away, he telephoned her frequently or sent Emails, usually made up of love notes which made her blush.

She was several months pregnant when, on the spur of the moment, she thought it was time to visit her grandfather. He had ignored letters, and appeared to have cut her out of his life. Not sure what kind of reception she would receive, she dressed discreetly, wore the minimum of make-up, and for jewellery just her wedding ring and a string of pearls with matching earrings. Her hair was in a *chignon* – a style Ben liked. Arriving in London, she hired a chauffeur-driven car, and enjoyed the luxury of the comfortable Bentley, dozing on the way. She timed her visit to when she knew the housekeeper was absent. It was some time before he answered her ring. He didn't recognise her and thought she was someone trying to sell him something.

"It's me, Grandfather. Ariadne."

He looked at her keenly, amazed that this poised, elegant woman was the shy, awkward girl he had seen every summer. If nothing else, her husband had done this much for her. He gruffly asked her in, and asked where Ben was. She felt she had to explain Ben's absence. "He is lecturing in America. As he has such an active brain, he needs the stimulation lecturing gives him. He doesn't charge for his time – only travelling expenses. The lecture tour he is on now was booked ages ago. It's about global warming and its effects on the oceans and climate."

The old man just looked at her, not saying a word. An embarrassed Ariadne sadly asked, "Am I so very different, Grandfather?"

The girl looked at her grandfather, but he gave no reply. Taking a deep breath, Ariadne told him she was three months pregnant. "So you see why I haven't gone with him."

He coughed and said dryly, "Well, I was beginning to wonder if it was all over between you."

Trying to keep her temper, she said, "We are both very much in love, and will never part. Tests show the baby will be a boy, and we are the happiest parents-to-be, I can assure you. Ben is so caring, and couldn't do more for me if he tried. He is over the moon about the baby, and so am I."

She realised her grandfather was beginning to look his age and, hoping to lighten the atmosphere, said, "There is a case of your favourite whisky in the porch, which I hope you will accept and enjoy." Looking at her watch and realising his housekeeper must be due to return, she kissed her grandfather and made to leave.

"Next time you come, bring that errant husband with you."

Flinging her arms about him, she hugged him, agreeing to come when the baby was born. "I promise we will come as a family."

On the way back to London for her return flight to France it soon became clear to her that she had not been forgiven. She realised he hadn't even congratulated her, ignoring the fact the child would be his great-grandson. Even the mention of her pregnancy had not softened his attitude towards her.

After his granddaughter had left, the professor sat for some time thinking about her and the man she had married. He took out his laptop and soon found what he was looking for – information on Ben Haraldsson – and he was amazed. There wasn't a lot but enough for Ariadne's elderly relative to whistle in surprise. He was impressed with the number of awards bestowed on Ben, especially those given by France. It wasn't exactly a 'Who's Who'. There were certain things omitted, such as where he was born and family details, which the professor would have liked to have checked on, but enough to reveal his granddaughter had married a very wealthy man. No relatives were mentioned, so when Ben died, Ariadne would inherit a considerable fortune, the coming child being the only other claimant to his wealth. The professor decided there and then to leave what he had to his housekeeper. Ariadne was a little late arriving back in France as fog had delayed her. Ben was already there, and frantic with worry. The note she had left had somehow blown to the floor. They were both tired, but when Ariadne started to prepare a meal, Ben stopped her and insisted they spend the night in their suite at The Merlin. It was one occasion when it proved its worth. Their meal was sent up to them and, to please him, the girl found a little appetite. In spite of feeling tired Ben was still eager to make love. He told himself he should soon put lovemaking on hold as Ariadne's pregnancy must have priority. She was soon asleep in his arms, and he gently stroked her hair. For him it was "shining like the sun" and always would.

Eight months pregnant and so looking forward to the birth of her child, Ariadne was counting the days, as was Ben. However, their peaceful world was soon to be severely shattered. A call came from the chateau telling them that Ariadne's grandfather was gravely ill and her presence was urgently required in England. The journey took several hours, and they arrived at the house in time to find Ariadne's grandfather was dead and his coffin was just being removed from the house. Ariadne was extremely upset. "Couldn't you have waited until I arrived? I am his only close relative."

Mrs Kitchener the housekeeper sniffed, saying, "It is what he wished."

She then started emptying the larder and filling her basket. Ben was furious and soon put a stop to her pilfering, saying,

"My wife and I have not eaten for some hours," and returned the food to the larder. Mrs Kitchener left in a huff.

On entering her grandfather's study Ariadne gasped. It looked as if it had been hit by a whirlwind. Papers were strewn everywhere. "I think she must have been looking for his will. There is one, and I know where it is." She pointed to a small picture over the doorframe. "It's hidden behind that."

Ben easily worked out the combination and on scanning the will, it was clear to him that Ariadne had never been forgiven by her grandfather. On being told that as far as she knew there was only one copy, Ben set about adjusting the money left in her favour. He had no compunction about doing this as Ariadne had told him she thought her grandfather's housekeeper had cheated him in more ways than one. The reason she disliked Ariadne was that when left to cater on her own, the girl always managed to cut the household bills considerably He was shocked to discover that the housekeeper not only inherited the house, but a large slice of the professor's financial assets. Ben, finding many as yet unpaid bills, grimly took out his own cheque book and paid them all.

The funeral was something of an ordeal for Ariadne, as being eight months pregnant she found standing for too long a strain. The service was well attended by both the local community and a large number of the professor's former colleagues. As they sat in the small church waiting for the funeral service to start, the girl thought of her grandfather and wondered why they had not got on better. She knew he had been difficult but always generous in his own way to her. She wished she had let him know how grateful she had been that he had paid for her education and always welcomed her into his home, at least until her marriage.

The service was soon over and both she and Ben were amazed at the number of learned professors who came and expressed their condolences. Several asked if there were any papers among her grandfather's effects that needed to be published. Ben said he would search for any relevant documents.

Whilst engaged on this task, Ben moved a heavy reference book and an envelope fell out, and he was surprised to see it was addressed to himself. Thinking it was from Ariadne's grandfather, he dropped it into his pocket and forgot all about it until several days later when, looking for a pen he had mislaid, he came on it again. He almost threw it away, and fervently wished he *had* done when he read the amazing contents. It was to be yet one more nasty surprise from a fate determined to make him suffer.

The letter Ben had discovered was not from Ariadne's grandfather, but from her mother. In the envelope, carefully wrapped in tissue paper, was the ring she had snatched off his finger all those years ago. Shaken, he forced himself to read:

> *Dearest Ben,*
>
> I tried many times to locate you, without success. You promised to return. After two months had gone by I was frankly desperate. With no sign of you, and being scared, I took the only way out left to me. I married Armand Villiers Du Pre. I met him at the art school we were both attending. I wasn't in love with him. You were, and are, the only love of my life. You see, darling Ben, you left me pregnant. Armand cannot give me children. He had mumps when young, which has left him sterile. Ben, you and I have an adorable daughter. I have given her an unusual name "Ariadne". She has red hair – much deeper than mine – a turned-up nose, and green eyes. If this letter ever reaches you I hope you will meet. I am sure you will love her. She will be a beauty and break many hearts when she is older. Armand loves her but I fear his mother does not. …'

Ben could read no more. The words danced in front of his eyes. It hit him that his beloved wife was really his daughter. Tears poured down his face. He was screaming inside. Deny it he could not. He knew it was the truth.

Try as he might, Ben could see no way out of his dilemma. He staggered to his feet, threw his wallet on a table, and took all the small change he could find. Leaving the ship, he made his way to where he knew there were drinking dens – usually the haunt of the poorer members of the population. What was sold in them would not normally have passed his lips, but in his present mood he felt even poison would have been acceptable.

When he did not return for several nights the girl started to get worried. She finally contacted Pag, who fortunately was not on duty, and they decided he should search for Ben. Pag had a good idea where he would find his friend. He thought, 'He's gone on a bender.' He was proved right. Every bar he entered said the "big man" had been there at some time in the past three days. "Trying to get drunk," one barman said. Pag knew Ben could take a lot of drink and still seem sober. The third bar proved helpful. The owners said he had recently left, and they begged him to find the "big man" as he owed them money. Pag settled the bill, and found Ben slumped on the ground in a nearby alley.

"Come on; let's get you cleaned up." There was no word of reproach from Pag. He knew it must have been something terrible to have reduced Ben to such a state. Ben had not shaved for three days and, with filthy clothes, was a disgusting sight. He didn't seem to care, and just stared at Pag out of bleary, bloodshot eyes. He hiccupped and said, "Leave me alone. I'm not worth bothering about. You know, old friend, it might be best if I got so drunk I killed myself. I just can't see any future for Ariadne and myself."

How Pag managed to get Ben back to the ship, he never knew. It was a struggle. Fortunately it was not market day, and it was lunchtime, when most of the shutters on shops and houses were closed against the heat, so few people saw them.

Once on board Pag asked Ariadne to make some strong hot coffee. Ben was got into the shower but was unable to help himself. With a sigh, Pag undressed and got into the shower with Ben. He felt it was the least he could do. Then he gently undertook to make Ben respectable, including washing his hair. However, Ben's hands were so unsteady that Pag himself proceeded to get rid of Ben's beard. All the clothes Ben had been wearing were fit only to be burnt. Ariadne had laid out fresh clothes and, without a word, took the dirty things away. His boots and his leather jacket were, luckily, retrievable. Ben drank the coffee without a word and as tears rolled down Ben's cheeks, Pag waited to learn what terrible thing had occurred to reduce his friend to this state of despair.

Ben clutched Pag's arm. "Please don't let Ariadne come near me until I've told you what horrible thing I have uncovered about our relationship." Looking decidedly better, Ben asked, "Can I have a decent drink?"

He was handed a good measure of brandy, which he drank in one go. His hands were shaking and he was reluctant to begin.

"What is the problem?" Pag was determined to get to the bottom of whatever disaster had overtaken his friend. He was sure it was something frightful. If he had to force it out, so be it. Sighing deeply, Ben handed him Miranda's letter, which Pag read in silence. He was horrified. How had this awful thing happened to Ben, usually the most astute and aware of anyone he knew? Ariadne entered the cabin. Seeing the look on Pag's face, she said simply, "Tell me. I want to know. If I am involved, please don't hide things from me."

"Yes, you have a right to know." Pressing Ben's shoulder and saying, "I am outside if you need me," Pag left them together.

"Come and sit by me, Darling. There is something I have to tell you. I had hoped it could wait until the child is born but fate has made it necessary to tell you now. It is breaking my heart. My darling girl, where on earth do I begin?" He poured himself another drink and, seeing her frown, said, "Sorry, Darling; I need a little Dutch courage." He took her hands and kissed them gently, then, bracing himself, said, "You know I love you very much. You do believe I would never hurt you deliberately, and that is the truth."

Ariadne, puzzled by his insistence, agreed. Stammering, Ben told her exactly what had happened: how he had met her mother, all those years ago, in almost the same spot on the beach as he and Ariadne met. At first she thought it was just the fact he had kept his meetings with her mother a secret, but there was worse news to follow. Poor Ariadne! Her world was shattered. Gently Ben explained to the girl that he truly loved her more than he could have believed possible, and how he and her mother had met. He explained how short the relationship had been. The shock was too much for Ariadne. She got up and fell into Pag's arms in a dead faint. A few hours later it was clear the baby was on its way. In spite of her protests Ben insisted in carrying her out to the car, and they drove in silence to the very expensive clinic where she already had a room reserved. Ben was offered an adjoining suite reserved for expectant fathers. He was delighted to accept. He joined two other expectant dads outside. They were all longing to smoke but there was a notice in French, German and English banning this. The two companionably accepted one of Ben's very expensive cigars and waited, each in their own way. In less than three hours, when the sun was just rising, a nurse brought out a well-wrapped bundle and handed it to Ben. Smiling, she said, "A lovely boy, Mr Haraldsson."

He was a beautiful child, full of energy, and obviously hungry. As Ben held him, a small hand shot up and a small nail caught his father a slight blow on the chin. It drew a drop of blood. Ben was rueful. "First round to you, Phillipe. If your mama has no objection I will add Tauran to your name. You have been born under the sign of the bull Taurus. What could be more fitting?"

Ben took his son into an exhausted Ariadne. "Ten and a half

pounds, I understand. I think he is hungry."

Ariadne turned her head away. "Please don't ask me to feed him."

His father was firm. "I have a room here and I'll hold him to you myself at feeding times if I have to. If necessary we can get a wet nurse later."

The room where the mother and child lay was quiet. Both were asleep. They were watched over by the one who was father of both. The girl he had made his wife was not aware that he himself was the result of genetic engineering performed on his ancestors with the specific purpose of ensuring any offspring would be born with no defects. The Old People, whom he led, had, in the past, inter-married, with the result that many children were born less than perfect. One pleasing result of the genetic changes was that their race had increased in brainpower and grown in stature. Ben was a prime example of this.

He wondered what Ariadne would think if made aware of this fact. She had been worried sick in case she gave birth to a brain-damaged or deformed child. Now was not the time to tell her. The doctors and nurses were amazed how devoted he was to the two of them. He was always there at feeding times and willing to change a nappy, which many fathers hesitated at doing. They worried about him as well. He ate little and slept hardly at all. The head consultant chided him gently. "You do know, Mr Haraldsson, there are nurses to look after your wife and child, and you have paid for their services."

Ben merely smiled and said he loved performing the little attentions he gave them. He would hold Philippe in his arms, talking softly to him while Ariadne slept. She was still in a state of shock at the discovery of their close relationship. Ben wondered if she would ever come to terms with it. He had accepted it after a fashion and hoped that, in time, she could also.

He found it difficult to look on her as any other than his "little wife". While she slept he would kiss her and stroke her hair. No one saw the pain in his eyes, or the tears.

When they left the clinic after three days, Ben did not make for the harbour but chose a different route, which Ariadne was not familiar with. "Where are we going?"

Ben expected her to complain but she merely looked out of the car window. He hoped she had not lost her spirit. She had little to say, and just sat waiting patiently for whatever he had planned. "Trust me, Darling. I hope you will like where we are going, and who is waiting there to greet you."

Soon seagulls were wheeling around and the sea was visible. On Ben turning the car into a sheltered cove, Ariadne saw a cottage. It was charming, and the anxious girl wondered if this was where she was to stay. A comfortable woman with rosy cheeks, and a pronounced accent that could only be from the Highlands of Scotland, held out her hand to Ariadne. "Welcome, Madame. Shall I take the wee laddie? I think he must be wanting a drink and a nappy change."

A smiling Ben said, "This is Nurse Shona McGee."

Ariadne held out her hand. "I do hope we can be friends."

The motherly woman looked at her, thinking, 'She will need a lot of help, but that's what I am here for.'

Ben, relieved to see that the two women had taken to one another, went on his lecture tour reasonably happy. He had had six candidates to interview for the post of nanny. The first five were, in his opinion, hopeless. When the last one entered the room he was using at The Merlin, he knew she was the right one even before she spoke. He liked her accent, which was soft and pleasant. When he asked why she was seeking the position she was open and honest, telling him in her lilt that it was on doctors' orders. The Scottish weather was giving her chesty colds, and she was advised to find a milder climate. He read her glowing references and engaged her on the spot. He was never to regret his decision.

When Ben and Pag met up again, shortly after the birth of Ben's son, it was obvious Ben had changed. He was now embittered and angry. He told Pag, who could only feel for his friend, "A cruel fate intent on making me suffer, has dealt me yet another spiteful blow."

The light-hearted Ben, who had always laughed at life and treated whatever it chose to throw at him with a degree of contempt, seemed to Pag to be completely shattered. He was now a stern, hard individual. "It's no good, Pag. I still love my darling girl and want her still as my wife. I won't touch her. Because of the boy, divorce, or annulment if more appropriate, is out of the question as far as I am concerned. My next lecture tour of the States is almost due. I will go and complete it, and see how the land lies when I return. If she still loves me, then it will be a different ball game. As you know, time is getting short and I must make a decision as to when we leave for the Two Islands. The launch of *Pegasus XIII* – the ship for the joint American and Russian expedition to Jupiter – is almost due, and I am away for the next three weeks. We both have a lot of preparation still needing our attention. I am afraid a lot will, of necessity, be in your hands. It is feasible for tentative plans to be made to take off at the identical time as the larger ship. All eyes will be on it. No one, hopefully, will notice our small vessels."

Pag agreed with his chief, and Ben said he would send him a coded message to come for a last-minute briefing nearer the time.

In the past Ben had always found his lecture tours a pleasant interlude; however, not this time. He thought constantly of Ariadne and their son. What did the future hold for them? He turned the question over in his mind, finding it difficult to concentrate on his usual meticulous preparation of his lecture notes. He ate and drank very little on the flight and tried to sleep, but this also was impossible. A chatty American soon got bored with trying to make conversation with his taciturn fellow traveller.

Arriving in New York, Ben contacted Doctor Weng, who had recently moved into new premises. He was delighted to invite Ben to meet him. He wanted to show off his new apartment and, although Ben tried to conceal his feelings, the kind older man soon detected there was something wrong. He looked on Ben almost as a son, and was disturbed at the look on the younger man's face. Although he drank little himself, he always kept a good supply for the many people who were always dropping in. He was popular, and his Chinese or American colleagues knew they were always welcome. Without asking, he handed Ben a good measure of whisky. "Tell me, my boy, what's wrong. I can see you are in trouble."

Ben fell on his knees and buried his face in his friend's lap. He was soon sobbing. He had kept tears at bay, but now the floodgates were open.

It took a while for the kind man to sort out exactly what was wrong. He didn't fully understand until Ben handed him Miranda's letter. Like Pag before him, he too was deeply upset. "What are you going to do? You know cohabitation of this sort is against all known laws."

Ben recovered his composure a little, and drank some of the whisky. "Will it shock you to learn I am still very much in love with my darling girl? She is quite an exceptional human being."

Dr Weng said nothing, but shook his head sadly. Ben checked his watch and said he would call a cab to get to the airport for the long journey across America to Seattle, where he was due to lecture.

Before he left Ben apologised to Dr Weng for what he called "my unseemly display of emotion".

The kind man brushed this aside, saying, "What are friends for?" The doctor owed a lot to Ben, for it was on Ben's recommendation that he now held his post at the United Nations. It was a 'without portfolio' position, but one highly valued on all sides. Dr Weng was a very useful go-between when the Chinese delegates were at their most intractable, as he was able to see both sides of a problem and was an efficient member of the Chinese delegation. The Americans needed a lot of understanding. At times they just appeared dense and unable to comprehend the

Oriental mind. This was where Dr Weng was invaluable. He usually managed to sort out the most difficult problem.

Ben found Seattle a delightful city, and soon settled in a comfortable hotel near the conference centre. The group he was to lecture to were mostly female, and they just drooled over him. He was always a little mocking but they didn't understand his sense of humour. He heard one young girl say "Isn't he just dreamy!" and another: "Wouldn't I like to go to bed with him!" Ben was amused, and wondered what they would do if he agreed to this. Probably run a mile.

Having had good night's sleep, he was surprised to find he had slept for seven hours. He had his usual light breakfast, and asked at the hotel desk if they knew of any riding stables where he could hire the use of a horse. He was directed to the Washington Post stables and was able to have the use of Mr Pepper, a large chestnut with a bit of a peppery temper, hence his name. Ben soon showed him who was boss, and enjoyed his ride. He felt refreshed and able to meet his audience on his terms. He telephoned France, and Nurse Shona sleepily answered the phone. He had forgotten the different time zones but was assured that all was well.

Fortunately, finding a wet nurse for baby Philippe was easily solved when Hortense, a local girl, was taken on to help with the cleaning of the cottage. She had given birth to a baby girl a month before Philippe was born. She came from peasant stock and was strong. She happily fed both babies, treating them equally, and Philippe was never left hungry.

Ben telephoned daily from America enquiring about his family, and was reassured. Ariadne told Nurse McGee she needed a break, and disappeared for two weeks. Her whereabouts were a mystery, and when she returned she looked far from well. Ben returned from his American tour feeling worn out, and he looked it. The flight had been delayed by bad weather, and his luggage took some finding. He kept his temper as he wasn't the only one suffering. He remembered with nostalgia the days when it took only a few hours to cross the 'Pond', as the Atlantic is famously known. A group of wealthy enthusiasts were hoping to raise enough funds to build a new, smaller version of Concorde for the use of business people only. He would have willingly added his contribution, but his plans lay in a different direction.

He stepped wearily aboard his ship and was surprised to find Ariadne there, leaning over the rail, looking seawards. She did not move until he gently took a strand of her hair and kissed it. On turning, she was genuinely shocked by his appearance. Taking his arm, she led him into the cabin and helped him remove his travel-stained clothes and his boots. He looked thinner, and she doubted if he had eaten or slept much while he was away. "Go and have a shower, and I'll prepare a light meal for you."

He ate the soup, roll and omelette she had prepared, in silence. She watched him. He was very near to having a nervous breakdown. She knew she had to do something. He moved an aching shoulder and she leaned over and started to massage it.

The problem with massage, Ben found, was it aroused him sexually. Ariadne often used massage to make him relax, but when she saw how he was reacting, she leaned towards him and kissed the nape of his neck. He groaned. "Don't you know what you are doing to me, girl? Stop, please stop."

Stroking him gently, she said, "Darling, I know what you want and need. I am here for you. You can't deny your feelings."

His head was in a whirl. Oh yes, he desired her. His body was responding to her touch. "Darling, don't you realise: if I let you talk me into having you, we will put ourselves outside the law? It is illegal, however we look at it." He still hadn't recovered from his journey, and was deadly tired. He swayed towards her. He so wanted to sleep but his need for her was strong. "How is my lovely boy?"

The change of subject was almost laughable. She did laugh. "He is going to be a big strong boy. He looks like you already."

She saw he was weakening. "You know, Sweetheart, you have always looked on me as your 'little wife'. Am I not still that?"

"Yes, oh yes."

"We, Darling, are answerable to no one. Come."

He said, "Like Hercules found with Ariadne in the labyrinth, you have the threads that lead me, my Ariadne." Not only did they lead him, he thought, they bound him as well. Whatever the future, he knew their lives were linked by a chain so strong only death would sever it.

They were still so much in love. It had to happen. Ben touched her hair, then her face. They kissed. Soon, between tears and laughter, they made love. Ariadne was happy to see Ben relax and the haunted look disappear from his eyes, but he felt guilty. Would Ariadne now decide to go with him? The voyage would be long and difficult, and he wondered if it was asking too much of her. There was also the child to consider. Ben was impatient to finalise the journey, and needed to have her decision. "Darling, you know I have a mission to go on. I must be away for some time. I would like you to accompany me but if you do, Philippe must be left behind. I have great faith in Nurse McGee's ability to care for our child, but when our voyage is over and we are back here you will have lost your baby, and a small boy will have taken his place. Can you face that?"

Ariadne was shaken. "Will it really take that long?"

Ben nodded.

"I am with you, but I must say goodbye to Philippe," said Ariadne. Ben was pleased, and felt the only person suitable to act as guardian was Lucien, who was delighted to become Philippe's 'uncle'.

Much against his will, Ben went to see the old lady at the chateau. He had a score to settle with her, and let her know in no uncertain terms that he was aware of her deceit by not revealing the relationship of himself and Ariadne. He asked her also to take care of Philippe when Nurse McGee felt the child was too old for a nanny. "I am taking Ariadne to my people, and we will be away for some time. They will accept her and look after her."

Feeling she had got off lightly, the old woman agreed to all Ben's suggestions. Ben inspected what had been Ariadne's nursery. It was cold and damp. Plans were left with Lucien Gervaise for a new nursery and central heating for the chateau. Ben told the old lady not to interfere with Nurse McGee's routine, and any rows would be referred to Lucien and the upkeep of the chateau and the vineyard would cease. On the way out he picked up an old teddy bear and some of Ariadne's books.

Ben hid the toy and the books he found under his coat, and bade the old woman a cool farewell. He didn't know it, but it was the last time the two would meet. There was no love lost between them. He could never forgive her, and she plainly hated him. She was envious of his virility and his ability to have such a beautiful child. She knew poor Armand had been weak, and she had had to lie and pretend Ariadne was his offspring. Only the local doctor knew, and he had sided with her in hiding the truth.

When Ben originally opened Miranda's letter he didn't at first discover the two snapshots of Ariadne, but found them later. One was of a lovely little one-year-old with a mass of red curls and a freckled face; the other of her at five years of age, clutching her fifth-birthday present. The writing on the back said simply: 'Ariadne with her birthday present. She has called it Pooh Bear and loves it to bits.' The books were dog-eared and tatty but still readable. When at his lowest ebb, Ben would take the snapshots out and gently kiss them. They were precious to him as the only link he had of Ariadne as a small child. Before he left, he made Lucien promise to take regular photos of Philippe and not miss sending him birthday and other presents when the occasion warranted them. Nurse McGee was asked to tell the small boy, when he could understand, that he was not alone, and had parents who loved him and would be coming back for him. Ben held Philippe in his arms and spoke softly in his own language. It was heartbreaking. As he handed Philippe to Ariadne he was blinded by tears. She was just as upset and he could see it was a struggle, for her loyalty was divided. Touching her arm, he took the child and handed him to Nurse McGee. He had to be brutal or she would never go with him, and decide to stay. "Come; there is a lot for us to do. We leave shortly."

They returned to the ship in silence, each with their own thoughts.

PART THREE

JOURNEY TO THE TWO ISLANDS PLANET

Chapter One

The Journey

It was time to go, and everything was ready. Ben asked his second-in-command, Captain Anion, to come to his ship in his space commander's uniform. When he arrived, Ariadne was asked to join them. She almost laughed when she saw their uniforms. To her they appeared to be dressed as in a *Star Wars* movie. The laughter died on her lips when Ben pointed to a small bible lying in front of her and said dryly, "I believe it is the rule on this planet to swear not to reveal secrets. Will you now please swear you will not reveal to any human being what Captain Anion is about to tell you. I could tell you myself but doubt if you will believe me. I have requested him to explain to you exactly who we are, where we are from, and where we intend to return. Please start, Pag."

Ariadne reluctantly took the bible and took the oath, repeating the words after Ben. She sat on the edge of her seat, and had no inkling of the bombshell about to be dropped on her unsuspecting head. Pag began as ordered by Ben. "Ariadne, you know Ben as Ben Haraldsson. This is not his real name. I have the honour to serve Prince Benon D'A-Huartan. As his daughter, you are entitled to be called Princess. We are from a distant planet. Yes, we are extraterrestrials. Our planet, known to us as Usaurius, was destroyed by several disasters, including meteors and, we think, an asteroid. Ben and his grandfather found what we now call home. It is a small planet – bigger than Pluto but smaller than Earth. There are not many of us left. Ben, myself and a few others came to Earth, and we have tried to find ways of supplying our small population with food. They are on the brink of starvation. What we take, we pay for well and, as you know, Ben is trying to impress on those on Earth who care to listen, the danger of global warming. Remember this when you reach what is now our home. We call it the Two Islands planet. When you see it from space for the first time, you will understand."

Ben interrupted at this point and asked Ariadne to make some coffee for them all. This took a little time, as fresh coffee beans were used and ground first. When she returned with the tray, she nearly dropped it. Both of them had shaved their heads. "Our journey is so long, it is necessary."

"You are not going to shave my head." Ariadne tossed her mane of red hair, of which she was very proud. Ben just nodded his head.

"Oh, no! Please." She was clearly upset.

Pag went on to explain where their planet could be found. "It is hidden by Sirius, the Dog Star. Radio signals and probes sent out from Earth cannot locate it."

Touching a switch, Ben displayed a map of the solar system. Pag went on to tell the bemused girl some basic facts of astronomy. Realising it was too much for her to take in at one session, the younger man saluted his chief, saying it was time for him to leave. His commander agreed. The two embraced, and Ariadne was left alone with her lover – he to fill in what was still to be explained.

"Ariadne, I think you need to think very carefully about what I have to tell you. Even in this modern age, space travel, especially the distance we must go, is not for the faint-hearted. For instance, the use of water is severely restricted. You will have to use body wipes to keep clean."

He then went on to paint a picture of hardship and discomfort. Ariadne said she did not mind. As long as she was with him, nothing mattered.

Ariadne found it a lot to take in. Ben told her she would

need to learn the language of his people, which he could teach her. "Oh, one other important thing. You will need to be able to pilot and navigate our spaceship."

"Where is it?"

Ben smiled. "You are in it." He went on to explain that their little ship could be converted in half an hour into a very efficient spaceship. The galley and sleeping quarters would remain virtually the same. The difference would be in the way the ship was fuelled. He explained that navigation would be controlled from a flight deck, and there was a viewing platform with a strong telescopic window to view the heavens outside.

Her next question brought a frown to his face. "Now that is a 64-thousand-dollar question." Try as she might to get more information out of him, he would not disclose any further details about his fuel source. She knew flights into space were rarely undertaken because of the billions of dollars needed for the special fuel required. Even the wealthiest of nations found it difficult to find the money required. Usually at least two, and sometimes three, nations would put political considerations aside and unite in a common cause – that of investigating space. Ben knew that countdown for the lift-off of *Pegasus XIII* would take place shortly, weather permitting. It was to be manned by three Americans and a Russian. Their mission was to find out all they could about Jupiter and its moons. Ben knew it would be a one-way mission if the crew were not extremely careful. He told Ariadne, "Jupiter is a giant and we, that is, my people, believe it was instrumental in destroying our previous home, the Usaurian planet, now a derelict shell. Some of them cling to the hope that conditions will improve, so they can return, but that is an impossible dream." He sighed, then remembering where he was and what there was to do, he told the girl he hoped to have lift-off at the same time as the larger vessel. "I have every intention of getting near Jupiter before the other ship."

Because he knew the girl was still uncertain, Ben elaborated on all she would be expected to do on the journey. He explained weightlessness, and that they would float around, the only exception being in the small galley, where food was prepared and eaten. He made her don what was once called a siren suit. It was soft and comfortable. Not so the heavy boots she was asked to wear.

These had magnets in the soles, which gripped the floor and kept the wearer from floating. "Don't worry; you will soon get used to them." She hoped so. He then produced a bottle of champagne and handed her a glass. "You are with me?" he asked.

She merely nodded her head. She didn't realise the glass contained a powerful sleeping draught, and she was soon asleep.

To save her distress he then cut her hair – not completely, but close enough so that she looked like a very young boy, not his beautiful Ariadne. He made a plait from the long tresses he had cut and, rolling it up in a scarf she had given him, put it in his breast pocket. He wanted to have this part of her close. In long sessions while he sat at his flight console he would look at it and kiss it gently. He longed to kiss her, but schooled himself to deny himself, and asked her not to touch him or show her body, knowing it would weaken his resolve. Here was neither the time nor the place. When she awoke she was rather groggy, and it was a few minutes before she realised her hair had been cut. Choking back tears, she asked where they were.

"Come and look." The Moon appeared to be almost at touching distance. "Do you see those men working in their space suits?" he asked her. She saw them, and asked what they were doing. "Searching for traces of Helium 3, which incidentally is what powers this ship. They will locate it in time. Whichever power succeeds wins the space race. They would probably shoot us down if they knew I was using it. It doesn't cause damage or pollution, as their rockets are known to."

Ariadne was stunned into silence. All the nations involved in space exploration and research were on the Moon or had staked claims there, with one aim: to discover a supply of what the scientists called the 'wonder fuel' known as Helium 3. If it could be processed successfully, it would make ordinary fossil fuel as dead as the dodo. It was more friendly to the environment, and possibly cheaper. Hopes were high. A small quantity had already been found, and was in the process of being tested in a laboratory. Ben explained this to a wide-eyed Ariadne. "Yes, it is what this ship uses for fuel, and no, I have no intention of letting you see what this fuel looks like."

A taskmaster he certainly was. The two of them had always been tactile and loved to touch. This was now taboo. He knew his resolve not to kiss her would weaken at the slightest touch.

Ariadne had a lot to learn. She found Ben, as he had told her, a 'hard taskmaster'. He pressed her hard. On her part she wondered where the happy-go-lucky lover had gone. He was stern and unbending, and orders were given in his strange, difficult language, and she was expected to reply in the same tongue. She was a good linguist but found it difficult to master. Fortunately she had a photographic memory, which helped. In this respect she was very like him. She felt weak at times but was determined not to let him see it. Like him, she had her 'comforter'. She slept with the blue merino wool scarf he had given her when they first met. It was usually on her pillow while she slept, and sometimes she clutched it to her. She was unaware Ben knew she had it. Seeing her tear-stained face next to it almost broke his resolve. It was all he could do not to kiss his darling, but he reminded himself of his vow. Touching was *verboten.*

They had been in space nearly eight months, when Ben sprang a surprise on the girl. He ordered her to go to the viewing station. This was a raised platform with a telescopic glass screen used to inspect the outside area in detail. He ordered Ariadne to "pick a star". Feeling rather foolish, she pretended to pick up a star from the galaxy in front of her. Gently he then said, "Now your left hand," and she was then led to the 'safe' area. When he actually kissed her, she was stunned. What was going on? His next words explained it. "Happy birthday, Darling!" She had not been counting the months, and had no idea. "You are no longer a teenager," he teased her. "Come and see your cake." This made her laugh. "Oh, I nearly forgot." Into her astonished hands he pressed two beautiful diamond-and-sapphire earrings. The cake, about four inches square, had a solitary candle, which he lit, asking her to blow it out and make a wish.

Impulsively she flung her arms about him to kiss him before drawing back in dismay. He was not angry. She declared it was "the best birthday ever". Shortly after this they reached the vicinity of the great planet Jupiter. Ariadne awoke after her rest period to find everything was glowing a fierce red. Ben said, "I don't want to frighten you, but come and look at the 'Destroyer'. This is our name for Jupiter. It was responsible for the destruction of our lovely planet." It was an awesome sight. He then said, "Just imagine placing a bus in its centre. That is roughly the size Earth would appear if measured against such a giant."

He held her close. She dared not break the spell. "It won't be long now. Darling. You have been just wonderful and I have, from necessity, been an absolute brute. Can you forgive me?"

She could and would. She knew he still loved her, and nothing else mattered.

The long journey was nearly over. Not long after her birthday Ariadne awoke after her rest period to be immediately ordered by Ben to the viewing platform. "Look down there." He wanted her to see the Two Islands planet from space.

She gave a delighted gasp. "Oh yes, I can see it, and there are two islands, just like you say, and as shown on your badges." Ariadne was to discover the larger one was mostly desert, with very little water, whereas the smaller one was almost tropical. Both she and Ben hoped they could find enough land suitable for sowing crops, which were badly needed, otherwise the small population would starve. The people she would come to love had no knowledge of agriculture and land management. Ben had tried in the past to teach them about agriculture, with little success. Ariadne hoped she could succeed, and was determined to try. Ben was dismayed to find they were a canister of oxygen short, and when he started to look ill Ariadne was terrified. He managed to gasp, "You must land the ship on the blue arrow. Please, girl. I can't."

He started to ramble and hallucinate, and his nose bled. He was an awful colour and his breathing was laboured. He managed to gasp two more words: "Space bends" before passing out. Ariadne tried to remember all he had told her about the condition. Their ship was now near enough for communication and she called Pag Anion, praying he would answer. He did, and she explained the position, saying she thought Ben had "space bends". She was trying to give Ben the kiss of life and pilot the plane at the same time. She told Pag she was going to come in to land, and on him asking her if she wished an escort she tersely replied, "No time. Just have your decompression chamber ready."

Pag watched her come down. His heart was in his mouth as he watched an incredible feat of flying. Suddenly she was there, and Pag took over. Ben was quickly seen to and the doctor sent for. The Space Riders were amazed a mere girl had been flying the craft, but what a girl! And one with red hair.

Chapter Two

The Two Planets

Lying in the quiet hospital room, Ben felt he was being kept unnecessarily. He knew he had a lot to do. He fretted and was worried about Ariadne. How was she? He wished Pag would come to see him. Dr Fuharan watched his patient. Ben had been put in a beautiful, comfortable room. He had nothing to do but rest. The journey had told on his usually strong constitution. How could the doctor tell someone like Ben that age was starting to catch up with him?

Meanwhile Ariadne was paying her respects to the head of the clan, Prince Bron. He was always referred to as the 'old prince'. In fact he was just sixty-five in Earth years. He looked sternly at Ariadne and fired a series of questions at her. Where, he wished to know, was the male heir he had been led to believe had been born. Ariadne's look was defiant. The Prince almost laughed. She was so like her father. Clearly he would have known, even if a disconcerted Pagan had not told him. She reminded him of Ben when he was the girl's age. That look was the sort of defiant look he had received on many occasions. He hoped she would not prove such a problem as her father had been when young. Ben had always been a law unto himself. Ariadne tried to sidestep the old man's questions about the male heir. She told him simply the child was too young to make the journey. The next question was more difficult to deal with. "His mother?"

"Oh, she is of no consequence".

Bron could get nothing more out of her, and dismissed her

with a wave of his hand. He felt there were questions he would ask of Ben, and get answers.

Glad to escape, Ariadne made her way to the hospital – the only building not enclosed in a cave. It was cool and surprisingly modern. It could have held its own with the best in Europe. Ben was delighted to see her. "Have you had the third degree from the old man?" he wanted to know. She assured him it wasn't that bad. "Please get me out of here, Darling," Ben said.

Dr Fuharan entered, and introductions were made.

Feeling his meeting with the girl Ben had brought with him had been less than satisfactory, Prince Bron made his way to the hospital centre to see Ben. The girl had been very evasive and the old man, astute leader that he was, in no way would be denied the truth. Did the pair of them think he was a fool? He had been warned by Doctor Fuharan that Ben was still in a very fragile state, and excitement of any kind was to be avoided.

"We shall see." The thought came to him that surprise was the best weapon to use. Taking his nephew's feverish hand in his own cold and wrinkled one, he said gently, "Your daughter is a delightful girl, but I want news of your wife. Why did you not bring her with you?"

Ben, trying to focus on his uncle through the nausea and pain he still felt, said wearily, "Cannot this be left to another time? I am still so tired." For once, the old prince was a little ashamed.

"Please," Ben whispered, "see Pag; he will tell you all you need to know." With this remark Ben's eyes closed, and it was clear he was asleep.

As he left the room where his nephew lay, the prince was gratified to see Pagan walking towards him. "Come, Pagan; I want a word with you."

Guessing what it would be about, Pag, noticing a small side room unoccupied said "This looks private," and drew the old prince into it. "I understand you are aware of the great secret that appears to hang over the identity of Ben's wife and the mother of his son. He says I am to ask you about it as you are fully apprised of all the facts. Is that so?"

Pag sighed and took a long breath. "Yes I do know, and it is a great tragedy for my friend Ben. He nearly went out of his mind when the truth came out." Pag then went on to tell the whole wretched tale. Prince Bron was shocked and extremely sorry for the pair of them.

Pag continued, "They are still so much in love. Ariadne made a big sacrifice coming here. It was a wrench leaving the child behind, but she will do anything for Ben. Her level head saved Ben's life. She is quite a superb flyer." Pag then explained how Ariadne had landed their craft exactly where it could be easily connected with the decompression chamber that helped save Ben's life. An admiring Pag said, "She is a girl in a thousand, and we should all be very proud of her."

The Space Riders already were. To them she was their "little princess" and they adopted her as their mascot. They were delighted when she offered to fly patrols with them when she had the time, and Pag said he would ask Ben if this could be arranged.

The old prince wasn't easily mollified, and was determined to keep the couple apart as much as he could. He arranged for Ariadne to work on the larger island; and Ben, when he was well and fit to work, to stay on the smaller island. This was quite the best plan, as the hospital and its facilities were near at hand if Ben needed help at any time. The prince expected a scene when this was explained to Ben, but Ben merely growled. He had his own plans, and nothing Uncle Bron could propose would alter them. Ben had already made his love for Ariadne known in the hospital, and news of it soon spread. Some – the females in particular – thought it very romantic, and some giggled over the implications. On the whole the male reaction was a little more guarded. Most felt it was his affair, and what had happened had been known to happen among their people in the past. A few, like Mu-Ani and her husband Prince Dron, were mildly amused and not a little pleased at the position Ben was in. "He is an arrogant bastard and just too full of himself. This cuts him down to size." There was no love lost between Prince Dron and Ben. They cordially disliked each other and this remark was echoed by Prince Dron's wife Mu-Ani. Meanwhile, in his hospital bed Ben continued to fret. He was frustrated by his physical weakness, and wanted to get back to his own quarters. He started to long for a drink and a smoke, but both were forbidden by a watchful Doctor Fuharan. He was on a course of tablets, and drink was strictly off the menu.

Ariadne was amazed when Pag proudly showed the suite of rooms Ben had provided for her. He had thought of everything. The bed was extremely comfortable and there were beautiful tapestries hanging on the walls. The floor was tiled, and with fluffy rugs in her favourite shade of coffee. Pag told her of the underground springs heating the complex, which kept it at an even temperature. She was dumbfounded when she saw the Jacuzzi in the bathroom. There was a large sitting room, which she was to share with Ben. There were Old Masters on the walls, and a drinks cabinet and a bar stocked with every kind of wine and spirit one could wish for. It was extremely modern. The only thing missing was a TV. There was a screen, which could be pulled down to show films, of which there was a good supply. Whatever the rest of the population went without, it was clear their prince wanted for nothing. A veranda was visible through swing doors, and the smell of his expensive cigars hung in the air. "Well, I don't know what to say. It appears Ben was expecting me to come here some time." Pag told her the room had been furnished from the date of their marriage, with items brought gradually over the year from Earth, "Usually by me," Pag added.

He left her to bathe and wash her hair. What a luxury! On entering the bedroom she found one of the ladies she had seen earlier. The girl was nervous. "I am called Antika, and His Excellency says I am to serve you, if I suit you, Madame." The girl then shyly asked if there was anything she could do for Ariadne.

"Well, I am rather hungry."

Ariadne was warned the diet was very limited on Two Islands planet, but she enjoyed the meats and fruits the girl brought. She knew she was going to miss bread, as there were no cereal crops grown. Flour was unknown, so, no bread. Ariadne made do with some biscuits she had brought from the ship.

The next few days were busy ones for Ariadne. Pag took her on a tour of the larger island. It was, as she had suspected, mostly a barren waste. She knew there must be water somewhere, otherwise how would the wild horses that lived on it survive? She was told it was believed there was a secret valley, where there was grass and plenty of water. So far no one had been able to keep up with the herds. Their stampedes raised dust clouds. When anyone bold enough tried to keep up with them the horses disappeared.

Returning once more to the hospital to see Ben that evening, she found he was restless and threatening to leave. He asked again how she was getting on with Uncle Bron.

"Oh, he's no trouble. I try to keep out of his way."

Ariadne sought the advice of Dr Fuharan. She suggested that Ben be kept under sedation for his own good. This was agreed and the good doctor marvelled at the girl's common sense. Ben was then sedated for a full day. It would give his body a chance to recover, they hoped. It had certainly taken a battering. He would never voluntarily give in to illness. Ariadne left and got on with the tasks she had set herself.

She took soil samples, and pegged and tagged certain areas. She was watched by a group of children and some adults, who asked questions. She patiently tried to explain. It appeared they had no idea how to work the land. She could see it was going to be hard work getting her message across. No wonder Ben said they were like children. There did appear to be two distinct sorts of people: the Old Ones, of whom Ben was the leader, and those they contemptuously called the Others. She felt she would need to start educating the children first. Some of them had asked intelligent questions. Perhaps they were not so stupid as previously believed.

The routine was gruelling, with rising at 4.00 a.m. Time was so different to Earth, the day being twenty-two hours long. The heat was too intense between 11.00 a.m. and 4.00 p.m. for anyone to work. The regulated temperature in the caves was welcome. The long siesta was used for eating and socialising. Ariadne chose to take a proper rest during this time. The food was starting to be very boring. She knew she should try to eat, but missed Ben's company. It had always been lively at mealtimes.

On the fifth morning she was a little late in getting up. She was half awake, aware her nose was itching. Trying to brush away what she thought must be a fly, she felt fingers. Her eyes flew open. Ben was there. "Coffee up!" He was smiling down at her.

"Have you permission to be out of hospital?"

"No. I just could not stand it another minute." He removed the light covering, which was all she needed, saying, "Now if you don't get up this minute I am going to get randy. You know what that will lead to."

She jumped out of bed, nearly spilling the steaming hot cup of coffee. "Be ready in twenty minutes. I have two I want you to meet," he demanded.

She was soon ready, and he led her to neat stables. He said, "I want you to meet Bramin and Bramina, my horses."

The larger of the animals was a big black stallion. Bramina, his sister, was smaller and gentler. The girl was enchanted. "Oh, they are just darlings." The mare was nudging her, and Ben, laughing, said, "Give her some of these sugar-lumps and she will be your friend for life."

It was a beautiful morning – the ideal time to take a ride, as the air was cool and fresh, with just a slight breeze. Ariadne found Bramina a delight to ride. After the cramped conditions on the spaceship it was wonderful to exercise again. Both she and Ben were enjoying their rides. Ben seemed to have recaptured his old *joie de vivre*. If caught in the right mood he could be a marvellous companion. The sun was rising a fierce red. As they came to the top of a hill, Ben suddenly ordered the girl to take off her riding hat. She did so. Leaning over, he took a strand of her hair in his hand. "See, Darling, your hair is the same colour as our sun up there. Now you can see why I say that for me it is always shining like the sun. Am I not right?"

They dismounted, and he found a patch of shade. He was just about to kiss her when the jingle of harnesses could be heard as two riders approached. They were the two people he disliked the most: Mu-Ani, to whom he had been betrothed, and Prince Dron. Mu-Ani had never forgiven Ben for not marrying her, and to shame him had married Prince Dron, known to all as the Dronk. He was a hunchback, and hated Ben. He found his wife a bit of a shrew, and it was clear who wore the trousers. Now Mu-Ani jeered at the two on the ground, who were standing rather close together. "Look. Benon's showing the sights to his daughter, or is it his lover? I'm not sure." Addressing Ariadne, she said, "Good morning, my dear. I do hope Benon treats you with more consideration than he has shown to me in the past." With a curt nod to Ben, she dug her heels into her horse's flank and galloped off. Prince Dron barely acknowledged them, and hastened after his wife.

The morning was spoilt for Ben and Ariadne. A furious Ben turned his mount and rode back in silence. The sun, as if agreeing with them, went in. One minute it was a beautiful red; the next, invisible behind a blue haze.

A furiously angry Ben, without a word, headed back. The girl was desperately sorry for him. It appeared their alliance was common knowledge. He disappeared when the horses were stabled. He went to confront Uncle Bron. He told him of the insult. His reply was typical. "You have only yourself to blame.

You did jilt her when you were betrothed. It is no wonder she likes to retaliate when the occasion arises."

"No I did not jilt her," was the furious reply. "She told me to stay here, marry her and give her children. I, as you know, had work to do, which kept me away most of the time."

The next three months were busy ones for both Ben and the girl. He had so many tasks that he had difficulty in keeping to a fixed schedule. Not only did he act as vet to the few domestic animals the people on both islands possessed, but shot deer and wild oxen, which would be salted and stored for future use. He kept an eye on the Space Riders, although Pag was now virtually in command. He had to endure endless sessions with the Council – made up of the ten members picked from Old People families. They were supposed to have brains. Ben lost patience with them. They took too long, in his estimation, to reach conclusions. He just pressed ahead and did as he wished.

The thing he did enjoy was helping Dr Fuharan with operations. The hospital badly needed additional assistance, requiring an extra doctor and more nursing staff. He was too busy to notice Ariadne was losing weight and not looking her usual happy self. She was just worn out. At night they were both ready for bed, and she was lucky if she received a hasty kiss on the cheek before they both collapsed in exhaustion. Ben liked to wind down with a drink and a smoke. He found he was now too tired to bother, and often collapsed fully clothed on his bed. In spite of being tired, Ben was finding it hard to sleep.

Uncle Bron decided to give them both a little respite. He suggested his nephew take his daughter to a small island, which if it grew any bigger, would mean the planet would need to be called the 'Three Islands planet'. It was thought deserted, but had a pool with beautiful clear water – an ideal spot for them to enjoy a bathe. It was lush, with plants; and a small animal akin to Earth's rabbit had been seen. Ben took his gun with them. If the chance came, he would shoot one and see if it was good for the pot. They spent a blissful couple of hours until the heat drove them to search for shelter. They found a cave and were just about to enter, when Ben said to the girl, "Keep quite still. Don't move a muscle."

She froze. The sound of the gun going off was like an explosion in the small space. Ariadne had never been so scared. "What is it? What kind of animal could live here?"

"I think it must be a wild dog. Some of our dogs escaped when we first settled here. I will have to arrange to get them shot. We had better get away in case there any more about."

Ariadne shuddered, looking with distaste at the animal lying at her feet. They had barely reached the small plane, when in the distance more dogs were seen. They must have smelt blood and were looking forward to a feast.

"The original dogs were beautiful animals," Ben explained, "but over the years the best had been lost and only the strong, wild ones survived."

Still shaken from the encounter with the wild dog, Ariadne was working on the large island, supervising the digging of channels to take irrigation water she had found by dowsing. She had not thought she could make it work but, to her intense delight, she had, and she hoped there would be enough to supply the crops she was sowing: root vegetables, including onions, potatoes and salad tomatoes, which she hoped would eventually be sufficient to supplement the very meagre fare composed mainly of dried meat, some wild fruit, and honey from the bees which, having no predators, had free range over the many wild flowers. The honey they supplied took the place of sugar. A kind of sugar was made from it but it was not processed as on Earth, though Ben had assured her it was just as good.

The day was extremely hot and Ariadne's water bottle was leaking, and she became dehydrated. Suddenly she called out to Pag, who was working near her, and she fell into his arms. When he realised it was not a simple faint he called Ben and Doctor Fuharan. On Ben's instructions she was taken to her own room. Ben was distraught, and blamed himself for her condition.

Doctor Fuharan took Ben on one side and asked when the girl had last had her monthly cycle. An embarrassed Ben said, "Not often. I was away and found her womb and an ovary removed when I returned. I never found out who performed the operation, or why."

Doctor Fuharan was dismayed that such an operation had been performed on a young and apparently healthy girl.

Slowly her strength returned. Dr Fuharan never told Ben how close he had been to losing her. When she regained her faculties, after what seemed an age to her lover, she was too weak to even smile. Ben worried as how to keep her happy and said anyone caring to visit her should choose the cooler parts of the day as she needed to rest. He had a bed-chair put in a shady spot where she could receive visitors, and many came, so he had to limit the number. The children were not restricted, and gales of laughter could be heard. Ben felt it wiser to keep out of the way when the children were there. They tended to fall silent at the sight of him. When she was allowed to get up she was, true to his promise, allowed to spend some time with the Space Riders. They still called her their "little princess" and went out of their way to spoil her. All much taller than her, they fussed over her until she called out "Enough!" in protest. She became their confidante, and listened to their problems. She soon found their main bone of contention. They often travelled with Pag to other space stations, where there was a good supply of things they knew their girlfriends would love: nylons, chocolates, perfume etc, but had no money to purchase. Pag always had plenty of money in various currencies, and out of the kindness of his heart would buy the odd item. Ariadne asked Ben why they were not paid, and suggested they should receive a salary according to rank and experience. "After all, Pag receives a good salary, as do all flyers, whether flying civilian or military planes."

Ben said he would consider this "when I have the time".

Ariadne's brain was still active although she was still physically weak. Ben was intrigued when he found her writing. "You are an industrious little thing. What is it all about? Do tell." But she wouldn't let him even glimpse at her scribbling, and kept it well hidden when he was around. It would all be disclosed at the appropriate moment.

She overheard Ben and Pag discussing the lack of some device for their spaceships which could possibly reduce the time it took to travel between Earth and the Two Islands planet. She had an idea and, while still fresh in her mind, quickly put it down on some graph paper she had found among her old school books that Ben had brought from the chateau on his last visit. She shyly presented it to them. She wondered if they would even look at it. They did, and were impressed.

The chief engineer was called to see it, and he was very excited. "Whoever thought up this deserves our thanks."

He hurried away, saying he would immediately make a trial pattern. When it was installed on their test plane the gadget, which incorporated an aileron, was hardly visible, and the structure of the plane was not altered. They hoped speed could be increased. Ben and Pag argued between themselves who should test it first. "You cannot, as our leader, be permitted to risk it," Ben was told, and Ben's reply was, "It is my duty, as leader of the Space Riders, to be the first."

Ariadne had just returned from patrol and she quietly put her helmet back on and slid into the test plane. She called the control centre for permission to take off, and was away before the two arguing realised what she was doing. They tried to stop her but she merely blew them a kiss and took off. Ben said afterwards he had died a thousand deaths. Laughing, Pag said, "My friend, you should have seen your face. It was a picture!"

Ariadne performed like an ace pilot. She knew what was required, and put the plane through every sort of acrobatic twist and turn. Ben rushed to help her out of the craft, saying, "I don't know whether to shake or kiss you," and did both.

First Pag and then Ben tested the plane with the new device, and both were satisfied with its performance. As Ben descended, he brushed against his transceiver. There was a loud atmospheric crackle and, to his surprise, a voice speaking with a cool American accent. It was an urgent mayday call for assistance from the spaceship *Pegasus XIII.* The caller was trying to reach one of Earth's space stations. Ben knew they were out of range. Looking at Pag, he said, "Yes, yes I know. We can't leave them up there. They may never get themselves out of the mess they are now in." Picking up his communicator, he drawled, "Your call for assistance has been heard. You are close to an inhabited planet and we are humanoid like you. You will be escorted into land. Please note the following..." Then Ben gave them technical data to assist their landing. "Oh, one other thing: no weapons of any kind are to be brought. I hope this is clear. The light here can be trying until you adapt. My advice is: keep your visors in place. You will also find the atmosphere a problem as the air is similar to that found in the Andes or the Alps on Earth."

The four who stumbled out of their spaceship were dazed and not a little nervous as to what kind of reception they would have. Was it a trap, and would they all be killed? They tottered a little on reaching the ground, and were like sailors coming ashore after a long voyage and needing to find the use of their legs. They were met by a line of uniformed, extremely tall men holding weapons at the ready. This was very unnerving, but Colonel Ed Godber held his head high. He was noticing a super-looking redhead standing by the one who must be their chief. The chief-like one didn't look pleased to see the four visitors from Earth but the sight of the girl cheered the colonel up. She at least was glad to see them, and was smiling at them warmly.

If she was aware of the colonel's interest in her, Ariadne gave no sign. He thought, "She must be human, not an alien like the others." He had noticed her French accent and her very human gesture when she tried to rub a smudge off her face. She was ordered by the tall leader to take the four visitors from

Earth somewhere. They all nervously followed her along a long corridor, which appeared to be carved out of rock. Her voice interrupted the colonel's thoughts as she said, "Please obey all orders he gives you. Is that clear?" It was; they were all aware he had saved their lives.

They were shown into a spacious suite of rooms next to Ariadne's own. There was some hesitation on their part when, not sparing their blushes, she requested them to remove all their clothing and place it with their footwear in a large container at the end of the room. She explained it would sterilise everything, and the clothes would be ready to wear again in about half an hour.

There was an alcove with a separate bed, and she suggested that the colonel, as leader, might like to use it. He thanked her for her thoughtfulness. She brushed his remark aside and turning to the Russian, said sharply, "Major, will you please give me the knife you have hidden. You will be in trouble if Prince Benon finds you have it."

The crafty Russian sheepishly handed it over with a grimace. When Ariadne left them he was firmly reprimanded by his chief. Ariadne returned with a pile of large towels and toiletries. "These are mine and, just this once, you may use my Jacuzzi. She showed them where it was and told the colonel he should be ready for debriefing in half an hour, and would be collected and escorted to the prince. "You will be met by one of our flyers. We call them our Space Riders, and they are the guardians of this planet." The four all looked at one another, not sure what to think of the strange situation they were in.

The four men from planet Earth looked with amazement at their luxurious apartment. It was not at all what they expected. From space, the planet they were now on did not appear to have much to recommend it, and certainly did not appear capable of providing such beautiful things. They had thought it merely a barren waste. Ariadne returned and, seeing their surprise, explained that what they saw had been brought from Earth over a long period. "Let me introduce myself. I am Ariadne Villiers Du Pre Haraldsson, and I am the daughter of Prince Benon. I consider myself French, as I was born and brought up there."

Colonel Godber introduced his crew. "This is Commander Tubbs, my second-in-command, and our ensign Milo Lawrence. He is due for promotion when we return, if he decides to stay in the service. I do know he wishes to continue training to be a doctor. He acted as our medic on the journey here." Then adding, "I'm Colonel Ed Godber and their leader."

The Russian snapped to attention, clicking his heels. Bowing low, he said, "I am Major Gregor Pavel Orlevski, and I think I have the honour of addressing Princess Ariadne. I am correct, yes?" He kissed Ariadne's hand and saluted.

"Yes, Major, you are correct, but please, no titles. Just call me Ariadne." When she heard the commander's first name was Tallyrand, she said with a smile, "Named after a famous Frenchman, of course."

His reply set her giggling. "Well, my mom saw it on a biscuit tin and kinda liked it."

Turning to the Russian, she asked, "What are you usually called, Major?"

She addressed him in Russian but he replied in fluent French, "Oh, I am usually called Pav, and I am a Cossack."

Ariadne clapped her hands. "If you are a Cossack, you must know all there is to know about horses. We have many here – some tame and some still wild. I am sure you could give us a lot of help."

The Russian beamed. "Show me the way."

Ariadne hurried away to let Ben know all she had learnt of their visitors, and how they could be useful.

The American colonel was nervous, and wondered what form his debriefing would take. He was surprised to see Ben wearing neat jeans, a pale blue silk shirt, and loafers on his feet. The colonel, however, kept things as formal as he could. "How do I address you, Sir?"

Ben raised an eyebrow. "Please just call me Ben. You may find on occasions I am addressed as Your Excellency. I wish to make this as easy as possible for you. Here. Help yourself." He pushed over a box of his cigars, in a generous gesture as they were his very expensive Havanas. "Would you like a drink? There is a good selection."

The debriefing, however, then began in earnest. "I assume you got rather too close to Jupiter. It can be unpredictable at times, and tends to retaliate."

Colonel Godber had to agree this was the case, but gave no names away. It had been the overenthusiastic Russian who was to blame, but the colonel was loyal to his crew, and did not name the culprit.

Ben was no fool, and a lot of technical data was then gone into, and the American was amazed at the other's knowledge. After an hour had gone by the man didn't know whether he was on his head or his heels. Ariadne came in with a glass of water and tablets. She frowned when she saw Ben had been drinking. "You know you are not supposed to drink when you are on these tablets."

Ben shrugged. "One must be hospitable, my dear."

She gave in but left the tablets where he could see them. Although tired, Ben saw the rest of the crew, and called Ariadne in to interpret for the Russian, but was delighted to hear he spoke fluent French. He was also pleased to hear that Major Orlevski was a Cossack and knew how to handle horses. "I gather Madame has told you we have many wild and tame horses here, and could do with your expertise."

The Russian agreed, and said he would be delighted to assist in any way possible.

Commander Tubbs was the ideal person to team up with Ariadne. He was already an experienced rancher, and used to dealing with problems as they arose calmly and simply. He could find water where no one else suspected it could be. He adopted an avuncular attitude towards Ariadne, and the girl teased him, calling him Uncle Tally, which he took in good part.

Doctor Fuharan welcomed the assistance Milo was able to give, and the two found they worked well together. Ben was well pleased, and hoped Milo would remain on the Two Islands planet and think seriously about staying. Ariadne spluttered with laughter when she discovered Milo's real names were Michaelo Angelo Fidelio Zola Lorenzo. "Now you can see why I changed it."

She agreed, and made him promise not to divulge that her baptismal names were Ariadne Delores Diana Francianne Nicolle Maria Hildegarde. She told him she thought even Ben was unaware of all her names.

Colonel Godber worked with Ben. There was much to be done before the Earthlings' craft – a large shuttle – could be considered safe to launch into space again. Ben told him it would take several weeks working round the clock before it was ready. The colonel accepted this with dismay, but realised they were lucky to have such an able leader as Ben to provide the help they needed.

Meanwhile Major Pav, as he was soon called, was delighted to be working again with horses, and was willing to share his expertise with anyone interested.

Ben and Ariadne could not have chosen four more capable men to assist them. Both Ben and Ariadne were delighted with the four strangers from Earth. They discussed how the four could be used to help them as they relaxed over their simple evening meal. Ben was in a strange mood, and Ariadne thought she recognised the signs. They had both been too busy for more than the odd kiss or caress. It was clear to the girl that he now wanted something more. She thought he had accepted she was his daughter, but it was obvious he had not. He took a strand of her hair, saying, "Always shining like the sun." He kissed it, and then the nape of her neck. He knew how to arouse her. He told her, "I still look on you as my 'little wife', and that will never change." Powerless to resist him, she let him make love to her. He was very demanding and amorous. "This is how a Usaurian makes love to his woman," and it left her completely exhausted. He was puzzled. "Don't you love me any more?" Oh yes she did, and he knew it. When she at last broke away from him, he followed her into her bedroom. The feverish moodiness of the previous hour had gone. "Shut your eyes, Darling. I have a surprise for you. An old friend you haven't seen in years is here."

Wondering what he was up to, she was led to her bed. Opening her eyes, she saw a strange little figure sitting on her pillow. "Why, it's Pooh Bear!"

It was indeed. Ben had asked Antika to make a kind of uniform for it, after giving the bear a good clean. He said with a sardonic grin, "I think Pooh Bear had better act as referee. When I desire to have my evil way with you and if you desire my company, sit him on this chair. If not, take him to bed, and I will know what your feelings are."

With this final remark he turned and left the room. She knew he was proud and would not beg for her favours. It took Ariadne a while to realise Ben must have picked up the toy on his last visit to the chateau. She hadn't seen the small elegant chair before, and had to smile at his sheer nerve.

One morning Ben arose, feeling that all was going to plan, when he heard a commotion outside his quarters. On investigating, he found one of the young Space Riders nearly in tears. When he made sense of the boy's rambling explanation it was to find, to his dismay, that his ship had been damaged in the night. It was fortunate he had taken the precaution of locking it so the inside was still secure. The damage meant the return to Earth would be further delayed. The work on *Pegasus XIII* was nearly finished and he didn't think Colonel Godber or his crew would be pleased either at the extra delay. He had an idea who was responsible: Mu-Ani or her husband. The Dronk, he knew, was quite capable of such an act of vandalism. Pag was asked to double the guards, but Ben thought bitterly that it was shutting the stable door after the horse had bolted.

To cheer them up he suggested a dinner be given for the four visitors, and Ariadne was asked to prepare a menu for his approval. She was dismayed, as their fare was so limited. Milo came to the rescue. He was in charge of stores on his spaceship, and gave her a tube of cream, some butter, and a roll of bread in a tube. This was a rare treat and was easily heated. If nothing else, it would help eke out their own limited supplies. Ariadne found some wild mushrooms and made a soup, adding some of the cream and a herb like garlic. The meat was beef, and the first vegetable crop was now ready for use. New potatoes and runner beans were available. The dessert was compote of fruits, with the remainder of the cream. Ben approved, and the girl breathed a sigh of relief.

The dinner given in honour of the visitors from Earth should have been a success. When Ben saw the gown Ariadne was wearing, he looked extremely angry. Only Tally saw the little exchange. The girl flushed, stammered "Excuse me," and fled. When she returned, looking absolutely fantastic in the traditional Chinese cheongsam, Ben was even more angry, but because of his guests he controlled his temper. The robe was slit to the knee on one side. On the other her thigh and panties were clearly visible. The Russian openly leered. Milo just said, "Wow." The two senior members just stared. They couldn't take their eyes off her. Her father had been annoyed because, her having lost weight, the gown she originally wore was badly fitting and revealed far too much from the neck downwards. The Chinese costume fitted her well. The material was silver brocade with a dragon's head in front, and finished off with a dragon's tail at the back. All picked out in red. She had dressed her hair so it came down over one shoulder. It was odd but it brought back memories to Ben of Fanny Su. He recalled she had worn her hair that way. It made him even more angry. The four guests could sense the tension but went out of their way to praise the meal. There was one further moment of embarrassment when Ben asked his daughter to say grace. She, feeling miserable, could not remember the words required. All she could think of was the Latin grace she said at school. She used this. Everyone held their breath. Ben was an affable host but anger was seething. When the meal was over and the couple were alone, he could contain his anger no longer.

He followed her into her bedroom. Her chin was up in the manner Uncle Bron would have recognised as being so like her father. They glared at one another, and Ben grabbed her by the shoulders, shaking her severely. Still she said nothing. Enraged, he said, "Take that thing off, or I will take it off for you." The zip stuck, and he tore the dress almost in pieces before it came away, and she stood before him like a naughty child. In that instant she really became his daughter. Throwing her over his lap, he gave her four smacks where it would hurt.

It was her turn to be angry. "You brute! I hate you." Sobbing, she snatched up a robe and ran from the room. She met Antika on the way. She had seen the assault on her beloved mistress. Coldly she addressed Prince Benon. "Excellency, may I show you something?" Not waiting for his assent, she went into Ariadne's bedroom and pulled back a curtain, which hid some clothes and boxes. There was very little there. No evening dresses, apart from the despised blue and the ruined Chinese dress, now merely a heap of rags on the floor.

Ben was aghast. "My poor baby, what have I done?" When he could not find his girl he turned to Antika. "Come. I have something I would like to show you." He took her along a passage she had never seen before. It was cold but not damp. Unlocking a door with a key from a high shelf, he disclosed a large cavern. It held several trunks. Opening one, from masses of soft paper a roll of the most beautiful material was revealed. It was in a soft shade of ivory, and had once been white but time had turned it into a soft creamy colour. The material was covered with elaborate scrolls, mainly of butterflies and leaves, all picked out in gold. "Can you and your sewing ladies make a dress for Ariadne out of this? I don't think it has perished."

Antika beamed. She would, with great pleasure.

The making of the dress was carried out like a military operation. Guards were set to make sure Ariadne was not around while the work was in progress. Surprisingly, it was the Russian who was the most helpful in its design. He had a relative in Paris who was in the 'rag trade', and the major was often sent the very latest fashion magazines. He was really well informed as to the very latest trends.

There was to be a state dinner with Uncle Bron, and all the Council members and their partners. The Dronk and Mu-Ani had to be included, much to Ben's disgust. Ariadne was occupied in working out a menu that was not a replica of the last occasion. She was lucky in finding someone on the larger island who knew where edible crabs and a kind of shrimp could be found. Her planting of salad crops was just about ready. The main course was meat from wild oxen, and new potatoes plus green vegetables were also available. She begged some shortbread biscuits from Milo's store and, with some fresh fruits, was able to make a reasonable dessert. Ben provided some excellent wines, and there was also coffee and spirits to finish what was quite a feast.

The evening of the banquet was pleasantly cool. There was great excitement to find out what Ariadne thought of her gown. She had been expecting to wear the blue dress and was pleased she had managed to put on a little weight. After a shower Ben told her there was a surprise for her. "Shut your eyes, Sweetheart."

She did so, thinking he was up to one of his tricks yet again.

The gown lay over a chair and Ben gently led her to it and placed her hand on the soft material. "Now open your eyes."

Ariadne simply gasped, "Oh, Ben, it is just beautiful. Is it really for me?" The design, picked out in gold, comprised butterflies and the outline of leaves. A smiling Antika came forward and helped Ariadne dress, and Ben did her hair. Ariadne went to a drawer and brought out Ben's decorations. "You must wear these. It is usual on state occasions." Ben was wearing his space commander's uniform, the only relief being his collar, with the four diamond stars on each side. With all his decorations, including the Legion d'Honneur, the grey uniform was quite a sight.

The four travellers from Earth also sprung a surprise. They had smuggled their dress uniforms on board their shuttle. Ed had said, "If we do meet aliens or any little green men and have to die, at least we will represent Earth properly attired." They were given seats of honour next to Prince Bron and Ben. When Ben led Ariadne in they caused a sensation. Ed said, "Look at Cinderella. All we need is Prince Charming."

Milo said, "You are looking at him." Then he went on to explain how they had married and later found out Ariadne was his daughter. Dr Fuharan had told him and asked him to explain the details to the others. "It is very sad for them. Ben almost went mad at first, and it hasn't quite sunk in yet. I think they are still lovers. They have a small boy whom they had to leave behind to come here. It was a big sacrifice for Ariadne but she will do anything for Ben. Further children are out. They have had no news of their boy, and are anxious to get back to see how he is."

The secret of Ariadne's writing was about to be revealed. She asked those attending the banquet not to leave as she had some surprises for them. Uncle Bron looked at Ben but Ben merely shook his head. He was as mystified as everyone else. From a box brought in by the head printer, Ariadne took out what looked like a pile of manuscripts. She gave a copy to each of those present, starting with Uncle Bron, then Ben, and each of the visitors from Earth. The ten members of the Council were next. She hoped she had enough copies, and had fortunately judged it just right. "These are the history of the Usaurian people as told to me over the months I have been here." There were copies in English for the Americans, and in French for the Russian and Ben. The cover was made from the only material available for printing on the Two Islands. The result was a cross between parchment and material, and was quite strong. The pages were from some paper Ben had brought with him. He had nearly thrown it away but Ariadne had come across it and put it to its present use. Everyone was delighted with the book. Uncle Bron rose to his feet and thanked her. "You have given us back a little of our history." Indeed she had, in no small measure. Ben was near to tears and unable to speak. He too was so proud of her. There was movement behind the curtain at the end of the room. Ariadne rose to her feet and at her signal the curtain was drawn back. There were gasps of surprise. The children of the colony were about to entertain them. She had taught them songs in their own language, and also in French and English. There was a small band comprising drums, penny whistles and triangles. Their audience was enchanted, having no idea the children could perform so well. Ariadne had done it all by love and example. They were introduced by little Annalisa, a favourite of Ariadne's. She must have been about the same age as Philippe. The Earth visitors led the applause, and each child was given a bag of sweets by Ariadne before the curtain came down.

A few days after the state banquet Ariadne regretfully put the lovely gown away. She had admired the style and the workmanship, wondering if she would ever have the opportunity to wear it again. The Russian had been a great success with the wild horses. He caught one and managed to join the herd on one of its mad stampedes. He returned triumphant and told Ben he had found the Secret Valley. Pav had actually ridden the horse bareback to what sounded like a dream location. It seemed the larger island was not entirely a barren waste. There was plenty of grass and water. It was like finding a new planet. Time was running short and though he hated to say so, Ben regretted he would not have the opportunity to see the valley. It was named the Russian Valley after the man who found it. The time for departure back to Earth was now getting close. Ben had not been well and Milo suggested all the flyers, including Ariadne, should have a medical. He was worried about the headaches Ben had been suffering. It gave Dr Fuharan and himself the chance to check Ben thoroughly without it appearing too obvious. The two doctors looked at the X-ray. It was as they had feared. There was a slight growth – possibly a tumour – in an inoperable place behind one eye.

They asked Ben to see them. When he saw their grave faces his reaction was typical. "Now you two; come out with it. Don't lie to me or disguise the situation."

There was an uncomfortable silence in the room. Neither of the doctors appeared anxious to open matters. At his most imperious, always the autocratic prince of the Usaurians, Ben said, "Well, gentlemen, will one of you please tell me what you are obviously reluctant to, or do I have to knock your heads together. Uncle Fu, I promise I won't wreck the place," using his childhood name for his dear friend who had been more than a father figure to him.

The doctor had tears in his eyes as he replied, "Sit down, Benny boy, please." He turned to a monitor behind his desk, and two X-rays revealed the outline of a skull and the right eye. "You can read X-rays as well as I can. What do you make of these?"

Ben leaned forward, and wasn't long in finding the source of an obvious problem. Picking up the doctor's pointer, he unerringly placed it on a spot behind the eye. "Well, for a start, that shouldn't be there."

Now the ice was broken Doctor Milo took up the details, and they were a shock. "It appears you have a growth, and we are not sure whether it is malignant or not. It is the reason for your frequent headaches. Hopefully it will disappear, but it could extend to the brain." There was no need to go further. Ben knew what his chances were. Milo continued, "You have another problem. Your body cannot risk taking in any more radiation. If you decide to make the journey to Earth you had best go in the better-protected vessel, namely the shuttle. I know your craft is lighter and faster, but it is open to radiation seeping in."

Ben said nothing, but moved to the window. He wasn't seeing what was outside apart from the fields of potatoes and root vegetables he and Ariadne had helped to sow. He knew the people would soon have maize and be able to enjoy corn on the cob. He saw the neat dairy where they could now make butter and cheese. His job was done, and he must leave. He so wanted to see his son again, and was determined to get back to Earth. Abruptly, without another word, he left and made his way to his own quarters.

There was still one last task for Ben to complete. He knew as soon as it leaked out he would not be returning to the Two Islands, the fate of his two well-loved horses would be sealed. Meat was still a luxury, and horsemeat, when it could be obtained, was fiercely fought over. No way was he going to let his two darlings suffer that fate. He was left with only one option: to have them put down. He would do this himself, although it almost broke his heart. He had loved them and cared for them over many years since finding two little orphans whinnying their distress over the body of their dead mother. It had cost him a lot of arranging to ensure they were well guarded and well fed. They would be a prime target for anyone daring enough to steal. He could just see the Dronk and Mu-Ani licking their lips. The two horses were in their prime and still only middle-aged in horse years. He could, of course, turn them out to join the wild horses, but knew they were so well conditioned to the softer life in warm, comfortable stalls where they were well cared for, they would probably try to return to what they knew. Also Bramin would have to fight to hold a place among the wild horses. The leading wild horse would add Bramina to his harem as his right. The ferry had an outboard motor and Ben soon reached the other island. He took oats and a supply of the sugar-lumps both horses loved. While they enjoyed their treats he dug two holes deep enough to take them. The pistol he had brought with him had a silencer, and he checked to make sure it would work. He led Bramin to the edge of one pit and gently stroked his nose. The horse nudged him, which he did when he was trying to coax more sugar from his master. Ben gave him a handful and gently told the big horse how much he loved him. While he still had the courage he pulled the trigger. As planned, the horse fell sideways into the pit. It was the work of a few minutes to cover Bramin with a horse blanket, over which he scattered a white powder.

The soil had been easy to remove as the area had been tested for its possible use as a potato field but turned down as too stony. Leading Bramina to the other pit, he said his goodbyes and she also fell, her head facing towards Bramin's. She too was covered with a blanket, over which the same white powder was sprinkled. It was lethal, a deterrent to any would-be scavenger. Ben was not known to be sentimental but he placed the remains of the two bags of oats in each grave saying, "For your journey into the spirit world." He saluted his well-loved companions and, hoisting Bramin's saddle to his shoulder and carrying Bramina's halter, trudged back to the ferry. There were no tears. They would come later.

Back in his own quarters Ben quickly emptied a crate he had previously packed and placed the saddle inside, managing to fit in several of the things he'd removed. Pag could collect the rest as and when he could.

He was exhausted and would have fallen asleep, but a gentle tap on his door was made. It was Dr Milo. "You left before we could give you these." In his hand were two packets. "These contain two sets of patches: one white, the other pink. You are to use one of each every time you rise after your main sleep, and destroy the two you remove. Place them just above the elbow on each arm. Do you understand?" Ben did, but wanted to know more about them. Dr Milo smiled. He knew Ben was no fool. "The white ones will give you protection against any radiation you may take in. They act like chemotherapy, which should assist your eye condition and, as the medication is in the patches, there will be no sickness, as can often occur. The other patches contain vitamins and minerals which we hope will improve your general health. This is a one-time-only treatment and couldn't be used should you try to return here." He paused and Ben thanked him. "Oh, before I forget, you are to continue to take your other medicine," and, with a smile, he left Ben to take it all in.

Tears rolled down Ben's face, and on entering his suite Ariadne went to him immediately and he fell into her arms. She didn't need to be told. The saddle in the crate and the pistol which he still held explained it all. Gradually she got the whole story. He explained that the grim end his two much-loved horses would have faced, and the way they would be butchered, was too horrible to contemplate. Even Uncle Bron couldn't stop such a slaughter. He was a pragmatist and would agree meat was meat whatever guise it came in. He had always felt Ben had lavished too much attention on his horses. To him they were simply a means of moving about.

It was eight hours to lift-off and there was still a lot to do. She saw Ben needed rest and as the Jacuzzi was still working Ben bathed, and she rubbed him down with oil and massaged his body. He soon fell into what she hoped would be a long restful sleep. She was hoping for his assistance in helping her check her spacesuit. She laid out all the equipment they would need, and proceeded to make coffee – the last for a long time. Something woke Ben, and he soon made it clear he wanted to make love and wouldn't take no for an answer. It was the one thing she knew that would calm him, and it did. Afterwards he was quite different, and eager to get going. Without her asking, he carried her to the Jacuzzi and they both washed again. They drank their coffee, still in their bathrobes. He then quickly began to check their spacesuits and equipment. He was the first to arrive at the launch station, where Milo, Uncle Bron and Dr Fuharan were waiting to say their goodbyes. Ben had asked the two doctors not to tell the old prince he would never be returning to the Two Islands, until after lift-off. He felt his uncle might try to stop him leaving, and he couldn't bear an emotional scene. After leaving their suite of rooms he sealed them with a secret code. If Philippe ever came to the Two Islands and used them, they would be ready for him and nothing would have been removed, as might otherwise happen.

The four Earthlings were called together in a group and told they would be helped to return to Earth provided they kept secret, as far as it was practical, the existence of the Two Islands planet. Ben appreciated NASA, and probably the President would need to be told, but that was all. They gave their solemn promise, with one exception: Milo hung back, and did not appear so willing. Ben drew him aside and asked if there was a problem he wished to share. "Yes, Sir, there is. Doctor Fuharan is badly in need of assistance and I am willing to stay behind and work here with him. He says he will pay for me to return to Earth at a later date and complete my medical training."

The doctor was one of the few people on the Two Islands who received finances. Ben saw he had plenty of money to pay for supplies from Earth, and he had investments in his name under the auspices of Lucien Gervaise, who often wondered who he was as any information came always through Ben. This was what Ben had been hoping for. With a twinkle in his eye he said, "I believe a certain young lady – one of the nurses at the medical centre – has also caught your eye. Am I not right?"

Milo gave a sheepish grin. "Yes. Nurse Marika. I would like to court her. Have I your permission, Sir? I understand she is an orphan."

Ben was only too willing. Colonel Godber wondered how they would explain Milo's absence to NASA but he was wished well in his new venture by all his fellow travellers. They knew he had no close relatives back on Earth, and hoped things worked out in his favour, although their feelings were decidedly mixed and all felt he was being very courageous.

The old man and the younger one, whom Prince D'Abron looked on almost as a son, embraced and bade their final farewell to each other. All was ready for the return journey to planet Earth. The Russian had taken Ben aside and asked in French, which he spoke with ease, if he could some time in the future return to live on the Two Islands. He said it made him feel safe. He was not always looking over his shoulder and watching to whom he spoke or what he said. He admitted he had sometimes not always been careful in this respect. He knew he had been sent on the mission to see Jupiter to get him out of the way. Ben asked if he had no family back in Russia. "*Non. Ma femme est mort.*"

Ben asked, were there no children. Again the answer was in the negative. "See Captain Anion. He is easily found, either in Milan or Rome, working as he does for Air Italia." The Major knew this, and vowed to contact him.

One small person was crying to Ariadne, "Don't go. Please don't go." It was the little girl, Annalisa. Ariadne talked to Ben. "We must have her with us in the future when she is older. Perhaps she could go to my old school." He promised to think about it. "She has no close relatives here. Her mother is dead. Her father is unknown." He promised, and she had to reluctantly drop the matter. Ariadne had taken quite a fancy to the little one. She had been able to give her some of her frustrated mother love and was extremely fond of the child. It was decided Ben was to accompany the colonel and the major. Commander Tubbs was to be Ariadne's companion.

Dr Milo was sorry to see his fellow crew members depart. He felt he was burning his boats, but did not change his mind to remain.

PART FOUR

RETURN TO EARTH

Chapter One

The Journey Back to Earth

The two crews of the spaceships waved goodbye and tried to settle down for the long journey ahead. They all had reasons for getting back to Earth as soon as possible. Ben and Ariadne were anxious to see Philippe again, and they both needed medical attention. The colonel was keen to start his campaign for the chance to become President of the USA. Ben told him he had a very good chance. They would be looked upon as heroes, and people love heroes. He just could not fail. Commander Tubbs was hoping to become a senator. He was also anxious about his wife Ellie Jane, and how she had managed the ranch in his absence. As for Major Pavel Orlevski, he just hoped to be accepted back into favour again. Ben spent most of his off-duty hours sleeping. He found it very therapeutic and, strangely, his general health improved. His companions fell in with this, and everything ran like clockwork on *Pegasus XIII.*

On the smaller craft Commander Tubbs was finding the lack of space a trial. He was, like all of them, tall. He wondered how Ben had coped, and said as much to Ariadne. She tried to make things easy for him but it took time for him to settle down. He was not used to working in such close proximity to a female. It didn't take the girl long to become aware of this. "Try and look on me as a male. Ben did on the way out. My hair was cut like a boy's, and I was called Ensign Henri." To ease the slight tension she offered to teach him the Usaurian language.

The commander was pleased to be travelling with Ariadne. He had a small guitar and when the occasion arose would strum it quietly, playing 'The Yellow Rose of Texas' and other American airs, which she greatly enjoyed. Ariadne appointed herself cook, and tried to make the very boring food at their disposal interesting. Her hair was cut short but she had refused to let Ben near it. She didn't want to look like a boy again. Fortunately water was not such a problem. For a start, a lot of their heavy original luggage had been left behind on the Two Islands. The blue dress was left in the care of Antika, and the books she had so loved reading to the children were given to little Annalisa. The little girl was still too young to read but she took the books to bed and loved looking at the pictures of Winnie the Pooh, Paddington Bear and Mickey Mouse. It brought her princess nearer, and the little one wondered if she would ever see her again. Tallyrand Tubbs told Ariadne about his life in the Naval Flying Corps, and that he was going to retire if they got back to Earth safely. He told Ariadne of his hopes of becoming accepted as a senator. She told him he would make a fine senator, and wished him well. He enjoyed learning the difficult Usaurian language, saying it made the time pass quickly.

When they were about halfway to Earth, and nearing the American space station, a signal came from *Pegasus XIII*. Ben was going to try the impossible and use his knowledge to 'bend' time. If successful, it would reduce their travelling time. He explained to his bemused crew members Albert Einstein's theory regarding time, and he asked them if they were happy to let him try. Of course they were, and if successful, it would reduce their time in space considerably. They were all anxious to get back to terra firma as quickly as possible.

The two ships were ready, and Ben issued the order for all of them to lie on their couches, ensuring they wore their helmets and all were securely strapped in place. He warned them to expect turbulence, and they got it in no small measure. Ariadne moaned to Tally, "We must have been mad to agree to such a hare-brained scheme."

He agreed, thinking of the meal they could now be enjoying

on the space station. Suddenly it was all over. "Madame and gentlemen, look at your watches."

They did, and were amazed. They all wore special space watches that not only told the time but gave other useful information such as the phases of the Moon, and the weather on Earth. Their time in space had been reduced by three months at least.

Not long after this they were in sight of Earth's moon, whereupon Ben decided it was time to rejoin Ariadne. It was a slightly complicated procedure as both he and the commander were still wearing their full space suits and they also had to transfer their personal gear. He thanked his fellow travellers for their help, and changed places with Commander Tubbs. Ariadne in turn thanked the commander for his support, and wished them all "Godspeed."

Ben added, "Safe landing."

When he had removed his space suit he took Ariadne in his arms and kissed her. "It has been so long, Sweetheart."

They let the other vessel get well ahead, before setting course for a sea landing, dropping gently into the sea off the coast of Cyprus. As Ben anticipated, NASA and the whole of America went crazily mad with delight at the return of *Pegasus XIII*. It had been thought lost, but by some miracle it was safe. He wondered just how they were going to explain the non-return of their medic, and wished he could be a fly on the wall to see how they dealt with the problem.

Chapter Two

Home on Earth

The *Sirius* splashed down off the coast of Cyprus unobserved except by a goatherd, who thought he must still be suffering the effects of imbibing too much ouzo the night before. Ariadne went to the nearest bakery, where she purchased a large supply of bread, and then to a supermarket to replenish their almost empty stores. She was soon eating a large slice of bread and butter. Ben remarked she would get fat.

"No I won't; I am naturally slim."

The next three weeks were spent getting themselves fit, acquiring tans, and generally feeling much better. Ariadne found a good hairdresser. Seeing her looking so smart, Ben leaned over and kissed her. "Do you realise what you are doing to my sex drive, Darling. You have no idea. No idea."

Trying to take his mind off the subject, Ariadne waved a piece of paper under his nose. "You can't miss this. It is an appointment for you to see a doctor in Paris the day after tomorrow. It will give us a chance also to see Lucien and ask about Philippe, and get your affairs sorted out."

Regretfully they left Aphrodite's island, and made their way to see what fate had in store for them.

Paris hadn't changed much, and they made their way to see the specialist, who was renowned for not dressing things up. He looked at the X-ray Ben produced, his only comment being, "I thought this type of X-ray went out with the Ark." When he saw them again after Ben had an in-depth scan, the man was smiling. "It isn't often I can give patients good news. This time

I can. You, my dear Sir, are in total remission. Come and see me again in six months' time."

As the two left the specialist's consulting rooms they laughed, kissed and danced their way to their car. Watching them, the consultant sighed. He wasn't at all sure that all was well with the tall man. His name seemed familiar; he was possibly a flyer or a sailor. The blood tests were inconclusive, but being of a compassionate nature the specialist, to be certain, felt further tests were required. He thought his patient had been in contact with radiated material at some time in the past and was keeping it a secret from his companion. They appeared close partners. He had said, cheerfully enough, "The tumour has shrunk to almost nothing," but instinct made him cautious. Meanwhile, let them enjoy life a little longer. Ariadne also saw a doctor and was delighted to find that a course of HRT made her feel a hundred per cent better.

Lucien was taken aback when the couple arrived at his offices. These were now in a very select area of Paris, which was reserved for brokers and bankers at the top of their profession. Ariadne summed it up as "very classy". Ben was astounded to learn he was now a multi-millionaire to the tune of twenty-five million euros. He also had nearly ten million Swiss francs in a separate account in Zurich.

He asked Lucien if there was any news regarding Swanbrook Hall, and if it was on the market. Lucien was pleased to say it was up for sale, but only just. It had been sold but the purchasers backed out when they found so much work was required to be done. Ben put an offer in, but in Ariadne's name. They felt it was wiser. They left Paris to see Philippe but did not announce their arrival. They wanted to surprise him.

There was one episode of their stay on Cyprus that Ben had to laugh over, and enjoyed telling those of his friends he could trust not to spread the details. He had found a delightful little cove with a small beach that could only be reached from the sea, and made a raft to carry the few things they needed to the beach. The *Sirius* was anchored a little way offshore. They saw no one for almost three weeks and got a little careless, treating the beach as if they were nudists. They had been thinking of leaving the next day, and were making plans to go to Paris. Ariadne was bare to the waist and lying face down. Ben had just finished rubbing sun cream onto her bare back. He rose to his feet and was naked. Suddenly voices were heard. A little girl asked, "What's that between his legs?"

Her companion, a boy a little older than her ten years, said, "I think it's his willy, although it is a bit big."

"What's it for?" was her next innocent remark.

"Well, I think all boys and men have one. It helps them pee."

"Really? I'm glad girls don't have one. Ugh! We don't need that."

Ben by this time had snatched a T-shirt and was struggling into his swimming trunks.

"Some boys in our school call it their winkle."

The girl was laughing. "You are funny."

The boy got a little cross. "Well, at least we don't have boobs when we grow up."

At this the girl started pushing him. An adult's voice was then heard. "Master Nicholas and Miss Jenny, what I'm to tell your mothers I don't know. Running away like that."

The two children forgot Ben and started teasing their nurse. She, poor girl, was flushed and held her side as if she had a stitch in it. Ben came to her rescue. "Here. Buy those two imps some ice cream and get yourself a cooling drink." With this remark he handed the nursemaid a handful of euros. The children were now running back the way they had come. The girl shyly thanked him, and wanted to know the name of their benefactor.

"Oh, just say Mr Willy Winkle."

The girl sped away after her charges. Ariadne, having hysterics, said, "We had better leave, pronto."

They did.

Chapter Three

Meeting Philippe

On the way to meet their son, Ariadne quizzed Ben about several things that had been on her mind since landing back on Earth. "Tell me how you managed to 'bend time'. Did you?"

Ben laughed. "Now if I tell you that, you can do a 'Back to the Future' book or go on TV and become famous." He was, she saw, quite serious. When she asked him what Ed and Pav thought, he merely said, "Oh, I just told them I pulled a lever in a series of bursts, and they believed me."

She gave up, knowing that if he didn't want to tell her he just would not. "There is one more thing. I suspect the specialist was a little puzzled by your blood test. There were signs he wasn't sure about, but you gave him no lead. Have you taken in more radiation?"

He sighed. "Full marks for woman's intuition. Yes, a little, I think. Don't worry; I am not going to drop dead. Not yet."

He was giving her one of his lopsided grins. It was her turn to sigh. When they reached the cottage, Philippe was nowhere to be seen. Ben got out of the car and walked round to the back of the building. A small boy was just dismounting from quite a large pony but he controlled it easily. Ben was bursting with pride. Philippe had grown into a tall, handsome three-year-old but looked much older. For once in his life Ben couldn't think of anything to say. Two pairs of grey eyes looked at one another. "Hello, Philippe. I guess you are wondering who I am?"

Philippe stood with his arms straight at his sides and his fists bunched as if to throw a punch. "No. Unfortunately I do know of you, Father."

Ben felt as if he had been punched in the stomach. It seemed Grand-mere had done what he suspected she would do: poison the small child's young mind against him. Philippe faced his parent. "Grand-mere said you took my mama away. There was never anyone to meet me when I came out of nursery school – only Nanny Shona. The children said I was born under a gooseberry bush. Where is my mama now?"

Ariadne heard the small boy angrily accusing his father. She saw the hurt written on Ben's face, knowing it was totally unfair. One day she would make her son understand. This she promised herself. Softly she called him. "I am here, Philippe."

The child turned. He gasped with delight. No one had told him how pretty his mama was. He ran to her, burying his face in her welcoming arms.

The mother looked at her boy. Like Ben, she had not expected him to be so tall. Her baby had disappeared. "Your papa is buying a big house in England. Wouldn't you like to come and live with us there?"

The child looked at her. "Will *he* be there?" His father was now sitting miserably in the car.

"Why, yes, of course."

He gave her a little push. "Then I will stay here with Grand-mere in the chateau, and you can come and visit me. You will, won't you?"

Much against their wishes, they had to give in. Nurse Shona told them, "That old witch has taken him over. She spoils him and gives him too many sweets. I tell her they are bad for his teeth, but she ignores me. Tells me I am just a temporary servant." There was obviously no love lost between them.

In the car Ariadne cried quietly, for Ben as much as for herself. At his request she reluctantly visited the old woman in the chateau. Ben's remark: "If I go, I will want to throttle her" didn't surprise her. Ariadne, however, was shocked by the older woman's appearance. It was obvious drink was ravaging her, and it was possible she was damaging her liver. Arrangements were made for Philippe to live with Grand-mere. This pleased Grand-mere as a generous allowance would be paid, and Lucien would continue to be at hand to ensure Philippe never went without. Ariadne was annoyed to discover she referred to Philippe as "my grandson". Unable to resist having a dig at Ariadne, and always sharp of tongue, she told the girl she looked ill. Ariadne made arrangements to see Philippe once a month in France. She could not get him to agree to visit his father in England. It appeared he hated his father, and it was clear he had been completely brainwashed by the old woman. The child had believed all he had been told by Grand-mere.

Ben and Ariadne returned to see Lucien. They had fortunately bought new clothes so did not feel out of place in his very elegant offices. Both of them loved visiting Paris but as it was the holiday season, and the city was very hot, all who could leave had, like lemmings, departed en masse for the Riviera or the Atlantic coast – anywhere, as long as they were out of the city. Fortunately Lucien had not yet left. As they sat in his air-conditioned office Ben asked anxiously whether the negotiations for Swanbrook Hall were any further forward. "Yes and no," was Lucien's answer.

Ben asked, were the vendors not happy with his offer. The sticking point was Ben's request that the family portraits plus two suits of armour and a refectory table be left *in situ*. He had already requested that only Ariadne's name be on the deeds, pointing out, "Death duties have crippled many an estate, and you are younger." Eventually things were sorted out, and Swanbrook Hall was theirs.

Chapter Four

The House

The day Clarissa D'Vane's grandson took possession of her home was one of those rare days, seen only in England. A hazy mist hung several feet over the countryside, not disappearing until late afternoon. It seemed to Ben to lend a magical air to everything. From his vantage point overlooking what was now his estate, the Hall did seem magical. On the west wing there was a mass ofVirginia creeper. It was just starting to put on its autumn shades of red, yellow and brown. Soon, as the sun set, the windows on the west wing would glow red, orange and gold.

The gates leading to the drive were in need of repair. Security seemed to be totally lacking. Ben made a mental note to replace the gates with a high-tech security system.

The deer park contained a flock of healthy looking sheep. A few of the deer needed either medical attention or otherwise being put down. The big man was used to this and was skilled in the veterinary field. What the local vet would say, he didn't speculate about.

The house too was in need of remedial repair, though not too much, he was pleased to see. On the way to the Hall he had noticed what must be stables, empty for now; but horses were a must, provided he could find one or two to accommodate his size.

He found the estate office and the tack room both very neat and uncluttered. Someone had obviously been delegated to look after things. The gardens around the Hall also looked well cared for. What he required was an estate manager to get things organised to his own high standards.

The door of the Hall was slowly opening. Ben had been advised that a skeleton staff had been asked to remain: butler, cook and jobbing gardener. He looked up to see who was welcoming him – his butler, he supposed. He fell back against his car in astonishment. They recognised each other immediately. It couldn't be, but it was. He looked at the tall man facing him. How many years ago was it? Ten at least. How he had searched for this man – in Marseille, other French ports, the coast of Africa – with never an indication he was still alive. The other man uttered two words: "*Mon Dieu*," being equally surprised.

Slowing mounting the steps, Ben said with a slight smile, "Doctor Livingstone, I presume?"

As he was unfamiliar with the quotation, his butler held out his hand. "Welcome to Swanbrook Hall, Sir."

Ignoring the outstretched hand, Ben pushed past, saying through gritted teeth, "Come and see me in the library in twenty minutes, and for heaven's sake bring something strong to drink. Where is Madame?"

Ariadne could be heard on the first floor, singing softly to herself. Ben ran up the stairs, two steps at a time. How he needed her calming presence. She was astonished to see he was weeping. "Why oh why, what could be wrong?"

He fell into her arms, and she soothed him like a child. Gently she led him to a large room she thought he must like. It was the best bedroom in the Hall. There were windows on two sides: one overlooking the deer park, and the other the rose garden and lawns. He thought the bedroom just perfect, and told her so. The bed itself was large enough for him, and the carpet, although slightly faded, had come from China some time in the past, and the fitted furniture was not out of place. He knew it would be a restful place to retire to. Taking his arm, the girl led him along a dark corridor. At the end was a portrait of a young girl – Clarissa Costello D'Vane – so like Ariadne.

She said, "*Voila! C'est moi, oui*?" It could have been her. It was of Lady D'Vane dressed as when presented at court.

Jean-Paul Raban, known as John Rivers – no one being aware he was a Frenchman – made his way to his own quarters to pick up the spirits Ben had requested. He thanked his lucky stars he had had the foresight to get in a good supply. The encounter had shaken him badly. He asked himself if he would be told to leave. His feelings towards Ben had not changed over the years, and he knew they never would. He loved him, and wondered how Ben was feeling. There was a young lady whose position in the household he had yet to uncover. She had introduced herself as Madame Du Pre. She was very young to be Ben's wife. He told himself that no doubt all would be revealed in time.

Jean-Paul was an extremely handsome man and, apart from a slight limp from an old injury, was supremely fit. He went over in his mind how he and Ben had first met and what had happened between them. He had joined the French army at an early age, much to his mother's relief. Some of his friends had got into bad company and the last thing she wanted was her only son to turn to crime. He made a fine soldier, rising to the rank of sergeant in an elite parachute regiment. Unfortunately he had a temper, and it let him down. He was brought before his colonel for punching a fellow sergeant. The sergeant had called Jean-Paul's mother a whore. The colonel was tired of brawling, and being in a vile mood, decided to make an example of the unrepentant young sergeant. He was sentenced to serve six months in the French Foreign Legion, with, of course, a loss of rank.

Capitaine Jan Van Den Hoof was an easygoing leader, too soft on the raw recruits usually sent him. He groaned when told of the latest arrival, but brightened considerably on meeting his new 'batman'. He taught Jean-Paul to wait at table and the Capitaine knew a lot about wine. Jean-Paul was soon a reasonable butler. The *capitaine* found the youth had the gift of leadership, which he would put to good use.

When it was agreed he could be the 'new' sergeant, Jean-Paul was in his element. He was moderately successful, but one recruit – an Englishman – resisted all his efforts to train him. His commander had a bet with Jean-Paul – although bets were strictly forbidden – that if he could make this rebel into anything like a legionnaire, he could have whatever he wished for, within reason. New boots were his first choice. Boots wore out quickly. He wasn't worried about clothes, but boots were a different matter.

The problem soldier in question, the disgraced son of a wealthy English Peer, said, "If I can teach you English within two weeks – and you must speak it without a French accent – I'll do anything you ask of me." They shook hands, and everyone looked on to see what would happen. Bets were taken and Jean-Paul, already fluent in Arabic, won hands down. The Englishman was truly amazed. The English accent was faultless. Jean-Paul found he quite enjoyed showing off skills he had kept hidden. He was already a first-class shot, and could ride a horse or act as mechanic with equal ease. One sweltering afternoon, the company were having a short siesta. Trouble was not expected. It was so hot even the guards were finding it difficult to keep awake. The drone of a light aircraft – a Cessna – could be heard. It appeared the pilot wanted to land. Henry Berringer – the Englishman – said, "Look at the markings. Don't shoot; I think he is French."

The first thing they noticed was the pilot's boots as he swung his legs out of the cockpit of his plane. They were fantastic. It was clear he was not an Arab. They were not known to have such fair hair, almost white. The company, now fully awake, soon got the message from this blond man that they were in danger. A group of terrorists were minutes away from launching an attack on them.

Van Den Hoof tossed a rifle to Ben and cocked an eyebrow at their saviour. Would he care to join in the fight? Ben needed no second invitation. The fight was short but bloody, and the surprised terrorists fled in confusion. Ben introduced himself, and a grateful Van Den Hoof invited him to join him for a meal. They got a little drunk, and when a challenge by Van Den Hoof to exhibit his ability with a sabre was issued, Ben just couldn't resist the chance to show off. To make things worse, the blades were sharp. It could have ended in disaster but for Jean-Paul stepping between them and getting a cut on his left cheek for his pains.

The fight wasn't over, as the terrorists regrouped. As dawn broke, they came in again, with reinforcements. This time the legionnaires were not so lucky – three dead, including their medic. Ben showed he could give injections of morphine where required. He looked for Sergeant Raban and found him lying in a pool of blood, not entirely his own. A young recruit of not more than seventeen or eighteen lay on top of him. "Poor little devil. I think he's had it," said Ben.

The sergeant looked at Ben. "My kneecap has been hit." It had, by a ricocheting bullet. Ben could see it was quite a mess, and spoke to Van Den Hoof. "He needs to get that knee attended to as soon as possible. With your permission, I will try and reach your base hospital. I can take him in my Cessna. There is only room for one other besides myself."

Permission was immediately given.

To Ben's dismay his plane had also been hit by bullets. He wasn't sure he could complete the journey, and took some morphine in case it was required. He told the *capitaine* he hoped to reach at least the first oasis – roughly half the distance. The plane got off the ground, but it was clear it wasn't going to get far. Ben reached the oasis and used his radio to report their position. He was told they couldn't be picked up until dawn. Ben lifted the injured man out gently, and made an improvised shelter for the night.

Although in a lot of pain, the sick man tried not to show it, but beads of sweat gave the game away. Ben brought water from the oasis well and gently washed away as much as possible of the blood that still clung to the body and clothes of his charge. Jean-Paul sighed. "Do you know, I don't even know your name."

Gravely they introduced themselves. Ben leant forward and carefully wiped Jean-Paul's face. Without warning the legionnaire reached up and pulled Ben's face down and kissed him full on the lips. When there was no immediate response he said, "Sorry, friend. You are just so bloody wonderful to me. I don't normally kiss a man. I am not one of those…" He grinned, and it made Ben realise that a rather frightened but naive boy was seeking what? He wasn't sure. He had called the type of man looked down upon by his fellow soldiers the rather rude French name which is best not repeated here. Ben realised he was attracted to him, and in his turn took Jean-Paul in his arms and kissed him. One thing led to another, and soon the pair indulged like naughty schoolboys in a heavy petting session. The night was cold and the two clung together, not sleeping, but gaining comfort from holding each other. They exchanged snapshots of themselves and promised to keep in touch. The morning arrived too soon, and they had to part. The drone of the rescue ambulance plane could be heard. Ben never forgot Jean-Paul, but try as he might to re-establish contact, the two never managed to meet up. Ben discovered later that Jean-Paul had been flown back to France for treatment. His leg was slow in healing, so he was given an honourable discharge from the army, with a small pension and a medal for his bravery. Now, after many years, the two had come face to face. What strange tricks fickle fate can play! All this was on Jean-Paul's mind as he hurried to see what fate had in store for him with Ben. He knew he still loved Ben, and always would.

When Jean-Paul reached the library Ben was already sitting behind a large desk – one of the items of furniture that had proved too large to move. Ben glanced at his watch. Jean-Paul was a little annoyed. "My living quarters are outside the main house. I apologise if you have been kept waiting. What would you like to drink?" He indicated a large tray, which held, besides the usual selection of spirits, an ice bucket containing a bottle of vintage champagne. "I thought Madame would prefer champagne."

"Yes, indeed." Ben looked at his new employee. "I assume you bought the champagne and spirits?" The other nodded.

Ben wished to know who had been looking after the estate after the previous residents had moved out. Jean-Paul, quite unabashed, answered, "I did. My duties as butler were no longer required. I was bored, and someone was needed to take charge."

Again not satisfied, his new employer asked who had paid him. Had he been left a float? When Ben realised everything had been paid for out of the other man's pocket he immediately took out his wallet. "I am now responsible. Will this cover it all?" The cheque he pushed towards Jean-Paul was large, and more than enough. "Would you be prepared to take on the duties of my estate manager and work for me? Your salary will, of course, be increased in line with what you will be required to do. Believe me, you will earn it. I have very high standards. I consider this will be enough to start."

The younger man gasped at the amount. Yes, he would really work for this amount.

Their discussion was interrupted by Ariadne joining them. When she had tasted the champagne she clapped her hands, saying, "*C'est tres bon.*"

They drank a toast to their future at Swanbrook Hall. On learning from Ben his butler had been offered the position of estate manager, Ariadne insisted he join them in their toast.

"First things first, my dear. He hasn't yet accepted the job." Ben was pleased when he saw the man hesitate. "Let's say we give him a month's trial, eh?" So it was agreed. "The first thing you can do is perform a small service for me. In the Long Gallery there is a portrait of my grandmother Lady Clarissa Costello D'Vane. Please have it removed and cleaned, and if possible, reframed in a more modern style."

There were tears in Ariadne's eyes. When she had first pointed the picture out to Ben he had merely said, "It appears my late grandfather and I possess a similar taste in women." At the time the girl had found the remark somewhat hurtful. She had immediately realised the portrait bore a remarkable resemblance to herself at the same age – the age when she and Ben had first met.

Jean-Paul soon found that working for Ben was far from easy. For a start, he found Ben was a very early riser, and he would be expected to accompany him riding every day. The problem was where to get horses to suit two such large men. "Let's leave that until another time."

Having seen Jean-Paul's work, observed him, and taken in things about him he had not previously noticed, Ben felt he needed time to get to know him better. Did they have a future together? Could or would they become lovers? He had no idea. Perhaps fate would, as in the past, take a hand. What would be, would be.

Feeling tired, Ariadne went to bed early. She was also anxiously wondering what life would be like in Swanbrook Hall. She had just undressed, when she realised Ben was in the room, and he was obviously in a romantic frame of mind. "Darling girl, I intend to treat you as my wife, which, in truth, you are. No one knows of our little problem." When she started to protest, Ben put his fingers on her lips. "I still look on you as my wife. Is that clear? I will never divorce you, and annulment is out of the question. Do you want Philippe to be looked on as a bastard?"

She gave in. Loving him as she did, and not wanting him to find comfort elsewhere, she did whatever he demanded of her.

Ben realised Jean-Paul could not be expected to run both the house and the estate, so he asked the younger man if he knew of anyone in the village who could act as housekeeper and become a friend to Ariadne.

"I know just the person. She is a lady, not one of the local gossips. A childless widow. Her husband was killed in a bomb attack in Beirut. He was in the diplomatic service."

Ben thought for a minute. "Hmm, she sounds ideal. How old is she?" Geraldine Tabitha Tidymann was the right side of thirty. Not especially a beauty, she was considered a 'handsome piece' by the locals. She was not stuck up, and always friendly when she used the local shops. She patronised them instead of the supermarket in the local town.

Ben interviewed her, and was impressed. "Do you think you will like taking on what is, after all, a menial position?"

She told him she was bored out of her mind and was not worried about the scale of her salary. She told him that as long as she had enough to keep her little cottage, where the few friends she had could be entertained and stay for visits, she would be content. Ben thought Ariadne would like her, and hoped she would enjoy working at Swanbrook Hall.

It was suggested she might like to go away and think about it. "No. I'm sure I shall be happy here." What she could have added but didn't, was that she was in love, so in love and always would be, with the big Frenchman.

Ben was delighted when she confirmed she was a fluent French speaker. "That's good. Madame Ariadne was brought up in France, and considers herself a Frenchwoman." He thought for a few moments, then with a smile, added, "Do you mind if your forenames are shortened. How does Genta sound to you? We already have a bit of a mouthful with Ariadne's name." He was also interested to know how or when she became aware Jean-Paul was a Frenchman.

"I have a good ear, and don't forget: I lived among French-speaking people. You know my husband was in the diplomatic corps," the lady replied.

When Ariadne came in shortly after this, the two women clearly liked one another. Genta she became known as, and in time no one thought she had ever had another name. She liked the quarters she was given: a comfortable sitting room with a bed settee should she need to stay overnight.

Having settled the staffing inside the house, Ben turned his thoughts to the stables and outside staff. He told them their work would be rewarded with very good bonuses. He saw some of them pull faces when they found out who their boss was. "You will take any problems to Mr Raven. Is that understood?" They got the message. "Don't bother me." Ben then added, "We have still to find horses. Petrol is too expensive to use just to run around the estate."

Jean-Paul agreed.

From the outside, Swanbrook Hall appeared a Georgian gem from its rose-coloured facade and stone steps leading to the entrance, to windows set symmetrically on two floors. Ben had already discovered, to his delight, an ample stable block plus the estate manager's office. He decided to leave the attic and cellar for inspection at a later date, for now concentrating on the interior of the hall, which was not entirely to his satisfaction. Over the past fifty years remedial work had been carried out amateurishly and badly. He considered the worst act of vandalism was the staircase. It was modern and didn't blend at all with the long hall and portrait gallery on the first floor. The portraits badly required cleaning. Ben sighed. Having purchased his ancestral home at a figure he thought of as a bargain, he soon realised he would have to spend a considerable sum to restore the interior to the standard required of a Grade II listed building. He wondered why the errors had not been picked up when the property was first put on the market. He intended to have words with Lucien, who had negotiated the purchase for him. He would also see that the surveyor was informed. The next few months were busy ones for them all. Using catalogues of sales around the country, Ben was able to purchase the perfect staircase for the Hall, and quickly had it in place. This led to further decorating, and again Ben was lucky in acquiring several rolls of William Morris wallpaper that had lain undiscovered for many years in a shop, the owner of which had gone bankrupt. The one room he left alone was the library. He made this his study, regretting he had to have modern office equipment and a number of telephones installed. He wondered if he would ever find the time to look at the books which lined three walls. There were even some first editions, and a wide choice of subject.

The more Ben saw of Jean-Paul, the more he liked him. He was a worker and keen to show he could do what was required of him to run the estate competently. The question of finding horses to suit two such tall men bothered Ben. He knew he would also need to employ a lad to do the mucking out that an efficient stable needed. Jean-Paul must have read his mind. He brought Ben a list of all that was required, and the names of several lads, the choice of whom Ben wisely left to Jean-Paul. The stables recommended by Jean-Paul were run by a Miss Amy Stamford. She was well known at equestrian events and known to run her stables efficiently. "What are we waiting for?" Ben wanted to know. Stable lads were interviewed and Ben approved of his estate manager's choice. Harry was a cheeky sixteen-year-old who loved horses, and his eyes grew round and his cheeks flushed when told the wage offered. It was far more than he expected, and he gladly took the job. Ben discovered he lived in the village with his widowed mother and had had difficulty finding work with horses. Ben told him he was small enough to be a jockey.

The boy sighed. "That is my ambition, Sir." He looked up admiringly at the tall man. Ben had collected another fan without trying, but took it as his due.

"Can you drive?" Harry was asked. He was, of course, too young. Jean-Paul offered to teach him when he was seventeen. Meanwhile, he would have to use his bicycle to get around. An efficient fodder merchant was also found, and his first delivery made.

It was a crisp Autumn morning when Ben and Jean-Paul made their way to Miss Stamford's stables. Jean-Paul assured

Ben he had ridden her horses and was certain they would find what they were looking for. Miss Stamford was a friendly, jolly, middle-aged lady, and Ben immediately took to her. He was impressed to see how well everything was run, and she was very brisk and efficient, not wasting time on idle chatter.

Miss Stamford smiled at Ben. "Come and see a most difficult horse. He is well over sixteen hands high. I won't deny he is a problem. You look as if you might be able to handle him."

Ben looked at the animal, which was eyeing him suspiciously. He liked what he saw. Entering the box, he offered the nervous animal some of his special sugar-lumps, at the same time stroking him and talking quietly. "What do you call him?"

Miss Stamford laughed. "You know, he had been called a number of names at different times, but he goes officially by the name of Black Knight. Well, he *is* black all over."

Ben said he would have him. Jean-Paul settled for a smaller horse, called Kipperell, and they decided on a frisky little mare 'Nara' for Ariadne.

Feeling pleased with their purchases, Ben suggested they call in and introduce themselves to the landlord of the Royal Oak, the local inn. When they entered they caused quite a stir. Jean-Paul had not patronised the inn before. He felt his position as butler rather stood in the way. The locals were just a shade suspicious of the Hall. They had disliked the previous residents, but were willing to give the two tall men a chance. The pair settled for two lagers and found a corner, where they conversed quietly in French. It was a typical village pub, not seeing many strangers, and the food was mainly of the pie and chips type. They both liked the atmosphere, and Ben nodded to the landlord as they went out. The local drunk, Ollie Hobson, got up and managed to spill a large tankard of ale, most of it going on Ben's immaculate riding habit. Ben was furious, and the landlord apologetic. Glaring at the culprit, Ben said in French, "Who is that oaf?"

Jean-Paul grimaced. "Oh, he is the local pain in the proverbial..."

Ben retorted, "Remind me to keep well out of his way in future."

The two would meet again, facing one another in the nearest magistrates' court, where Ben would show extraordinary leniency.

The mare bought for Ariadne delighted the girl. It was sweet tempered and easy to ride. Usually Ben and Jean-Paul rode out together, but there were occasions when they made a threesome.

Ben took to life in the Hall as a duck to water. He met all his tenants. Their farms were not overlarge and they all seemed happy apart from the usual grouses about the cost of farming materials, the price of diesel etc. He was shocked to find that none of the tied cottages had indoor toilets or bathrooms. He immediately called them all to the Hall to discuss this. They were all gratified when he said this would be put right, possibly before winter set in.

When the restored portrait of Lady Clarissa was returned, Ariadne was dismayed to see it was even more like her than before. She pointed this out to Ben. "It is clear I must be a descendant. You will have to say I am your daughter. If you don't, then I will."

He could see the logic of this but was reluctant. However, his wish to honour his ancestor overcame his desire to have the girl he loved still known as his wife.

When Jean-Paul and he were next alone he took out Miranda's letter, saying simply, "Read this, and perhaps you will understand why I hope we two can forge a partnership. I do need a companion, and I feel we are growing closer all the time. Tell me how you feel."

The letter was read without comment, and to Jean-Paul it explained many things that had puzzled him. "What a horrible thing to happen. Come to my quarters this evening, and we can have a long discussion."

When it was nearly midnight Ben left the Hall and took the short walk to Laurel Cottage, which Jean-Paul had taken over from the previous tenant – the recently retired head gardener. They talked for several hours, Jean-Paul telling Ben of his time as a mercenary in North Africa, the Congo and Somalia.

Jean-Paul had left his employment serving as a mercenary, richer but disillusioned. He was frankly horrified by what he uncovered. He told Ben of young boys not more than twelve or thirteen years old being taught how to use rifles and machine-guns or knives. The more handsome had been repeatedly raped. He had heard some of them crying in the night, and managed to assist a few to escape, but realised he was suspected of helping them escape. Fearing for his life, he did not renew his contract, terminating it, saying his family in France needed him. Ben had brought with him a box of his rather select cigars, and the two smoked together for a while. Suddenly Ben rose and, moving quickly, started silently to undress Jean-Paul, then himself. The two looked at one another. Ben grimaced. "One can hardly say either of us is fat." He was proud of his leanness and was almost a match for his younger companion. "Do you know something? I think my manhood is bigger than yours."

They both laughed as the younger man retorted, "Ah, but I am taller than you, so I think we are quits." With this remark he threw a packet on the couch. "Condoms or a sheath. Interested?"

Ben said, "Let me fix it for you." Soon, inexpertly at first, then with growing confidence, they made love. It was an amazing experience for both of them. Jean-Paul told Ben he had loved him from their first encounter in the desert but wanted to know where Ariadne fitted in with Ben's new relationship. Thinking for only a few seconds his lover replied, "If you can stand it, part of me I must keep for my darling girl. I am still in love with her, and always will need her. Do you understand?"

Although it hurt, Jean-Paul did understand: he felt half a loaf was better than none. He appreciated that if they were to continue as lovers, Ben would not make physical love, but the nights were solely for him to show his love for Ben. In the day their approach to each other was to be strictly on the formal side.

Genta was a great comfort to Ariadne. She felt very lonely and shut out from Ben's life. He was absorbed with so many things she wasn't allowed to share. She and Genta enjoyed chats over coffee but the days seemed overlong to Ariadne. She was used to a routine, and now had little to do. She had not found anything in common with the local villagers. They thought her 'Frenchy' and a bit aloof. The Jurassic Coast – their part of Dorset – was enjoying an Indian summer. The days were very warm but the nights reminded Ben and Jean-Paul of the coldness of Sahara nights. The antiquated central heating system of the Hall was waiting to be updated. Because it was a Georgian Grade II listed building, planning permission for the solar panels Ben wished to install were refused. They had an ample supply of logs, so made do with these and electric fires until the heating engineers got round to installing the central heating.

On one such cold night, Ben and Jean-Paul decided it was too cold to use the cottage for lovemaking. Jean-Paul made up a fire in the small room off the library. He piled cushions on the floor, and the pair of them settled down for one of their sessions. In her bedroom Ariadne was also feeling the cold – so much so, she decided to make herself a warm drink and find a blanket. She made a mental note to remind Genta to bring out warmer duvets. They were still using summer-weight ones. Hearing sounds from the small room off the library and thinking the TV and light had been left on, she made to push the door open. She heard Ben's voice and Jean-Paul's. They were swearing, and it was frankly obscene. They were vying with each other to find words from all over the world which conveyed the sexual act. It was a shock to the girl. She heard Ben say, "My dear Jean-Paul, there isn't a word to match the good old Anglo-Saxon f★★k," at which remark, they both laughed.

Two men can share a questionable joke that women can't. Ariadne's ears and face were burning. She had already covered her mouth with one hand. Opening the door slightly, she looked in. It was all she could do not to scream. Jean-Paul was making love to Ben. For a few seconds, like a rabbit caught in headlights, she was glued to the scene.

All she could think was, how had he let this happen. He, the most fastidious being she knew. She almost hated them. "Why? Why?" She asked herself if Ben had ceased caring for her, and how long it had been since he and Jean-Paul became what she knew was called 'an item'.

Sleep was out of the question. Rising very early, she packed a small case and went to her little office, where she wrote letters and saw to menus and other minor household tasks. She wrote a brief note to Ben, and then rang her bell for her breakfast. Jean-Paul brought it. He looked as if he hadn't a care in the world. "How long have you and Ben been lovers?"

He put the breakfast tray on a side table and almost insolently took out his wallet. He placed two snapshots on the table – he and Ben, taken when both much younger, with Jean-Paul wearing French army fatigues, and Ben immaculately dressed, as usual, in smart jodhpurs and a white shirt. "We met for the first time nearly twelve years ago. In the desert. We were lovers briefly. Circumstances kept us apart. We were both shaken to meet up again here after such a long time. Madame Ariadne, I must tell you I love Ben very much. I don't think he loves me. He loves only you. He has told me of your extraordinary relationship, and is fearful for you. He says he has a genetic attraction towards you which is very strong. Please see that being with me is his way of trying to distance himself from you."

The expression on Jean-Paul's face told Ben there was trouble in the air. "She knows about us," he blurted out in one gasp.

"How?"

"Last night she came down and heard us."

Ben acted quickly. "I assume she is not here?"

The other nodded, handing her note over to his angry lover.

"Give me your keys." Jean-Paul looked blank. "The keys to the Land Rover." Snatching them up, Ben quickly left. He knew where she would go: the place they called "our beach". He was right: she was sitting gazing out to sea. He came and stood behind her, and she knew he was there. The smell of aftershave, the one specially prepared for him, wafted towards her. He placed one hand on the back of her neck, and took one of her hands in the other. He held it tight, at the same time rubbing the back of her neck. "I am sorry, little one, that you had to find out about Jean-Paul and me. You know why. You and I are not meant for each other, but every day without you here beside me would be a living hell. You know I still love you, and always will. Please, darling girl, come home where you belong."

She looked at him and said not a word. Then he kissed her. It was a kiss full of the most intense passion. She didn't protest as he lifted her bodily and carried her to the Land Rover. Shakily he fixed her seat belt, and went to attach her little car to the towrope used for jobs about the estate. He was interrupted by the village policeman. The policeman dismounted his motorbike, saluted smartly, and offered to help. He had noticed the sullen girl and thought to himself, 'She looks very angry.' Winking at Ben, he whispered, "Daughters can be a problem. I know. I've one of my own."

Thanking the man, who, after all, meant well, Ben drove back to the Hall. Ariadne spent the rest of the day in her room. Genta, not aware of what was going on, assumed Ariadne was ill.

The two people who meant a lot to Ben were openly at war, so it seemed to both he and Genta. After a week Ben had more than enough. He called them in to his sanctum and read the riot act to them. "Will you two stop tiptoeing around one another, and shake hands. I will decide with whom I spend my time and how. Is that clear?"

They shook hands reluctantly, and Jean-Paul left the room. Ariadne was ordered to remain.

"You are falling down on certain duties. Do you realise your fair hands have not deigned to touch my computer since we moved here?"

"Maybe I haven't. You could have asked me before, and there is no need to take that sarcastic tone."

Ben loved to see her in a temper. It made her very attractive to him. "Come here, you little devil."

He grabbed her by the shoulder and swung her around. He tried to undo her bra, but she pulled herself away. "All you ever think about is sex."

He was grinning. "Well, as you well know, I am highly sexed."

Genta was aware of tension between the three of them, and worried about it. She was fond of Ben and Ariadne, and frankly adored Jean-Paul. She was relieved when there was a lightening of the atmosphere. This was helped when Ben brought two new members into the household. He bought two dogs: a big Irish wolfhound for himself and, for Ariadne, a little Yorkshire terrier. She brightened considerably and had only one name for it: Pookey Two, named after her beloved Pookey of the past. Ben called the big dog Brutus. The big dog was surprisingly gentle with his much smaller companion. Fortunately they were both dogs. Her previous pet had been a lovely little bitch. When possible, the big dog was with Ben constantly, becoming his shadow, companion and guardian.

The Hall was warm after the heating engineers had done their job, and Ariadne looked forward to their first Christmas together in their home. It did indeed feel like home to her. She and Jean-Paul searched the estate, looking for holly and mistletoe, if available. They were lucky, and found both. Ben was not so pleased. "What on earth is all that?" he asked.

The tradition of Christmas and all that was expected of him as 'squire', Ariadne explained to him as patiently as she could. A couple of Douglas firs were dug up. The larger one was put outside, with lights and candles on it. The smaller one was placed in the main hall near the stairs. Ariadne set about turning it into a tree no one would ever forget. The colour scheme was gold and white. Presents were placed at the foot. Everyone who worked on the estate, as well as the tenant farmers and their families, was remembered. Ben wrote cheques for the latter. He consulted Genta as to what presents Ariadne and Jean-Paul would like. In turn, he asked the girl what he should give to Genta. They were all pleased with his choices. Carol singers came, and the evening was enjoyed. One elderly singer said, "Like the old days, when the 'family' had owned the Hall." This made Ben cross. "Don't they realise I am part of that same family?"

Ariadne hushed him. "Please don't spoil things. It will take time."

Soon it was New Year. Ben was still enjoying his role as 'squire'. He felt Ariadne needed more to occupy her very lively mind. He and Jean-Paul were riding one crisp morning in February, when they were aware of being followed. Brutus gave a low growl. Peter Purvis, the son of the village general store owner, was stalking them. "Come out, you young monkey."

The boy revealed himself, grinning widely. "I was only trying to take in what you were saying. You see, I want to learn to speak French."

Ben said, "Go and see Madame. I am sure she will be pleased to teach you."

Twice a week Peter cycled up to the Hall. Ariadne made a good teacher, as Ben anticipated she would. He and Jean-Paul conversed together in Arabic whenever the boy was about. "Little pitchers have big ears," was his comment. Soon Peter was quite fluent. He confided his ambitions to Ariadne. "I want to get into the Foreign Office, or perhaps the Diplomatic Corps."

She was sympathetic but pointed out he still had a few years to go before he could even consider it. "Don't forget, there is university first."

His face fell. "I'm not sure my people can afford to send me."

She spoke to Ben about it. "You do seem to collect lame ducks," but he did promise to give it thought at the appropriate time.

He and Jean-Paul went riding one morning to a site

adjoining his property. The plot was for sale. Ben wondered if it was possible to turn it into a vineyard. "I think it would be another interest for Ariadne. The soil would have to be the correct type. I've never felt Le Papillon vineyard has the proper soil for grapes."

The ground was surveyed and the soil tested. Both were to Ben's satisfaction. On Ariadne's twenty-third birthday she found a bunch of keys on her plate at breakfast, beside other presents and cards. There was no card from Philippe, but he was still too young, she supposed. "What are these for?"

Ben took her hand, telling her to follow him as he had a surprise for her. She was puzzled when she saw the field. Her mouth flew open when it was explained she was looking at the site of her very own vineyard. Ben gently closed her mouth and hugged her. "You can decide on the name and labels. In fact it will be your very own 'baby', Darling."

Climate change was a hot topic in more ways than one. Ben's lectures on the subject had always been popular, especially in America, and once again he was much in demand. He told Ariadne and Jean-Paul it made sense to have a base in New York. He had never made a charge for his lectures but the rising cost of travel and hotels, where he always demanded the best, was becoming difficult. They were not to know he had another reason for wanting a permanent base. He was often invited to Dr Weng's home and was attending a reception with his mentor when the good doctor took his arm, steering him towards a lady whose back was to them. "Come and meet my niece Suella. She used to live in China but lost everything in the 2008 earthquake." The lady turned, and Ben caught his breath. He couldn't believe it. It was Madam Fanny Su. She was also stunned. Her eyes pleaded with him, "Don't give me away," as if he would. Introductions had barely been completed when someone caught Dr Weng's arm, and he left them alone together. She had certainly changed. Her clothes were more modern and westernised. Her eyes were different. Ben wasn't sure whether she had had them operated on, or her skill with cosmetics had produced the change. She still looked marvellous. It turned out life had not been kind, her money being lost through the machinations of a Chinese mafia boss. He had wanted her to work for him. She managed to get out of Hong Kong by the skin of her teeth. Ben knew a lot of her clients had been members of the diplomatic service and he asked her, "Tell me, are you not afraid of being recognised?"

She laughed. "Some men don't look at their whores, especially if Chinese. To them, we all look alike." She said her uncle was not aware of her double life. She had always been the soul of discretion.

"Is it still not a bit of a risk?" he asked her.

She smiled. "Oh yes, but all the more exciting." She asked him to accompany her home. This was to a fairly modest apartment, not to be compared with the luxurious one she had owned in Hong Kong. There was, of course, no maid. With a rueful sigh she said, "As you can see, I have come down in the world."

She made coffee, as she had done on that previous occasion. Ben wondered what she was expecting from him. "Before you get any ideas, I am not looking for sex," he said.

She pouted. "No? I thought all businessmen played away from home." She accepted his statement with a shrug, but was clearly disappointed. "I know you have a woman now. I told you of her. I hope she is all you need. Something tells me she is not."

Ben had no intention of discussing his love life with this passionate woman but before he left, took her in his arms and kissed her. She sighed. "There. I knew it. You do want me."

Slowly he released her, and left.

Feeling lonely on returning to his hotel, he decided to call Ariadne. He knew he just longed to hear her voice. He knew that UK time was five hours ahead of New York time but she was glad to hear from him, and very relieved when he assured her there was nothing wrong. "I will be returning on the next available flight." She promised she and Jean-Paul would meet his plane. "You know, Darling, I am tired of jetting about the world. There is no place like home." Ariadne was pleased to hear this. "Goodnight, Sweetheart." Feeling comforted, he fell asleep as soon as his head touched his pillow, ignoring the dull roar of New York's traffic.

There was a six-hour delay in Ben's flight to Europe. He hated hanging around in airport lounges and just couldn't stand angry passengers plus their screaming children. On the spur of the moment he decided to return to Madam Fanny's apartment and spend some time with her. Perhaps they could go out for a meal. He had asked her to give him her telephone number, and when he explained the situation she was more than happy to meet him. It was lunchtime, and they enjoyed a delightful meal in an Italian restaurant. He had expected her to suggest a Chinese meal. There seemed to be something on her mind. He could sense she wanted to tell him something, but he didn't press her.

On returning to her apartment she offered him a drink, which he accepted. They had just settled for a chat, when a key was heard in her apartment door. An American voice called, "Hi, Mom, I'm home – a day early, I know. Hope there's some food in the place, as I'm starving."

Ben looked at Fanny. He still couldn't get used to calling her Suella. She was sobbing and there was a look of fright on her face. A young man entered, throwing off a baseball cap, and he stopped in surprise on seeing his mother had company. Ben looked at the young man, who was about twenty-two years of age – about ten years older than Philippe. Rage filled him. He turned to his companion, saying, "Why was I never told?" He took Fanny by the shoulders and shook her. "Introduce us, if you dare."

Speaking with difficulty after her shaking, she said dully, "This is Michael Woo, my son."

Ben glared at her. "Don't you mean *our* son? Deny it if you can."

She couldn't. Ben was beside himself. He had by a cruel fate been denied the childhood of all his children. Michael looked at his father. "I told Mom we should meet, but she is so proud."

Ben recognised his son as a typical Usaurian. He was like a lot of the Space Riders: tall, athletic, and very intelligent.

Michael's hair was slightly darker than Ben's. His eyes were the same grey, and although he was not quite as tall, no one could have doubted their kinship. For a start, they shared the same sense of fun. They laughed at the same jokes and were both great teases. They were the two halves of the same coin. Once he had recovered from the shock Ben forgave Madam Fanny. With tears in his eyes, he thanked her for giving him such a wonderful son. He made arrangements to move them to a more salubrious neighbourhood. When in New York he treated Suella – he had gradually got used to her new name – as his wife, and bought her a wedding ring, which he insisted she wore.

At Swanbrook Hall things were not quite so happy. Ariadne discovered perfume and lipstick on Ben's shirts. She asked Pag if he knew what was going on. He himself had only a vague idea. Ben was now spending more time in the States than had been his practice. Ariadne kept her discovery to herself. One evening she caught Ben making a long-distance telephone call to New York. He was laughing with someone he called Michael. Surely he hadn't started another *affaire*. He certainly seemed much happier when he returned from his now-frequent trips. Jean-Paul, meanwhile, remained blissfully unaware that anything was wrong in his relationship with Ben. Ben arranged for funds from his Swiss bank to be transferred to Michael's account with the Bank of America. He told Ariadne he intended acting as sponsor to a boy called Michael Woo, whom he had met in New York. She decided to take the bull by the horns. "Ben, what exactly is your relationship with this boy? And please, don't lie to me."

He sighed. "I wondered how long I could keep it secret." Briefly he told her of his meeting with Suella, and that her son was also his son.

A snapshot was pushed towards Ariadne. She caught her breath. The boy was so like his father, or like him when younger. One thing worried her. "He is, of course, your first son, and should be your heir to the Two Islands, or have you other plans for him?"

His father did not answer immediately. Instead he picked up the snapshot and put it away in his wallet. "When we first met I thought he was about twenty-two years of age. He is a little younger, but a very mature twenty, and struggling to pay his way through university. I will of course assist him. He will not take Philippe's place. You know he is destined for Two Islands one day. Michael is interested in law. I think he has the makings of a very able future district attorney. If you agree, I would like him to visit us here, perhaps when Genta and Jean-Paul are away. Next month I will arrange for Genta and Jean-Paul to have arrangements they really can't cancel."

Ariadne knew what Ben wanted Ben got. She realised with a shock that Michael was her half-brother, and wondered what he would make of her.

Chapter Five

The Half-Brother

Ariadne walked slowly down the wide Georgian staircase of Swanbrook Hall to greet the young man gazing up at her with admiration written all over his face. He hadn't expected his half-sister to be so lovely. For a start, her hair was such a simply wonderful shade of red, and he felt tongue-tied. Ben looked on with amusement as the two sized each other up. They seemed to like one another. Ben was pleased he had arranged the meeting which, he much regretted, would have to be kept short. He was determined to have at least one ride around the estate with Michael. As his eldest son it should be his inheritance, and Ben decided he would see he was made aware of the fact before he left. Ben knew the estate and house were in Ariadne's name so he would need to tell her, and also, of course, his solicitor.

The dress Ariadne was wearing didn't seem familiar to Ben at first, but one's memory can play strange tricks. He saw her in his mind's eye, as she had worn it when, with obvious delight, she had paraded before him like a model in the new clothes she and Lucien had purchased from the fashion houses in Paris. How long ago that now seemed – an age. Ben knew, with a sickening jolt, he still loved and wanted her. Pulling himself together, he steered Michael towards the picture of Lady Clarissa. Michael was puzzled. "Is that a portrait of Ariadne?"

Ben smiled. "No indeed. Read the inscription." Michael did, and gasped. Ben continued, "Yes, as you can see, Ariadne is very like our esteemed ancestress." She was, and was wearing the two diamond-encrusted combs Lady Clarissa was shown wearing in the portrait. "The combs you see Ariadne now wearing were given to my grandfather, and have eventually come down to the only one who can possibly do them justice."

The evening meal, which Ariadne had taken particular pains over, was enjoyed, but Michael was showing signs of jet lag and was obviously very tired. Ben bade him goodnight, and Ariadne showed him to the main guest room, rarely used. Ariadne had gone out of her way to make it as welcoming as she could, but Michael was too tired to appreciate the bowl of fruit and flowers or the drinks tray. On going to her own room she was surprised to see Ben there. He helped her remove the marvellous dress, and before she could stop him, he had thrown her almost violently onto her bed, face downwards. Quickly she scrambled to the other side of the bed, and to Ben's surprise, he was gazing at a small pistol she held in her hand.

"No, Ben. Take me if you must but the only way you will ever have me, otherwise I will kill us both." He wanted her so much he had to agree, and he made love a little carefully, aware of the pistol. He cursed himself for a stupid error of judgement, but still loved her.

It was a bleary-eyed Michael that stumbled into the stable block, where Ben was busy saddling the horses. Ben, as usual, was fully dressed and shaved, his French aftershave making Michael a little ashamed of his stubble. Ben smiled. "I suppose I have to thank Madame Ariadne that you are here at all. Is that not so?"

Michael had to agree ruefully, yes it was so. Ariadne had brought a steaming mug of hot coffee into his bedroom and stood over him until he had drunk it and got out of bed. When she was sure he was fully awake she stripped the bed. She wasn't going to have him sneaking back to bed when her back was turned.

Father and son rode in silence for a while, and when Ben was sure the boy was fully alert, he explained the estate and how it worked. "My estate manager is away in France at the moment but, as you can see, everything is so well run he can afford to take a few days off." Michael was impressed, and said so. Ben continued, "I am telling you and showing you everything, as one day, if you want it, this estate will be yours. There is also a title to go with it. I am taking steps to have you declared my legal son and successor. If you want it, you can one day be Sir Michael Haraldsson D'Vane." Michael was silent, trying to take in all he was being told. His father continued, "Your brother had been promised what by right should go to you, but that was arranged before I knew of your birth. I think, however, you are better off here, and where Philippe is to go might not be to your liking."

Michael asked, "Where is Philippe to go? Are you willing to tell me?"

Ben sighed. "It is better you don't know. It is a little complicated. Perhaps one day Madame Ariadne will explain."

The boy turned a little angry on his father. "Tell me one thing: why do you call my sister Madame all the time. Why can you not address her by her first name?"

Ben rode in silence for a time, then, making his mind up, stopped his mount. It was dawn, and a little warmer. "I have something to tell you about Ariadne and myself. You may end up hating me, but please, no pity."

When he dismounted Ben swayed a little and seemed to be in some pain. Michael was concerned. "Dad, are you OK? You seem ill."

Ben took some pills from his breast pocket and swallowed them with the help of a flask of coffee in his saddlebag. "Yes, but please don't tell your mother. I don't want to distress her. What I have to tell you, I find very difficult, and it upsets my system, which is not as it should be."

There had been no rain for several days and as the ground was dry, Michael led his father to a grassy bank, where Ben was grateful to lie for a few minutes. Michael was glad when a little colour returned to Ben's face and, sighing, Ben said, "I have wrestled with myself as to whether you should be made aware of certain facts, but I feel honesty, however distressing, is the best policy. I noticed you were very taken with Madame. I saw it almost as a sexual attraction." Michael flushed, and Ben laid his hand on his son's arm. "Please, don't worry: she has that effect on people. It isn't deliberate; she can't help it. I have a letter for you to read but I will explain how it came into my hands, and the unhappiness it brought."

Ben then told of his meeting with a beautiful young girl whom he fell deeply in love with, and how she returned his love. He explained how happy their first year had been, and how overjoyed he was to learn of her pregnancy. He knew it would be a boy, and now his only relative, his uncle, would at last stop pestering him to acquire an heir. He handed the letter to Michael, who read it in astonishment. "Now you can see why she is Madame, and not Miss."

Michael embraced his parent. "I take it you are both still in love?"

Ben sighed. "Yes, we are still lovers at times, but I have a male lover, as I try not to touch my darling girl except when I am driven to distraction with my need of her."

The pair rode back to the Hall in silence, where Ariadne had an American-style breakfast ready for Michael. She was surprised when Ben said he would join Michael for the meal. As a rule he only drank a cup of coffee and a little juice.

After breakfast it was decided Ariadne should take Michael to the airport. It took a while, as Michael had arrived at Heathrow – some distance from Dorset – but it gave Ariadne a chance to talk to her brother. Michael had little luggage, so Ariadne chose their comfortable Mercedes for the journey. On the way, taking all her courage into her hands, she said casually, "I assume Ben has told you about our relationship? I suppose you are shocked. Don't worry; I can understand if you are. Believe me, I also find it difficult. Ben has tried to distance himself from me, but it is impossible."

Michael was silent for a while, and Ariadne wondered whether perhaps she was wrong and should have kept silent. Michael, trying to find the appropriate reply, said, "I have been told to show no pity, but I feel for you both. You are so perfect for each other. I know Ben is fond of my mother but I can see it is you he really loves. I will keep what I've been told to myself. I will tell no one. I feel it is a very private and precious confidence. I know he is a very special person, and I am extremely proud to be his son and your brother."

Ariadne was almost in tears by now, and it was fortunate they were on a quiet stretch of road as her driving was a little erratic. She stopped the car and, wiping her eyes, said simply, "Thank you, Michael."

They stayed silent until they reached the airport. Michael insisted she did not hang about so she made the solitary journey back as quickly as possible, driving a lot faster as she was anxious about Ben.

The light was on in the library – Ben's sanctum – and she saw Jean-Paul talking with him. When Jean-Paul left the room he wasn't aware of her presence at first, and she saw him go to the drinks cabinet and pour a large whisky, which he swallowed at one go.

"Why, Jean-Paul, whatever is the matter?"

He glared at her. "Ben says I should ask you about your visitor."

Adriane had to laugh; the buck had passed to her. "Oh, it was just a one-off visit from a friend." She said no more, and he had to be content.

Ariadne decided to confront Ben and, if given the chance, give him a piece of her mind. He was obviously expecting to hear what she had told Jean-Paul about their visitor and was standing in front of his desk, with one long leg crossed over the other, enjoying a smoke, having taken to preferring, in place of larger cigars, the very latest and most expensive cheroots, which just fitted into his very elegant holder. A brandy was freshly poured but he ignored both smoke and drink on seeing Ariadne's face. "Now what has this old reprobate done to bring such an angry look to our little princess's face?"

She challenged him, "Is it your intention to put me down and place me in difficult situations at every conceivable chance you get?"

He shrugged. "*Non, non, pas de tout, Cherie.* I assume you look on me as a male chauvinist, *oui*?"

Her reply was equally non-committal. "*Aussi pas de tout, mais...*" Then she spoke in English, "If the cap fits, wear it."

This remark made Ben extremely angry. He gripped her right shoulder and used such force she had to gasp at the pain, but wouldn't let him see how much it hurt. She saw that underneath his open shirt he was wearing the insignia of the D'A-Huartan clan. It meant he was still, in his mind, the prince of his people and could do as he wished on any occasion. She saw in a flash of insight that it was where Philippe had got his cruel streak: he had inherited it from his father. Lifting her off her feet, Ben carried her to the little room next to the library. Ariadne was dimly aware of a swish and click as the blinds were drawn and the room locked. She was alone and at his mercy. He showed her none, but made love; angrily disappointed she didn't respond. Afterwards he carried her to her bedroom and bathed her and dressed her bruises, knowing this time he had gone too far. He made her a light meal and forced her to eat, but it was days before she finally recovered. She asked herself why she still loved him, but had no answer.

Six months before deciding finally to return to Europe for good, Ben asked Suella to marry him. He had set the scene for a romantic evening at one of their favourite restaurants in Greenwich Village, celebrating her fiftieth birthday. He had ordered champagne, kissed her, and laid her present on the table. "May I open it now?" she asked.

"Of course, and I hope you like it."

Suella gasped with delight at his gift. His taste was always excellent, and the earrings would match the bracelet he had given her so many years before. There was a small orchestra in the rather avant-garde restaurant, which had a reputation for being spotlessly clean and attracting a good cross- section of New York's diverse population. It boasted there was nothing they couldn't supply, and had so far never let a client down. When they were enjoying their coffee, Ben's mood suddenly changed. He took Suella's hand and asked, almost diffidently, "Will you marry me, Suella?"

She was silent for a minute, and Ben saw she had tears in her eyes. She leaned towards him across the table, and very gently touched his face. "Ben, my dear, I am afraid the answer is no I will not, no matter how many times you ask me." Her head was shaking sadly. He tried to interrupt, but she went on. "Michael has told me of your lovely home in England, where you are a kind of lord, and there are pictures of your ancestors on the walls. Your grandmother was a titled lady. Can you really see me fitting in there? I am afraid the shadow of Madam Fanny, as I once was, still hovers. Remember Hong Kong was once controlled by the British, and there would always be the chance we might come across someone who knew of my reputation and profession. I could damage your name. I would not want to be just your 'American wife' tucked away out of sight."

Ben sighed, knowing there was no hope of her changing her mind.

Ben visited Suella for five years, treating her as his wife, never neglecting Ariadne or Jean-Paul, but the strain told on his strong physique. He saw that Michael had plenty of funds to see him through university, and it was with much pride he accompanied Suella to see Michael graduate *cum laude*. This led to Michael being taken on by a very respectable law firm in Boston, where his ability was soon apparent. Ben took life a day at a time and when he was approaching what he termed his sixtieth birthday, never being sure of the exact date, he felt he needed to return to Swanbrook Hall for good. Suella was busy at a special meeting of the United Nations, where her interpreting skills were much in demand. Ben felt he couldn't stand an emotional parting so wrote her a brief note saying he needed to return to Europe on urgent business. He also wrote a note to Michael, going into more detail. He made things clearer by also removing all personal items from the apartment, explaining about his illness and how he had been struggling for years against the effects of radiation, and said, "I want to die in my own home. I've always said I will die there, and be buried next to my grandmother Lady Clarissa D'Vane. Tell your mother how much I love her and I will see she is well provided for in my will. Bless you, boy. Your loving father."

When Michael got the note he tried to contact first Ben, and then the airline. He needed to say goodbye at least. Ben, however, timed things to suit himself, and was already on his way over the Atlantic. He never saw Suella or Michael again. Suella was inconsolable. Like her son, she wished she could have said goodbye, but it was not to be.

Ben had to admit Suella was right. There was no way she would possibly fit into the life of Swanbrook Hall. He could imagine the scorn, the questions and the jealousy if she tried to usurp Ariadne and Jean-Paul. He told himself that once again he had let his heart rule his head. He knew his time in America was running out, but just didn't know how to tell either Suella or Michael. His son had settled well into his life with the Boston law firm, and also enjoyed a good social life. He made friends easily and was generally well liked by them. Ben returned to England refreshed and relaxed. He had enjoyed two days' sailing off Cape Cod, where he had purchased a small property for weekend use when he could manage it. Michael, like his father, was a good swimmer, and Ben taught him to be a good sailor. Suella was not keen on sailing, saying it made her feel seasick. Ben had enjoyed having Michael to himself, and knew he would miss him. Ben thought about his problem all the way back to England, but could see no way out. He detested scenes, and Suella might throw one. He knew that if there were tears he would probably give in and promise to continue with his visits. On his arrival back in Dorset he found a long letter from Dr Milo. He had completed his training, as Dr Fuharan had promised, and in the course of his work had come on a new drug which he thought could be very beneficial to Ben. He said it might prolong his life by up to five years, and wanted to know if Ben was willing to try it. Although the drug was still in the experimental stage there were very good reports on it. Ben was willing, and got in touch with his friend immediately. One good thing was that the nosebleeds that had plagued Ben were less frequent. He was not over-optimistic but he did start to feel a little less drained than previously, and not so tired. He was very good at taking the medication, and didn't need Ariadne to constantly remind him when it was due.

Before leaving America for the last time, Ben visited his old friend Dr Weng. He challenged him. "How long did you know about my relationship with Suella before you arranged that oh so casual meeting at the United Nations reception?"

Dr Weng looked just a little put out. "Not long, my friend. Suella got her job on her own and tried to keep out of my way. With some difficulty I found out her address, and you can imagine my surprise to see the boy. He reminded me of you when you were about the same age. After you told me of your dreadful discovery and your agony over your 'marriage' to Ariadne, I hesitated and debated whether it was wise to give you even more pain. I felt, however, that Michael was entitled to know his father, and you your son. I think I did the right thing, and some good has come out of it. Michael simply adores you and will be upset, as will Suella, on your decision to return to Europe for good."

Ben sighed. "Yes I know, but I need to put my affairs in order. I know I am living on what is known as 'borrowed time' and wish to die in my own home. You do understand. I know I'm a coward, but just can't face saying goodbye to them both."

He embraced his old friend, and left. There were tears in his eyes and he didn't look back. If he had, he would have seen the old man was crying also. The good doctor was on the point of retiring, and hoped to stay in America if he was allowed. China had had racial troubles in recent years, and there was a lot of unrest. If necessary he would apply for political asylum. He didn't think it would come to that and knew he could always find work part time, covering the subjects he had taught in Shanghai.

For Ben the worst part of the split, apart from not seeing Suella, was parting from Michael. Ben tried to remedy this by contacting him at his place of work, but this proved difficult. He tried writing but the letters were returned unread. In despair he contacted Dr Weng. "Please, old friend, can you get Michael to contact me by phone or letter? I'd like to talk to him," was Ben's frank admission.

Dr Weng sighed. "He is, of course, your *Doppelganger*, and as stubborn as you, but I will do my best."

Ben looked at Dr Weng speculatively. "Well now, I'm wondering if you are aware of how Suella earned her living before she moved to New York." The two friends were talking in a quiet corner of a lounge in the Ritz in Paris. Ben had thought it best to meet in neutral surroundings, and as the doctor was with a delegation visiting France, it was an opportune time to get in touch without causing too much speculation.

The doctor's gaze was unwavering. He sighed. "Yes, I am sorry to say, I did know. She must think I am blind. She had quite a reputation in Hong Kong and her mother, who was also a beauty, told me of it. She, poor lady, is now dead, but made me promise to try and get her girl away from that kind of life. Until they came to America, when Michael was thirteen, the two had not seen much of each other. As you must be aware, Michael adores his mother as much as he adores you. I think he was heartbroken when you decided to return to England."

This made Ben press his needs home. "All my letters to him

are returned unread. I'll accept it if he doesn't want to see me, but would appreciate the occasional telephone call or letter. Please tell him."

The older man patted Ben's arm. "I will certainly do that."

Ben was overjoyed when Michael started to write, and the pair never lost touch again.

Suella was devastated by Ben's decision to return to Europe. She was tempted to follow him there and try for work in Paris or Brussels, but Michael dissuaded her. How she missed Ben's visits and the way he would call out "Honey, I'm home" on arriving at the apartment. She missed his lovemaking, and, on finding a bottle of his very expensive French aftershave would put a few drops on the pillow he used, and pretend he was there. This usually reduced her to tears. Michael sought the advice of Dr Weng, who had kept away from the apartment when he knew Ben was there. "Tell me, Great-Uncle, did you know of mother's relationship with Ben Haraldsson, and that he is my father?"

The old man sighed. "Who do you think introduced them again to each other? I've known Ben since he was younger than you, my boy. I saw, when we first met on your arrival in America, that there was only one person whom you could claim as your father. Believe me, boy, he is a very special individual. He told me he hopes you will one day make your name in the legal profession. Yes, I also am worried about your mother."

Dr Weng visited the apartment and was very shocked to see Suella was letting herself go. "Snap out of it, Suella. I know all about you and Ben. He would be upset to see the condition you are now in. He left because he wants to save you distress. He is very ill, and has been for some time. He will require round-the-clock medical attention very soon, and frequent blood transfusions – impossible in this apartment. I know he hates hospitals, and is better off where he is. He doesn't think he has long to live. He told me this apartment is in your name and you have an income for life. Carry on and be a fighter like him; I know that is his wish for you. He loves you and Michael – remember that."

Suella did pull herself together, and went on with her work as normally as possible. Michael kept her informed of Ben's condition, but she never stopped loving him.

Jean-Paul was away in France, and Ben was bored out of his mind. The medication Dr Milo had prescribed for him had certainly made him feel better, and he was almost up to taking on his previous workload again. Ariadne felt it was too much but he told her, "I am never happy when I am bored. I'll know when it is too much."

She wasn't convinced, but knew he was a law unto himself and would do what he wanted no matter what she or his doctor said. He prowled around the Hall, driving both Ariadne and Genta mad. He was reading his daily papers, which were delivered every day and included French and English editions. He suddenly called out, "Ariadne, can you spare me a minute?" Resigned and wondering what mad scheme he had thought up, she found him with a broad grin on his face. "Darling, how does a trip to town feel. There is a rerun of *Les Miserables*, which I would like to see again, and I am sure you could do with some new clothes."

This last comment was true as since arriving at the Hall Ariadne had usually worn boots, raincoats and jeans. Clothes were not very high on her list of priorities. They decided to stay overnight at the Savoy, feeling it was central to the theatres and restaurants. Ariadne was pleased, as she had never felt at home in the Chelsea flat, always feeling it was Ben and Jean-Paul's domain. She spent a blissful afternoon restocking her wardrobe, and arrived back at the hotel with a number of boxes, including one for Ben. "You are not to open it until this evening," she told him. She had bought him a new dress shirt, and he thanked her. It was very elegant and, as she knew his taste, was a very welcome gift.

At the theatre they were lucky to get a box, due to a

last-minute cancellation, and both enjoyed the first part of the performance. At the interval they went to the bar. Ben was served quickly and had just put his glass to his lips when he froze, and Ariadne knew something was wrong. He looked absolutely furious.

Looking over the heads of those around them, Ariadne followed Ben's gaze. She was also astonished. Standing, with one arm carelessly flung around the shoulders of a younger man, was Jean-Paul. Ben elbowed his way towards them. His voice was like ice. "Won't you introduce your friend to us, Jean-Paul?"

To give him credit, Jean-Paul kept cool. He was formal. "Certainly, Sir. This is my cousin, Henri Caron."

The young man was about twenty-five and, seeing the discomfiture on his cousin's face, hastened to explain, "It is entirely my fault Jean-Paul is not at this moment in France. He was about to board his flight when I got in touch to say I was on my way to England. We appreciate my dear cousin coming to us too often, and felt it only fair to take our share of the cost."

Only partly mollified, Ben insisted the evening's entertainment was over. He told Jean-Paul to get rid of his cousin and get back to his duties at the Hall as soon as possible. He turned and, without another word, marched out of the theatre. That night in their hotel room, he made love to Ariadne. It wasn't a very pleasant experience for the girl. She told him not to take his anger and frustration out on her. He didn't apologise but slammed out of the room. She assumed he would find somewhere to drink, belonging as he did to several clubs in town. Ariadne sighed to herself. He would be like a bear with a sore head in the morning. And there was still the journey back to Dorset to face.

When she awoke after a restless night, Ben was in the room. They drank black coffee together in complete silence. He kept the silence up all the way back to Dorset. There was the inevitable row when they arrived back at the Hall. Ben tore a strip off his lover. He was insanely jealous. He wanted to know if Jean-Paul's cousin was his lover, and if that was why he was making such frequent trips to France.

The atmosphere was electric as the two lovers met in verbal battle. Genta couldn't hear what was being said. She didn't need to. Their faces said it all. Without warning, Ben leaned forward and gave Jean-Paul a kiss on the lips. Genta gasped and, turning to Ariadne, asked, "Am I wrong, or was that a lover's kiss?"

Ariadne felt extremely sorry for her. "Yes, Dear. I am so sorry." She explained that they had been lovers since Ben took over the Hall.

Genta was devastated. She was in love with Jean-Paul. "They both appear so manly, not as homosexuals tend to look or behave."

Ariadne agreed. "They are what is known as bisexual. They can favour either sex."

Genta said, "I think it might be best if I left. I am not sure how to act towards either of them."

When the girl was able to get Ben on his own, she reported Genta's reaction to discovering about his relationship with Jean-Paul. He was upset, and went at once to her sitting room. He could be very persuasive, and laid the charm on thick. "What would we do without you Genta, Darling! You mean a lot to all of us. Who will make those lovely little cakes I enjoy so much, and the delicious coffee you brew for me all hours of the day. You are our friend. Ariadne would be lost without you. I think you deserve a holiday. Tell me where you would like to go, and I'll see you get first-class tickets."

Genta's reply was cold. "You think money solves all problems. Do you know the meaning of honesty and decency? Where do they come in?"

Ben left her impatiently. He decided to leave Ariadne to do the persuading, and she succeeded and Genta gave in. Genta having made Swanbrook Hall her home, she just could not face the inevitable question as to why she wished to leave. Genta knew Ariadne often sought her support, but was left far from happy. She decided to take the holiday, but insisted on paying for it herself.

Genta returned from her holiday, and on the surface everything seemed the same. But the old easy friendship had gone. She was now purely an employee. It meant she never addressed Ben by any title other than 'Sir'. She never lost her devotion to Jean-Paul, blaming Ben for having seduced him.

Life turned into a humdrum routine. Ben and Jean-Paul led their own lives, and the two women theirs.

One day there was an unexpected visitor. Genta knocked on Ben's door and for once forgot her aloofness. "There is a French lady to see you, Sir."

Ben was intrigued. "Well, let's have her name." He had no idea.

"It's Madame Nicolle Chevalliere – the ex-wife of the former French president."

Ben whistled. Why was she calling on him, and for what reason? When Madame was ushered in she soon made clear the reason for her impromptu visit. Ben greeted her like an old friend. So she remembered him. Ever the gallant, he kissed her hands and both cheeks. When formalities were completed he ordered coffee and waited to hear what she desired from him. He was astonished, and not a little amused. She was running for President of France, and wondered if he would care to manage her campaign. "Madame, my life is here in England. I think you would make a formidable president. If you care to telephone me any time to seek my advice, I shall be delighted to give it and assist you in any way I can. Perhaps a cheque to assist your plans is acceptable?"

It was, and kissing him on the lips, as she had done all those years ago, she left. He and Jean-Paul laughed over the encounter. Jean-Paul hit the nail on the head. "I have the feeling that it was funds she was really after, not your expertise, *mon ami*."

"I am feeling so much better," Ben was able to tell Ariadne, and to demonstrate just how well he felt, decided to go riding again. Ariadne knew it would be useless to try and dissuade him but she insisted he had a good rest after lunch. He had safely returned from his ride, accompanied, at Ariadne's insistence, by one of the grooms as Jean-Paul wasn't free, when he received two surprises. The first was the arrival of Dr Milo. He was now the senior physician on the Two Islands, as Dr Fuharan had retired. "Yes, it would be nice to have some extra help but where it is to come from? You tell me." He was delighted to see Ben appeared to have profited from use of the new drug, and said he fully expected Ben to live a good deal longer than previously thought possible. They enjoyed a delightful lunch but because Jean-Paul was also present, had to be guarded in their topics of conversation. Later, the doctor was due to meet Pag, who was returning with him to the Two Islands. The second surprise was a telephone call from Michael. At first Ben thought there was something wrong with Suella. She was upset, as was Michael. He had forgotten that now he was an American citizen he was liable for military service if found fit. The military had been looking for a Michael Wood. His father told him, "Why not accept that as your name? It might save a lot of hassle."

Michael was mainly upset because he was just getting himself noticed for his ability at work, though his firm was willing to accept him back after service. He was considered too tall to fly fighter planes – his legs were too long for this to be done safely. When it was revealed he was a linguist, he was posted to Intelligence. He would later join the Advocate General's office. He proved an able cadet and was awarded the sword of honour. It was presented to him by the former president, Ed Godber. Looking at the younger edition of Ben the ex-president thought, 'Well I'll be damned; not another one of yours, Ben?' Ed smiled as he said to Michael, "When you next see Ben, remember me to him." A startled Michael had but to agree.

Gradually Ben and Jean-Paul resolved their differences. The latter continued his trips to France. His mother had got into financial difficulties and her son was determined to "keep an eye on managing her money". He continued at his work as estate manager and, like Ben, was respected for his ability and fairness. Colonel Morley, known as Colonel Fitz – his full name was Fitzroy Hammond Morley and beside being a colonel was chair of the local Watch Committee – called on Ben and asked if he would care to be a relief magistrate and then take over when the present official retired. Ben was intrigued, and said he would consider it an honour. He sat in on several sessions, and was pleased to join the two ladies already there. He sat between them, as if he was in charge, and soon showed them he knew as much, if not more, of the legal system than they did. They were impressed, and often let him deal with difficult cases. One such case was Ollie Hobson. Ben looked at the rascal – not a pleasant sight. After a night in the cells he needed both a shave and change of clothing. He had been up before the Bench on several occasions, usually for poaching. This time the charge was 'Drunk and Disorderly'. Ben looked at him and recalled the last time they had met – when Ollie had ruined Ben's riding habit in the Royal Oak. "What have you got to say for yourself, Mr Hobson?" Ollie shifted uneasily. He didn't think he could con this chap, like he could old Mr Jepson. Why did the old fool have to retire? Ben continued, "I understand you have four children, and your wife is expecting another shortly." Ollie agreed this was so. "If you go to prison, even for just a short time, your family will suffer; and you, I know, are short of funds. I'll give you one last chance." He turned to the two ladies. "If you agree, I will give him a job on my estate. He will be strictly supervised, and any lapse will be dealt with severely."

It was agreed. The new gamekeeper was supervised, as Ben had promised. Jean-Paul undertook his responsibilities in this direction very seriously. He told Ollie, "Let down Mr Haraldsson when he has been so lenient, and you will answer to me. I will have your guts for garters. Is that clear?" Ollie merely grunted. "You will address me as 'Sir'. Is that also clear?"

It was. Ollie made a good gamekeeper and showed a flair for the work, as long as he kept off the drink.

One morning Ben woke with a strange presentiment something was going to happen. Pag arrived at the Hall in a terrible state. He fell into Ben's arms, sobbing hysterically. When Ben and Ariadne had the full story they were also very upset. Pag's wife, the beautiful Dorita Maria, was dead. She had been struck by a hit-and-run driver, and died on the way to hospital. "My boys. What can I tell them, and who will look after them?"

Ben gave Pag a sedative, and while he recovered his composure Ben and Ariadne discussed how to best help their friend. "Pag has his work with the airline and what he does for me."

When he was more himself, the sad pilot apologised for burdening them with his problem. Ben said, "Nonsense! What are friends for? I have an idea. Tell me what you think." He outlined a plan which, if considered feasible, would provide a home for the two boys, now sixteen and twelve. It would take care of their future. Ben proposed they went to their maternal grandmother in Italy for three months. She was the one to give them the love and support they would need to get over the shock of losing their mother. Ben said, "Ed Godber owes me a few favours. Now is the time to call them in."

Ed had served as President for two terms – a popular if not brilliant president. His main interest had been the exploration of space and how it could best help mankind.

Ed Godber was delighted to use his influence to get Georgio into the International Space School. When he mentioned the boys' plight to Senator Tubbs he also offered to assist, and arranged for Sandro, the younger boy, to live on his ranch. Being mad about horses, this suited young Sandy, as he was soon known, down to the ground. He was able to continue his education besides being near to where Georgio was training. Mrs Tubbs was pleased to have two boys to mother. Georgio spent off-duty time there also. A very relieved Pag was able to continue his work knowing his boys were in safe hands.

Things had started to settle down again at the Hall, when Ben made an astonishing discovery. He and Jean-Paul were out riding, when Ben bent his head under a branch of a big oak. The oak snapped back and hit him on the face. Not thinking, Ben uttered an old Usaurian oath, exclaiming "Bakra, bakra" several times.

Jean-Paul looked at him strangely. "If that is a swear-word, I've heard it before. I am sure my father used it on several occasions. Where did you pick it up?"

Ben went cold. He passed it off by saying he frequently picked up odd words. He had been around quite a bit, hadn't he now?

On returning to the Hall, he went to his computer and checked all the information he had on Jean-Paul. He tried to trace his family tree. He could find his mother's line but there was a blank when it came to his father. He went to his laboratory at the top of the house. He took DNA from everyone. It was surprisingly easy, and no one was aware of it. He already knew his and Ariadne's were different to Genta's. His hands shook when he came to check Jean-Paul's. There was no doubt about it. Jean-Paul had Usaurian blood. He was Uncle Bron's grandson.

Should he tell Jean-Paul they were cousins? Ben decided it might not be the best policy.

"Why ever not?" Ariadne wanted to know.

"Well, just suppose he blurted it out to someone. He does get drunk sometimes. We must be careful. May I ask you to tell him only when I am dead?"

This upset Ariadne and she burst into tears. "Please don't talk like that."

Ben tried to comfort her by saying, "Remember, I am that much older than both of you. I've told you many times I don't expect to live to be very old. I quite expect Uncle Bron to survive me. I have a special request that I wish you to honour. When I do die, I would like my heart removed and placed in this casket." He indicated a beautiful casket made of gold, which was in his safe. Ariadne was still upset, and to show he still loved her, Ben took her once more into his arms, and they made love. This happed so infrequently that Ariadne did not protest, but accepted they still meant this much to each other.

Ben contacted his solicitor and altered his will. He left a sizeable sum of money to Jean-Paul, and also the flat off King's Road, Chelsea, that he had purchased for their now-frequent trips to town. Both he and Jean-Paul were ardent rugby fans, especially when France was playing. In the summer months they and Ariadne were keen racegoers. They often met up with Sheikh Kassim, who would invite them to join him in his box. He and Jean-Paul were old adversaries. He roared at the younger man, "You can't throw me out of here, like you tried to in the desert. I know you were acting under orders but it was, and still is, my country."

Jean-Paul would grimace, and try to keep out of Sheikh Kassim's way. He would often disappear, saying he was going to place a bet on at the tote.

Three months after starting as relief magistrate Ben was offered the position for as long as he wished. Everyone was impressed with his way of carrying out his duties, and he was soon extending his circle of friends. It also led to him being offered other positions in their small community. Ariadne told him he was taking on far too much, but Ben was enjoying life and, as usual, did as he wished. His first encounter with Millicent Dackett didn't impress him. She appeared before the three magistrates accused of shoplifting. She was nearly eighteen, and a probation officer was asked to investigate her circumstances. His report shocked Ben. He was on his own the second time she was brought before the court, and he was dismayed to see how much thinner she was and how she appeared completely cowed. She started to sway, and Ben asked her when she had last eaten.

"I had some bread and water before I came out."

The court was stunned into silence. Both the bailiff and clerk of the court just gasped. In their day and age even prisoners were no longer fed such meagre fare. Ben frowned and, beckoning a police sergeant, who had just entered the court, ordered him to take the girl to the court canteen and find her something to eat. "If there aren't sufficient funds in the court charity box, I'll pay."

When she returned a half an hour later there was some colour in her cheeks. Ben had read the report with dismay. She pleaded guilty and he felt he could quite easily discharge her with a small delayed sentence or put her on probation. Her parents, he read, were strict chapelgoers and the girl not only had, until her dismissal from work, cooked and cleaned the house for her mother, but helped out working on the smallholding they rented. The father, the probation officer considered, was a bully, and he had seen bruises on the girl. Her mother spent all her time working in the chapel. Everything the girl earned was taken off her, and she was allowed the fare to work one way only, and only a small amount of money for a meal.

"You have pleaded 'guilty', so the court is inclined to give you a chance to turn your life around. You will serve a month doing community service. I will ask the local meals on wheels service to take you on twice a week to help them deliver meals to the elderly and housebound. Do you understand?" The girl was now crying, and removed her glasses to wipe her eyes. "Do you really need to wear those? They don't really fit you."

The girl replied through her tears, "My father bought them for me."

Ben asked, "Have you seen a qualified optician?" She shook her head. Ben felt he would like to wring the neck of such an uncaring parent. He drew a card from his pocket. "I would like you to go and see this lady, and say I sent you. She will, I hope, be able to help you." On the card Ben had written "*Cherie*, see what you can do to turn this ugly duckling into a swan. I feel the poor girl needs our help." He directed her how to get to

Swanbrook Hall and thought with a wry grin, 'Now Ariadne will say "It's now your turn at helping lame ducks, like you accuse me of always doing".' Ah well, what will be will be!

Feeling content and happy with his decision, Ben carried on, and the rest of the morning was routine and uneventful. Millicent found Swanbrook and nervously handed the note to Ariadne, thinking to herself, 'What a lovely lady!' Ariadne looked, with not a little dismay, at the state of the girl. For a start she was much too thin – almost anorexic. But Adriane liked a challenge. "How are you usually addressed? Milly, I suppose?"

The girl shook her head. "No. It is always Millicent at home, but I rather like Milly."

So, Milly it was from then on. Ariadne found some of her own clothes, which fitted Milly as they were much the same size, and as tall as each other. Milly enjoyed a bath in the Jacuzzi – the first time in her life she had used one – and the scented oil she found pure heaven.

She didn't give a thought about her parents and what their reaction would be. She just didn't care. She was happy where she now found herself.

Ariadne washed the girl's hair, but realised the 'brassy' look would have to go. The local hairdresser's, known as Hair Today, could fit them in, and it was known Madame Ariadne was a good tipper. It was a unisex salon and well patronised, not only by the local community but by people in the surrounding district. Carole the owner could have gone to London but preferred the quieter life, where she was well-known and knew her customers' likes and dislikes. Milly's hair was lightly washed again, and cut. Carole suggested the light ash blonde colour it now was would benefit from highlights, and these were added. Milly's eyebrows were also plucked, and her nails manicured. The transformation was now complete. Ariadne thought Ben would approve. He did, and whistled in sheer surprise as he had no idea the girl was so lovely. In French he said quietly, "Madame, you have worked a miracle, as I knew you would."

He saw Milly blush, and quickly realised she had understood. "You speak French?" he asked her.

Milly hesitated. "Well, not very well, but I did pass my first grade French."

Ben was pleased. "French is the first language in this house, so we will have to see what we can do to make you speak it as we all do. Even Madame Genta is fluent. We use English, of course, outside with the stable lads, but even they are learning."

Milly was only too willing to learn, and Ben was delighted when she told him she was a competent computer operator. "I learnt at school, and only need slight revision."

Ben asked the girl if she would like to act as his PA. "I could do with some assistance now Madame is so busy elsewhere."

"I had no idea you actually lived here," Milly added. "Is it OK for me to stay here with you?"

Ben said, "I am ready to challenge anyone, even your parents, if I have to."

Milly said she was sure her father would have something to say. Ben had a note sent to her parents, on official paper as if from the court, stating he was acting *in loco parentis* while Milly was under his care for 'training'.

Her parents responded quickly, and turned up together to challenge Ben personally. Ben looked at Milly's father and quickly saw, as the probation officer had stated in his report, he was a bully. He saw Milly tremble, and vowed to himself that whatever happened he wouldn't permit her to return to such a vile man. "You are aware I had Milly examined by the police doctor, and he found bruising consistent with a beating. I see you wear a heavy leather belt. Should you wish to challenge me in court, I will have evidence against you that could possibly give you a prison sentence."

The man blustered, "My girl is not yet eighteen, and she is needed at home."

Ben sighed, and pushed a paper towards the man and asked him to read it.

"What's this?"

Looking with ill-concealed contempt at the man facing him, Ben said, "It is a statement by me, as a magistrate, declaring I do not consider you are a fit person to have care of a juvenile."

Milly's parent went white with rage, and for a minute Ben thought he was going to lash out, and was ready for him. Milly's mother had been silent during the encounter, and now laid a restraining hand on her husband's arm. "I don't think the wicked girl is worth bothering about."

Ben rang the buzzer on his desk, and Jean-Paul entered. Ben spoke to him in English. He was asked to show Milly's parents out. He was of course younger and stronger than Ben, and said coldly, "This way, Sir and Madam."

They went quietly enough but Milly's father uttered one final threat: "You haven't heard the last of this; not by a long chalk."

A few days later Ben received a summons to appear at the county court and explain things. He was happy to do as asked. The relevant documents he already possessed, he felt sure, would vindicate him. The contrast between the two men couldn't have been more marked. Ben was wearing freshly laundered linen and a new dark suit. He looked every inch the gentleman, whereas Horace Dackett looked what he was – a man of the soil. Ben chose to affirm not take the oath, but stated his case clearly. "Miss Dackett now works for me as my PA. She is very competent, and her abilities are far above the career her parents have wished on her as a shelf stacker in a supermarket." He then went on to give a detailed account of how he had first met Milly and the reasons for her appearing in court. He did not elaborate, but brought out documents proving the reason for her lapse from grace arose from sheer parental neglect. "Can you believe that a girl of nearly eighteen has never worn make-up or owned a pair of nylons? In summer she went without, and in the winter months she was wearing a pair of thick scratchy rough socks – the type seamen wear. She had all her wages taken from her, and was only allowed the minimum fare to work."

He handed the probation officer's report to the residing magistrate, who asked to speak to Milly. The tall graceful girl was a far cry from the photo taken of her by the court photographer a short time earlier. It didn't take long for the case to be dismissed. The magistrate was very impressed by her and agreed that as she was nearly eighteen, she was quite capable of deciding where she could live and work.

Milly returned to Swanbrook Hall and told Ben she was happy to continue working for him as his PA. He was always busy either preparing his lectures, which he now gave nearer home, or searching the internet for data concerning the many subjects various magazines wished him to write about. It was very tiring, and both Ariadne and Milly tried to make things easier for him whenever possible. Ben found he no longer needed to rise so early, and often stayed in bed until six or seven o'clock. His horse – a new one called Magnus – was always ready, and he offered to teach Milly to ride, which she was delighted to agree to and proved a very willing and able pupil. Things settled down, but as Ben had found many times, he dared not take things for granted. The smooth and contented atmosphere at Swanbrook Hall was to be disturbed yet again.

Four months later, after a busy morning sitting on the Bench, Ben was just about to sign off and retire for a well-earned cup of coffee, when he was aware of a heated argument between the bailiff and the clerk of the court. "Anything wrong?" he asked.

There was. "Your Honour, we have a problem. The County Court has requested us to deal with a group of men, believed to be Polish seamen. They seem to have no English, an interpreter cannot be found, and as you are known to be a linguist, they hope you can help out."

Ben sighed. "OK; wheel them in."

The bailiff, having got the gist of the matter off his chest, breathed a sigh of relief.

Ben did not look up immediately, and got a shock when he did. Four Space Riders – one of Pag's crack teams – stood before him. They were led by Orion, his companions being Krakan, Tresun, and the youngest – Serin. Ben controlled a desire to shout. He turned to the bailiff, saying calmly, "As this will be very boring for you, perhaps it is better if I deal with them on my own. Goodness knows how long it will take." The youngest Space Rider looked terrified, and the policeman who had brought them in patted him on the shoulder, saying, "Don't worry, lad, it's not a hanging offence. Mr Haraldsson is very fair," laughing at his own joke.

Ben added, "Please lock the door. I have a bell if I require assistance."

Reluctantly, as it was considered most unusual, the court was cleared, and only Ben and the four disgraced Space Riders remained. Serin bit his lip and trembled visibly. Ben read the report, which stated that the four had been involved in a pub brawl and had caused considerable damage to the property. Ben snapped, "Serin, explain, and don't give me a made-up story to cover yourselves."

When the young boy had finished, Ben realised it wasn't their fault, but they all knew the only rule they were asked to obey when visiting Earth was not under any circumstances to allow themselves in any situation they couldn't get out of with ease. "How much money have you between you? You will have to pay for the damage you have caused."

They emptied their pockets, and managed to raise sixty euros. Ben knew it wasn't nearly enough to pay for the damage, and realised he would have to top it up. "I will give you a conditional discharge, but you will have to see what punishment your commandant considers necessary." He beckoned Serin to approach him, and said, not unkindly, "I wish you to stay behind and work for me. Are you agreeable?"

Of course Serin was. Ben rang the bell and the court officials returned, much relieved Ben was still in one piece.

Serin found his way to Swanbrook Hall, and Milly was one of the first people he saw. She was in the garden helping Ariadne, and held a large bunch of flowers in her hands. He thought she was one of the most beautiful girls he had ever seen. It was a case of love at first sight. Milly was given charge of him and was asked to help him with his English, which needed improving, and generally tell him things he required explaining. Soon they were never apart, except when Milly was working for Ben. The one person who saw how things stood with them was Ariadne. She told Ben, who was a little piqued. He realised he had a rival. He was surprised to realise he himself was attracted to the girl, and told himself it was ridiculous at his age as he was now well into his fifties. Ariadne had warned him when he first decided Milly could work for him, not to get involved, and he had promised to behave himself. Gradually it seemed Milly was starting to care for Serin also. On her eighteenth birthday Serin asked her to be his partner. She was a little in love with Ben but knew it was a hopeless infatuation. What would a wonderful man like Ben want with a nobody like herself? Serin asked Ben if he could tell Milly about what he did and also about the Two Islands planet. Reluctantly Ben agreed. Milly was utterly enthralled. "Why isn't Ben there now?" she asked Serin.

"Don't you know about his illness?"

She had no idea, and almost told Ben she loved him. Serin had been given work cataloguing Ben's library. Ben said it would help his English but found, to his dismay, it brought the two young people closer together. Ben decided to send the ardent young lover back home but Serin said no, not without Milly, and she begged to be allowed to join him. Ben was forced to agree, and a farewell party was given for the pair.

Ben was in his bedroom, having left the party, saying he was tired, when there was a timid knock on the door. He was surprised to see Milly there, nervously smiling.

"Excellency, I know you are attracted to me, and I have discussed a proposal I have with Serin, and he is agreeable. I am sure you know the expression '*droit de seigneur*' and as Serin is, in a way, one of your vassals, I am offering myself to you before we depart."

To say Ben was dumbstruck was an understatement. He looked at the girl and realised she had very little on under her robe. What was he to do? If he agreed to her outrageous proposal he would be doing the very thing Ariadne had warned him about. If he sent her away she might feel humiliated and of little worth, and perhaps lose all the confidence she had gained since working for him. "Wait here," he ordered, and disappeared, first to make sure there was champagne in his private refrigerator and, secondly, to contact Serin to see if he really did agree to Milly's proposal. It appeared he did, and Ben took two large glasses of champagne back with him. He found Milly a very sexy partner, and she stayed the night with him, and he knew Suella could not have made love better when she was plying her trade. Where had the girl Milly learnt so much? She did everything he asked of her, and he felt quite battered when she eventually left him. He told her that if there should be a child he wished Serin to be declared the father, and he didn't want any news of it. Milly promised. In the morning Pag came to collect the two, and with dry eyes Ben saw them depart and wondered if he would ever see either of them again.

It was Pag who told Ben that Serin was dead. He had died bravely, crashing his craft to save others. Milly was returning to Earth, as she was homesick. Ben wondered how they would react if they did meet again, and chuckled at his recollection of their last meeting.

One warm summer's day Ben was taking his siesta in the garden of Swanbrook Hall and was half asleep, when he felt someone was standing near him. He opened his eyes and saw a lovely little girl no more than two or three years old. She was touching his face and holding a rose out for him to smell. "I picked it especially for you. You can kiss me if you like."

Ben picked her up and sat her on his lap. She turned her

face and his heart nearly missed a beat. Her eyes were grey. The grey of all his family. He looked around wildly and saw her mother Milly, wearing her Space Riders uniform, coming towards them. He mouthed silently over the little head, "Mine?"

Milly nodded agreement. He knew he had asked her not to tell him if there was a child, but now words just failed him. "What is your name, little one?" he asked.

"I'm called Benita; I fink after my dada."

Her mother corrected, "Remember, it's 'think', Darling, not 'fink'."

Ben hugged his child and was so happy he could hardly speak. Like all children fathered by a Usaurian, she was tall and remarkably forward in every way. Her hair was the same colour as Ben's had been as a child. "Are you my dada?" Benita asked.

"I rather think I am. Do you mind?"

The little one put her arms round Ben's neck and hugged him. They seemed to bond immediately. Ben had missed the childhoods of his other children, and hoped he would be spared to share just a little of this child's babyhood, for she was indeed still a baby. One thing he was glad about was that he had told Ariadne of how Milly had offered herself to him, which he knew was a 'thank you' for all he had done for her. He decided to spend at least three months with Benita and her mother, but where?

As if in answer to a prayer, the solution was in a letter from Nurse Shona McGee. 'I have met a very nice English lady and she has asked me to spend the summer with her at her home in Bournemouth. I know you are far from well so please remember I will be quite close if you need me at any time.' She went on to give details of where keys were etc, and a pleased Ben decided to go there with Milly and Benita. They had three weeks to fill and Ben spent this time spoiling his darling child. He took her to the zoo and to several theme parks, and they had a whale of a time. Clothes were his next priority for the child as, with her being tall, baby outfits children of her age usually wore were out. He also bought clothes she could wear later on when she was a little taller. Also he had to think about her future, and put her name down at a very select girls' school. Milly protested, "Isn't she a bit young for you to be thinking of that just yet?"

Ben disagreed. "I don't think so." He went to Zurich and, using money in his Swiss account, set up a trust fund for Benita and arranged for Milly to have an income. One thing he did secretly, not telling Milly: he made holograms of himself and discs, to be given to Benita on each of her birthdays, starting with her fourth, as he knew he couldn't be with her. He did manage to attend her third-birthday party and she loved his gift – a gold bangle that would expand as she grew older.

The little French cottage had been left spick and span by a thoughtful Nurse Shona, and the weather was just perfect. Ben felt he should make love to Milly but wasn't sure he was physically up to it. She was understanding, and led the way and seemed to enjoy it. She told him Serin had been found to be sterile, so incapable of fathering a child. Ben felt this was just as well, as he wasn't sure how he would have known how to deal with another child, especially one that wasn't his.

The three months were nearly up when Ben realised he had omitted to take his usual quota of tablets. He felt he was likely to frighten Benita if he was taken ill, so with a heavy heart he left them. In the morning Benita wanted to know where Dada was. Milly was also upset but told the child, "Dada has had to go away."

"When is he coming back?"

How could she tell the child Ben loved so much that she would never see him again?

Ben just had time to return to Swanbrook Hall before collapsing with a heavy nosebleed. In a way he was glad of his illness, as he would have broken down if he had to say goodbye personally. He had a letter sent to Milly when he was a little recovered, saying she was to make sure Benita returned to the Two Islands planet when she was eighteen, and assumed her rightful title of Princess. He said he expected Philippe would be the leader by the time she was eighteen, and if there was any doubt of her parentage, there was a sample of his DNA to prove who she was. Benita had a constant reminder of Ben in the little bangle, and every birthday wept a little when she viewed her birthday hologram. Milly found work in the employ of one of Lucien Gervaise's colleagues, and from being a mere PA, worked her way up and became a director of the firm.

Ben never left Swanbrook again, and it was a caring Ariadne who continued to look after him.

When Philippe was twelve years of age, it was decided to send him to a boarding school in England. He wasn't very happy, and complained to his 'Uncle Luke', as he liked to call Lucien Gervaise. Ben and Ariadne, as his parents, were asked to go and see the headmaster to sort out the problem if possible. Ben was doubtful they could help. It appeared Philippe had been fighting, and when asked the reason why, he assumed a truculent air. After a good deal of probing the headmaster decided the only ones who could possibly sort him out were his parents. He was dismayed to find the boy was reluctant to see his father. The head was impressed with both parents. His mother was a good deal younger than her husband, and he wondered if that was the reason for his problems. Was the child jealous of his father? The mother was certainly a beauty. He sensed an air of mystery about them. It was known that they had left the child when young, to go away. No one appeared to know exactly where.

Ariadne took her son on one side and gently asked why he was finding things so difficult.

"They call me a frog because I am French. If I try to be friendly, they bully me."

This made his mother smile. He was far taller than his fellows. "Surely not, Darling." She also discovered it was the unwritten rule for tuck boxes to be brought every term. Philippe had not been provided with the essential 'goodies', and he was thought mean. She promised to see this was put right immediately. He put his arms about her and gave her a hug and a kiss on the lips. She felt he was too emotionally mature for his age but decided not to mention this to Ben.

Back at the Hall the vineyard was starting to take shape. Their first real harvest was expected, and this was causing quite a stir in the neighbourhood. On tasting the wine Ben's verdict was, "Not exactly Beaujolais, but not bad."

The quality of the wine was superior to that produced by Le Papillon. It was mellower, and suitable to drink either on its own or with white meats. Ariadne considered sending a case to her rival but Ben said a firm no, saying she would either throw it away or pass it off as her own. It was decided to call it simply 'Swanbrook', and sales were fairly brisk. Even the local beer-swilling customers of the Royal Oak liked it.

Ben did not see his son for several years. Philippe suddenly turned up at the Hall without warning, announcing the old woman was dead. He had been left the chateau and the vineyard, and wished to sell both. When asked where he would live he said he had arranged accommodation, but gave no further details. Ariadne was devastated to find her childhood home was up for sale. Ben contacted Lucien and asked him to negotiate the purchase of the property. On no account was he to let the boy know who the purchaser was. It was decided the best thing was to lease it out as a study centre and keeping a flat for family use. This side of the deal was not disclosed to Philippe, who was delighted with the price. There was a good deal of work required to put it in order, and it proved something of a headache keeping all the details of the purchase from Ariadne. On her thirty-fifth birthday she found the deeds on her breakfast tray. She burst into tears. "Darling Ben, what a lovely surprise!"

He gently dried her eyes. "Now, no tears on your birthday." But they were tears of happiness. Philippe, however, was not so pleased when he found out he had been tricked.

"Well, it is keeping it in the family and I paid more than it is really worth. It is costing me a small fortune getting the work required completed in time for the first students," was Ben's comment.

After some discussion it was decided not to purchase the vineyard, but allow it to go to a developer. Its sale would not interfere with the chateau; it was on a separate site. Ariadne found there was no one left there she knew, so it was not like asking people she could have employed being denied work. When the developers started there would be plenty available.

Ben realised he would have to resign from the numerous projects he had become involved in over the years. He didn't like to say no, and they had just snowballed, taking over his life. His doctor agreed, and he was cajoled into taking a long holiday. He took Ariadne, feeling Jean-Paul was needed to take care of affairs on the estate. It was certainly the wisest choice as Ariadne told him, "There is no knowing what the two of you might have got up to. It wouldn't have been a holiday. Certainly not the rest you need."

Ben pulled a face at her, but he was aware she was talking plain common sense.

They went to the Greek islands, hiring a trim little craft and the services of a small crew. After three weeks Ben started to get restless. This lotus life was not to his liking. He told Ariadne he wanted something to do.

"You are burning yourself out. I am not going to let you resume your old way of life. Remember, you are now past your prime."

He groaned. "Don't I know it!"

They finally returned to Swanbrook Hall and although Ariadne did her best, there was no suppressing Ben's restless spirit. She managed to persuade him to give up his position as relief magistrate, and put a firm veto on any more trips to America.

He retaliated by going for long rambles on his own. Following him once to see where he was going, she found that he was indulging in his lifelong love of birds. He was birdwatching.

Lying flat on his stomach, Ben motioned her to get down to his level also. The big wolfhound was by his side. There was no growl at Ariadne's approach – only a gentle wag of his tail.

"Look. I think that's a corncrake, very rarely seen except in Scotland. I wonder what it's doing here?" said Ben.

The grass was just a little damp, so she tried to get him away. His answer was to lean over her and start his usual kissing routine. Much to his surprise, she resisted him. He was irrepressible, and turned a little cross. Ariadne said, "Doctor's orders. No excitement of any kind."

They returned together but he had exhausted himself and would not admit it. She made him a hot drink to take with a sleeping pill. Ben slept for hours, and on waking barely remembered how he had spent the previous day.

Ariadne was nearing her fortieth birthday, and under the greatest secrecy a special treat was arranged.

The dress she had worn on the Two Islands was brought out of store. Genta was very taken with it. A message was sent to Major Orlevski, who contacted his relative in Paris. The dress wanted just a little alteration to make it more modern and fit better. Ariadne had put on a little weight, but still managed to look no more than thirty years old. Her hair was still the glorious red of her youth, and it never needed any dyes or colouring. Her skin was still peaches and cream. It was decided to send her to Paris for a few days. Lucien was in the plot, and a scheme was hatched which required her to also go to the chateau. There was a ballroom at the Hall, but how to get it ready without her knowing? It was hard work by all. Invitations were sent out and catering arranged. There was a good supply of wine already in the cellar, and champagne was also ordered. The dress arrived back, and all was ready for the 'belle of the ball'.

It was a success, due mainly to Ben's careful planning – he had anticipated well in advance all that would be required. He was assisted by Jean-Paul carrying out his orders faultlessly. The occasion was discussed for a long time afterwards. The women couldn't take their eyes off the dress. They had never seen one like it, and wanted to know who designed it.

"Now that is my secret." Ariadne was not going to give anything away. The guests were further intrigued by the arrival of Major Orlevski. He was bitter because although given a medal, as yet there was no promotion. He reminded Ben of his desire to go back to the Two Islands planet. They discussed this out on the terrace, where their conversation was drowned by the small orchestra engaged for the occasion. Ariadne joined them and talked freely in Russian to the Major. Pag arrived a little later. He was pleased to help with final arrangements for the Major to go with him on his next journey to the planet.

The guests were delighted by the lanterns that were strung along the drive. As dusk fell they were treated to a *son et lumiere* and laser display, followed by fireworks. "Everyone seems to have had a good time," Ben said after he was thanked for such a marvellous evening. He was tired, and starting to droop. Ariadne saw this, and ordered him to bed. He went meekly, feeling too tired to argue. She was worried about him, and voiced her concern to Genta. "Let's leave it until the morning, and see how he is then," she said. Only partly reassured, Ariadne and Genta made their way to bed.

No one felt like breakfast the next morning. Everything felt flat, and there was a feeling of anticlimax. Ben was nowhere to be seen, and Ariadne found him still in bed. He appeared to be in a lot of pain. The doctor was sent for immediately and, on seeing the condition of his patient, wanted to send him to hospital. A gruff voice from the sickbed said, "No, no. I refuse to go to hospital. I know I am going to die, and I wish it to be in my own bed, in my own home. Is that clear?"

Dr Sims gave in. He had met Ben on many occasions, and had no idea he was so ill. Holding Ben's hand, he said kindly, "OK, just as you wish, but Ariadne and Jean-Paul cannot look after you entirely on their own. You will need a nurse."

Ben turned to Ariadne. "Get in touch with Nurse McGee.

She promised to come if ever needed." He explained to the doctor how Shona McGee had been his son's nurse and was fully qualified, so she was sent for.

Dr Sims was delighted, liking her no-nonsense approach. He said to Ariadne, "If anyone can keep Ben in order and make him do as he is told, it is this Scottish lass."

She laughed. "Do you know how old she is?" He was amazed when told she was "pushing fifty". Nurse Shona soon had the sick room well organised, allowing Ben only a small TV, and she reluctantly allowed a laptop computer, limiting the use of this, much to Ben's disgust. When he found difficulty sleeping Ariadne brought his grandmother's bible. The print was too small even with the glasses he now had to wear for reading. She hoped it would change his agnostic frame of mind, and strangely, it did. Mr Kent, who had taken over the parish when Mr Childs retired, came to see Ben. They had many a lively discussion when Ben was feeling well enough, and the sick man was dismayed to learn he could not be buried next to his grandmother as he had never been baptised. He asked if this could be arranged. Not sure of Ben's commitment to the Anglican faith, the kind vicar did arrange this, and Ben said he now felt more at peace, and happier.

Ben hung on to life for another year. He had his good days and his bad. He still kept in touch with Lucien, and Pag brought regular reports from the Two Islands. A schedule of care was arranged, so there was always someone at hand if required. Before he was taken ill, arrangements had been made for Annalisa to come and be educated, as Ariadne had promised. She was away at school for most of the time, but spent her holidays at Swanbrook Hall. She was a great comfort to Ariadne, and Ben liked her. She would sit and read to him. She was fluent in English and French, and willingly read the most boring financial papers. She had grown into a lovely girl. She was known as their 'niece' but to Ariadne she was the daughter she could never have. She hoped she and Philippe would like one another. The thought came, not unwelcome, that she might one day be her daughter-in-law.

Ben was getting worse and at the end of the winter, just as spring was coming to their part of England, it was obvious he hadn't long to live.

One morning he asked Jean-Paul to fetch a little sandalwood box from his desk. Not suspecting anything out of the ordinary, the younger man who had been his lover did as he was bid. When he left, Ben wrote several letters, which he carefully placed in the box. From it he took a small pill. It would not kill him – just make his end a little more bearable. He found the normal drugs were having no effect, and the last thing he wanted was an undignified end.

He called them into him one by one, and said goodbye. Ariadne was the last. He took her into his arms. Kissing her gently, Ben said, "You have been wonderful to me, darling girl. You are my beautiful, precious, most precious daughter." In his dying breath he at last acknowledged she was his daughter.

Somehow Ariadne got through the next few weeks, though as if in a nightmare. Annalisa and Genta did all they could to comfort her but she mourned without tears, sleeping little. Their neighbours were astonished when they read Ben's obituary. It was in both the English and French papers. Madame Chevalliere sent a large wreath and a letter of condolence. The funeral was well attended. Colonel Van Den Hoof came; as well as Senator Tubbs, who represented the crew of *Pegasus XIII*. Philippe arrived late, and Ariadne thought for a time he was not going to attend. Ben was buried, as he wished, next to the remains of his grandmother, already moved to the family vault. Ariadne had secretly removed Ben's heart, as he had requested. She would transport it to the Two Islands, as he had asked. There were a couple of unexpected mourners. Ariadne saw Michael, in American captain's uniform, escorting a lady wearing black, and she knew it must be Suella. Ariadne went to meet them. "It is so good of you to come."

Suella bowed her head. She was older now, and grief was etched on her face. "Will you come up to the house?" Ariadne offered.

Suella shook her head. "Thank you but no." In her hand was a single red rose. "May I put this with the other flowers?"

Ariadne smiled gently. "But of course." She led Suella to the open vault, not yet closed. Suella stood for a few seconds, then Michael gently took her arm and they moved away. They got into a large car with blacked out windows, and departed as quietly as they had come. Philippe wanted to know who they were. Ariadne was not going to enlighten him, although sorely tempted.

Seeing her so wracked with misery, Jean-Paul suggested she went to the Alps, telling her the change would do her good. "I think there is still some snow there."

She was persuaded, and enjoyed five days of peace. It was helpful and, feeling refreshed, she was ready to return and face the world. Her case was in her car, and all she had to do in the morning was dress and head for home.

Fate, always considered by Ben his nemesis, was waiting to inflict in his absence a nasty blow to Ariadne. It was something she could not have imagined in her wildest dreams.

She had carelessly forgotten to bolt the door of the chalet, although it was locked. As she was just getting off to sleep she felt a draught on her face, and there was the sound of movement as the door opened. Someone was removing skis, and she called out, "Who's there?" There was no answer, and she sat up in bed, reaching for her robe. Then she saw who it was – Philippe. She had no idea he had a key. His eyes were glazed but he didn't appear to be drunk. He moved towards the bed and suddenly she was afraid, very afraid. She knew he had hated his father. Was he now going to punish her in his father's absence? Yes, it seemed he was, and she wondered if he was under the influence of drugs. Whatever he intended would soon be clear and she shuddered, knowing screaming at him would not change things.

The chalet was slightly away from the others, and any cries from her would be carried away by the wind. Neither of them spoke. Silently he swayed towards her.

Philippe's intention was clear to Ariadne. He was hell-bent on rape. It was in his eyes. Slowly he stripped and threw the coverlet off the bed, and ripped her nightdress almost to threads. When he saw she was devoid of hair in a certain area, his only comment was "Interesting". She knew he was strong, and his physique was so like Ben's that any attempt to resist him would be futile. His next remark shook her. "Well, my sister, let's see what our high and mighty parent found so attractive in you." She winced at this, and he laughed mockingly. "Oh yes, I know all about the two of you. Even when you discovered your close relationship you just couldn't keep your hands off each other. I heard all about it from the old woman. I was about twelve, and once when she was very drunk she spilt the beans. Well, it is payback time now." She bit her lip to keep from screaming. He was very rough and coarse. She told herself this was her son, but he was like a wild animal. She prayed for it to end. He slapped her face hard. "Keep your eyes open. I want you to see me enjoying myself." He humiliated her as much as he could. When she thought it was finally over he tossed her off the bed, kicked her and, forcing her legs apart, tore at her. She could stand no more, and blacked out.

Gradually she came out of the faint, having no idea how long she had lain there. The chalet door was open and the wind was blowing in, bringing in a slight flurry of snow. Thankfully he had gone. She dragged herself to the door and bolted it. There was a taste of blood in her mouth. The slap on her face had knocked a tooth out – one that had been bothering her. Medical attention was required elsewhere. She knew there was a mountain rescue station half a mile away. She would get there, or die in the attempt.

Lucien Gervaise was just enjoying a second cup of coffee, when the call came from the Beau Rivage Clinique asking him to come and see them on urgent business concerning Madame Haraldsson. He asked what it was about, but the matter was considered too sensitive to discuss over the telephone. Fortunately it was the weekend, otherwise he would not have been at home. Very intrigued, he went by car, which took several hours. Arriving not a little put out that the weekend had been spoilt for him, he was kept waiting even longer, until the specialist was free to see him.

"You are a good friend of Madame, are you not?"

Lucien agreed he was, and asked, "Is she here? Has she had an accident? I know she went to her chalet to ski."

He was deeply shocked to hear Madame was gravely ill following a brutal rape. The specialist said, "We think she knows her attacker. Often it is a family member who commits such an act. Have you any idea whom it might be?"

Lucien was careful not to let his face give him away. He shook his head. He knew the one and only person that hated Ariadne enough was Philippe. He knew there was love and hate in his feelings for his mother. He suspected the horrible old woman at the chateau was somehow involved. He had always felt that even as a child there was something odd about Philippe. There was a strong streak of cruelty, which had been there even when quite young. Lucien had seen him dissect butterflies and small birds while they were still alive. He shuddered, and asked if he could see Ariadne. He was allowed two minutes. He leaned over, asking her gently, "It was Philippe, wasn't it?"

She nodded. "He is a brilliant doctor, and capable of saving many lives. I cannot ruin his life and career."

Much against his better judgement Lucien agreed not to say anything to implicate Philippe. It was several days before Ariadne was well enough to travel back to her home.

Jean-Paul travelled to France by private jet to collect Ariadne from the *clinique*. He was a good customer of the small private airline, and they were only too pleased to accommodate him. He was shocked at Ariadne's appearance. All the spirit seemed to have drained out of her. She needed to use a stick to move around, and had aged considerably.

His eyes filled with tears. What would Ben think of his lovely girl now? More to the point, what would he think of his son? Horsewhipping was too good for the young swine. Ariadne whispered, "Please, Jean-Paul, don't condemn him. He has had a chip on his shoulder for so long. Perhaps I have now atoned for the wrong committed by his father and me. Perhaps we are the real sinners. I am aware Ben told you about us, but not where we went or why. I have some very important information to pass on to you. Ben made me promise to tell you after he was dead. I understand Mr Page, our solicitor, is coming to read Ben's will to us this week. It is quite complicated, hence the delay. Come and have a glass of something strong with me once I'm settled back at Swanbrook. I can assure you, you will need it. I have to tell you this news, as you are mentioned in the will. It will surprise you."

Back at Swanbrook, Genta was also dismayed by Ariadne's obvious frailness. She fussed around her and, for once, there was no protest. Jean-Paul brought a tray with a good assortment of spirits and sherry into the drawing room, where Ariadne now took a siesta after lunch. He waited patiently for her to begin. She told him that quite by chance Ben had found out that he and Jean-Paul were cousins.

"Are you sure?" he wanted to know.

"Oh yes. There is no doubt. He checked all our DNA. He was clever at things like that. There is no mistake." When Ariadne told Jean-Paul he had an aged grandparent, he immediately wanted to know where and when they could meet.

It took six weeks for Ariadne to start looking anything like her old self. She had been working on a way of getting Philippe to come and see her on the ship. Meanwhile she tried to avoid answering Jean-Paul's questions. Eventually she gave in and, calling him to her sitting room, asked him to swear on the Bible, as she had done in the past, not to reveal what she had to tell him, even to Genta. As gently as she could she explained who Ben really was, and how she had accompanied him to the Two Islands planet.

To say he didn't believe her was an understatement. He roared with laughter, thinking it was all one of Ben's elaborate jokes. Ariadne sighed. "Will you believe Captain Anion?"

"Is he in on the joke as well?"

She went to a drawer and took out a cassette. "Listen to this."

It was a taped message. It gave her a shock to hear Ben's voice. The message was addressed to Jean-Paul. It told him to take seriously what Ariadne had to tell him about himself and the Two Islands planet. It explained why he had remained on Earth, and if he had any doubts as to the truth of what was being explained to him, he should contact any of the three people had who returned to Earth with Ariadne and himself. Ariadne told Jean-Paul she was hoping to lure Philippe to her ship. "He is the Usaurians' leader now, and somehow I have to get him to accompany me there. It will take us six months, which is a good deal shorter than the time it took Ben and me on our first journey there."

Jean-Paul realised there must be some truth in what she was telling him. She smiled. "You and I are half ETs. Do you realise that?"

They proceeded to the drawing room, where the main benefactors were gathered for the reading of the will.

Mr Page the solicitor cleared his throat. He hoped all who had been requested to attend the reading of Mr Haraldsson's will had taken the trouble to attend. "Ladies and gentlemen, I wish to proceed, unless there are any objections. I do not intend to waste time waiting for anyone not here. The will is quite a large one, and extremely complicated."

Mr Page then handed envelopes out to the main group, comprising Ariadne, Philippe, Michael and Jean-Paul. "These are special messages from the deceased, and are for the eyes of the recipients only."

Philippe looked at the man on his left, and wondered who he was. He noticed Ariadne seemed to know the stranger, but hadn't thought to introduce them to each other. Ariadne had placed a glass and bottled water near the solicitor, as she understood he preferred this to spirits and liked to keep a clear head.

The will was certainly long. Everyone connected with the estate was left something – even the two grooms taken on when Jean-Paul found he required extra help. Suella, Dr Weng and Nurse McGee were left incomes for life. The apartment in New York and the property in Cape Cod were for Suella's use, but left to Michael. He and Philippe were left two million US dollars each. Lucien Gervaise was not forgotten, nor Pag. They each received one million euros. Swanbrook Hall and the estate were already in Ariadne's name, so this wasn't mentioned, except in passing. The rest of Ben's assets – after inheritance tax, about thirty million euros – were left to Ariadne. She also inherited a large collection of jewellery and the mine on Two Islands, but this was not mentioned, being explained in the letter left for her. There were also surprise bequests for Ed, Tally, Pav and Milo, although the solicitor was asked not to read these out. Sheikh Kassim was left two horses of his choice, to be purchased in Kentucky. Ariadne asked Mr Page if he would care to stay for lunch but he declined, saying he was pressed for time.

When the solicitor had left, presumably for another appointment, Philippe cornered Ariadne. "Who was that chap sitting next to me, and who is Su… whatever her name… that has been left so much in New York?"

Ariadne took a deep breath. Michael was in the room and looking at her, also with questions in his eyes. "Well, that is a little difficult to answer as it is rather personal, and we still have company. I don't want you to start throwing punches. Come into the library."

When she had seated herself in Ben's favourite chair, feeling it would give her courage, she looked up at Philippe. "Suella is the woman Ben looked on as his wife. She wouldn't marry him, even when he asked her to. Michael is her son, and your half-brother. Now do you understand?"

Philippe uttered one word, "*Merde*," and flounced out of the room. Ariadne quickly followed him. He wasn't confronting Michael, but had made for the drinks cabinet. He wasn't a heavy drinker but had poured himself a stiff scotch. He glowered at Michael but didn't approach him, much to Ariadne's relief. She fervently hoped he didn't intend challenging his father's wishes. She turned, to find Michael at her elbow. She knew he was not afraid of Philippe. He was the older of the two by ten years and the senior in more ways than one. Military service had made him supremely fit. She hoped any scandal could be avoided. Michael gave her a puckish grin, and it was so like the grins she had received from Ben on many occasions, it tore at her heart-strings. She tried to blink the tears away; it had been such an emotional day.

"Steady, old girl. Here; have a good blow," said Michael, handing her a spotless white handkerchief. Gratefully she accepted it, trying to smile.

The company was breaking up, and when the house was almost empty she tried to get the two to meet. They barely acknowledged one another. Michael looked at his watch. "I've got transport. Time I was off." He kissed Ariadne goodbye and left.

After Michael had left, Ariadne sat for some time, trying to come to terms with the responsibility of being left heiress of such a large sum of money. She knew she would continue to support the orphanage Ben had funded in China since the terrible earthquake in 2008. There were a number of other charities he was interested in, and they also would continue to receive support. She knew it was what Ben wished. She was mulling over the various bequests when a glaring omission struck her. Why had no mention been made by the solicitor of the legacies she knew had been left to Jean-Paul and Genta? After a search of Ben's papers she found a copy of his will. It was there in black and white; he hadn't forgotten them. The solicitor, when she eventually got through to him, was most apologetic. Yes, it was a mistake, and he would come and apologise personally. He had turned two pages over together. It was sorted out the following day and, to their delight, Jean-Paul and Genta had been left three million euros between them. Jean-Paul and Genta were to continue to look on Swanbrook as their home. Jean-Paul was given the stewardship of the estate, which he was to run as previously. A very relieved Ariadne then turned her reluctant attention to other delicate matters. Aloud, she said to herself, "What am I to do with your clothes and boots, let alone all the numerous other things you have managed to amass, Ben?" Perhaps she was being silly but talking to Ben as if he was still there helped. She made a pile of things she knew the two men in his life would like. What to give to Suella? She would leave that decision to Michael.

There were official robes and uniform, which she would take to the Two Islands. His boots, she knew, would fit Philippe. Shaking herself to keep tears away, she made a pile of things to be burnt. Once he had jokingly said, "When I die, perhaps I should copy the gypsies and all I own be put on a funeral pyre. Oh, and put me on top." She had told him it was a ridiculous idea. Now she was exhausted.

The letter received by Philippe puzzled him. It was not at all what he expected to receive from Ariadne. "Come and see me on my ship. I know you have never visited it, and I am sure it will interest you. I wish to discuss your father's wishes for your future. I am willing to forgive, if not forget what happened at the chalet. Believe me, this is not a trap. It is most essential we meet."

Both Jean-Paul and Genta were pleased to see Ariadne looking more like her old self. She seemed to possess a steely determination to do something, though exactly what, they were not sure. Jean-Paul and Genta came into her sitting room looking somewhat secretive. Genta took the lead. "Will it surprise you to know we have decided to get married?"

The smile Ariadne gave them made them laugh with relief. "It is what Ben hoped would happen," she said.

Jean-Paul was now in his early fifties; Genta younger by seven years. "We would love a family, but I suppose I am now too old to think of it." Genta was a little wistful.

"Nonsense! Women are having babies much later now." Privately she thought Genta was very brave to take Jean-Paul on. She wondered whether his liking for Ben had not given him a taste for sex with a different gender. The wedding was quiet, and the two left on a brief honeymoon, leaving Ariadne to make plans. She wrote letters, to be posted at a later date to all the places and people she knew Philippe was connected with. They were letters of resignation due to 'family circumstances beyond my control'. The letters said he needed to take a sabbatical for a year. Ariadne waited until the honeymooners returned before proceeding with the next stage of her plan.

It was the thought of seeing the ship that finally persuaded Philippe to meet Ariadne. He arrived on time and was surprised to see her looking so well. She invited him to look around the ship but impressed on him the danger of pulling levers or touching mechanical equipment. He was quite impressed, and said it must cost a packet to run and maintain. He was invited to have a glass of champagne, and wondered just what she had up her sleeve and why was she so affable towards him. He had expected her to spit in his eye at least. She removed his coat, and was not at all surprised to feel a pistol, which she deftly removed, throwing it into the harbour before he realised what she was doing. He had switched his glass with hers, but she had already anticipated this move. He started to feel hot, and asked if the cabin door could be opened. The next minute he was out cold.

When he finally came to, he felt he had been transported to a different place. Everything looked different, even Ariadne. She was wearing what appeared to be a uniform in mid-grey.

He found he was strapped onto a bench, unable to move. A gag covered his mouth. Her next move terrified him. Unsmiling, she undid the zip on his trousers and exposed him. There was a knife in her other hand, and he thought for a minute castration was intended. Smiling now, she said, "It is the law of your father's people that all boys are circumcised before they come of age. You are a little old, but I will do it for you now."

With a quick swish she brought the knife down. The pain must have been excruciating. He would have screamed but for the gag. Leaning over so he couldn't miss her meaning, she said, "We are quits now, OK?" Releasing one of his hands she placed a suture, needle and antiseptic into it, saying, "Just in case any repair is needed."

PART FIVE

RETURN TO THE TWO ISLANDS PLANET

Chapter One

The Journey

Feeling still a little unsure of things, and in some pain from the operation Ariadne had performed on him, Philippe tore off the gag with his freed hand. "What the hell do you think you are doing?" He looked anxiously at his damaged organ. He had to admit she had done the job competently and, with the few stitches required, he would soon be able to move and get away from her. He knew he should never have trusted her. Then he attempted to rise but the room spun and he fell back, too giddy to do anything but gasp, "May I have a glass of water?" She brought, it looking down at him warily. "You do realise this is kidnap."

"Oh yes, but it is the only way I can get you to accompany me to where I am required to take you."

"Oh, and where, pray, is that?" She indicated a porthole. He couldn't understand why it was dark, unless he had been out a long time. He looked at his watch. Four hours had gone. "Look out there." He looked, and gasped. Now he was really scared. "Yes, we are now approaching the Moon. We, dear Philippe, are in space." In spite of the water he had just drunk, his mouth felt dry. He felt he was going mad. "No, you are not dreaming. We really are in space. We are on our way to the Two Islands planet, where your father's people are. As his heir, you are now their leader. I think you will like it. There is a well-equipped medical centre, which is gradually getting up to Earth's standards."

"How about the people I am letting down back on Earth?" She explained that letters had been left saying he had been called away on urgent family business. "Where is this planet?"

She merely smiled. "You'll see soon enough."

When Philippe tried to grab Ariadne he found he was lifted off the floor. Ariadne laughed. "If you promise to behave yourself I'll give you a pair of special space boots. They have magnets in the soles, which will grip the floor. It takes time to get used to them, but will stop you floating everywhere."

He was still furiously angry. "I demand you return at once to Earth so I can get on with my normal life. I am not sure whether you have fed me a lot of tripe or I am hallucinating due to the drugs you have given me."

He would have said more, but she moved away to her console and adjusted some equipment. "We are now on our way to Mars. Surely you would like to see the Red Planet?" In spite of himself he was interested, and soon found that if the circumstances had been different he would have been enjoying the experience. Looking him full in the face she said, "If you as much as touch me, I have the knowledge and am quite capable of blowing this craft into smithereens. Is that clear?"

He realised he had a formidable opponent in this virago. She was different from the weak woman he had raped.

He came to the decision that he would comply with her wishes for the time being. He was brought back from his thoughts, as she was now telling him he would be required to help her fly the craft. "That's impossible," he snapped back at her.

"I know you can fly. Your father saw to that. I will show you. You will need to be an efficient flyer as there are several squadrons of Space Riders who are there and waiting to greet you. You have inherited the role of Space Commander-in-Chief. Captain Anion is their leader, but he will hand over command to you when we arrive."

Philippe started to feel he was in cloud-cuckoo-land. What surprise would she spring on him next? He dared not think.

The time passed surprisingly quickly. Negotiating the asteroid belt between Mars and Jupiter, which Ariadne had, unknown to Philippe, been rather afraid of, was without incident. He managed to learn a little of the Usaurian language and also how to pilot the ship. Like Ariadne before him, he was interested in the fuel they used. He had heard about the so-called 'wonder fuel'. Tests were still being carried out on Earth to see if it was feasible for everyday use, so far without any degree of success.

Jupiter was an awesome sight. "I had no idea it was so big."

He heard, without making further comment, how it helped destroy the Usaurian planet, and how Ben, when only a boy, discovered their present home and found the new planet able to sustain life, if somewhat meagrely, for his people. He named it Two Islands for obvious reasons. Not long after the two travellers sighted Jupiter, the Two Islands planet was clearly visible.

"So it really does exist." Philippe had only half believed all he had been told.

"Would you like to land the ship?"

He did this without any problem, and Captain Anion was there to meet them. He saluted Philippe, welcoming him warmly. This was generous of him as he was one of the few who knew about Philippe's attack on his mother. He asked if Philippe would like to inspect the Space Riders. Feeling a little out of his depth, he agreed. Philippe commented on how smartly they were turned out, and said how young they all were. He then went to pay his respects to Uncle Bron. He had been instructed how to approach the old man, and by now he was *very* old. Uncle Bron looked at Ben's son and thought, 'He is so like him but hasn't got the sense of fun that Ben always had. He is far too serious.'

Ariadne kissed the old man, and there were tears in her eyes. "Oh, Uncle Bron, it is so good to see you. I have brought Ben's heart, as he requested. I miss him so much."

The two people who had loved Ben went together to a small grotto which had been set aside as a burial chamber for the D'A-Huartan family. There was a place already prepared, and Ariadne reverently placed the casket containing Ben's heart there. Tears ran down her face but she brushed them away and squared her shoulders, and the two left in silence. It was the place she would return to whenever she had a problem. It was a peaceful spot, and she always drew comfort from going there. Meanwhile, Philippe inspected the small medical centre. It was hardly big enough to be called a hospital but he decreed it should be known as the Villiers Centre. He liked Dr Milo, realising the older man had more experience of likely problems. He smiled one of his rare smiles, saying to the older man, "I need to pick your brains as I am not sure how everything is run. I hope you won't object if I alter anything. Please feel free to let me know your views on anything I suggest. I don't want to cause friction."

Ariadne thought it a minor miracle they got on so well together. Dr Milo was glad to have such a competent companion. They apportioned the work equally. Philippe did most of the operations and Milo saw to the medical side. Philippe liked the Two Islands. It was better to be a big fish in a small pond than a mere nobody in one of Earth's big teaching hospitals. It would have taken him years to achieve anything like the position he now held. In time Philippe would be a respected leader, but never received the love that his father was given. Uncle Bron was glad to have someone to take over the reins. He was too old to make decisions, and there were plenty needing to be made, and quickly.

Ariadne sat at her dressing table preparing to go to bed, and knew with dismay she was not alone. Philippe was in the room. He stood behind her and, taking her hairbrush, started to brush her hair. He leant forward suddenly and kissed the nape of her neck. Huskily he whispered, "I don't know what your power is, little witch, but I love you." It was clear he was getting sexually aroused.

Trying not to panic, Ariadne picked up a small paperknife but he laughed sardonically and twisted it out of her hand and kissed her on the lips. Her reply was, "Stop this foolishness or I will scream. Antika is outside." Ariadne then touched a bell under her dressing table, and Antika was there within seconds. An angry and frustrated man was forced to withdraw.

There was no lock on her door as all doors were controlled by an electronic beam, so with Antika's help, she pushed a heavy ottoman from the foot of her bed to where anyone not knowing it was there would fall over it on entering. After a restless night Ariadne called Pag to discuss the situation. He was as concerned as she was.

"I think the best thing is for me to return to Earth and say I am going to collect Annalisa. It won't hurt to cut her schooling a little short. She is due to return here soon anyway." Ariadne suggested.

Pag entirely agreed. There was one problem: how to appease Uncle Bron – he was no one's fool. Pag said, "He is bound to be somewhat suspicious."

They decided to give the old man a watered down version of Philippe's attack on Ariadne. He listened in silence, and then his old cracked voice said, "I was aware there was some tension between the two of you, but I had no idea how big the problem is. By all means go and collect Annalisa. Leave Philippe to me; I know how to deal with him," and he did. He warned Philippe he was in danger of being sent back to Earth, never to return to the Two Islands planet. Philippe heeded the warning, and promised to keep away from Ariadne in the future.

Chapter Two

Back to Earth

Captain Anion handed over command of the Space Riders to Philippe, and made arrangements to fly back to Earth. Ariadne was to accompany him. As for Philippe, he began to realise what a fine leader his father must have been. He found it impossible to spend all his time on medical matters but discovered many other things with a call on his time. The Council, he decided, was in need of new blood. He would try and recruit some of the younger members of the community. As an incentive, they would receive a fee. This was a welcome innovation: there was some jealousy as the Space Riders were the only Usaurians to be paid a wage. Philippe hoped this new innovation would be the first step to everyone receiving money and sharing in the prosperity that was starting to take place on both islands.

Before Ariadne left, Philippe asked her to come and see him about a matter on Earth he wished her to attend to. Intrigued by this request, she agreed. He showed her some documents, which he said he carried about with him all the time. With them was a snapshot of a small boy about two years of age. "As you know, dear Ariadne, I am not a saint. I was married briefly to Duella Brogan, the daughter of the Texan oil millionaire. You may have heard of him. She was a spoilt little rich girl, determined to have me, but a nymphomaniac. I caught her twice with two different men. I was in the process of divorcing her, when she was killed in a car accident with another man. Her father's money hushed up any scandal. She left behind our son

Dune. He is now four years old and living with his grandfather on the old man's ranch. I dearly want to know how he is. I haven't seen him since he was a baby. Will you go and see how he is? He is, after all, your grandson."

Delighted to learn she had a grandson, Ariadne couldn't reach Earth quickly enough. She discussed the situation with Pag, and he was as intrigued as she was. It was convenient to land on Senator Tubbs's ranch as it was only a few miles from where Jake Brogan and his grandson lived. Landings were always tricky as they had to take place in an isolated spot. Fortunately there was a river running through the property, and the *Sirius* splashed down unobserved. As Pag knew the area well, he arranged for hire cars for himself and Ariadne, and left to see his sons. Ariadne made her way to the ranch owned by Jake Brogan. It was certainly big, and young Dune was heir to an immense fortune. His grandmother wondered what kind of reception she could expect. There was the possibility she might be ordered off the ranch. She would be asked why she had left it so long to contact her grandchild. Would it be believed when she said she had only recently heard of his existence? Arriving at the ranch house – it was a long one-storied building built in the Spanish hacienda style – she found no one about. Feeling foolish, she realised it was siesta time. A child's voice broke her reverie, and she turned to see Dune. It had to be him; he was so like his father at the same age. "Who are you? This is private property. Are you lost?"

Ariadne wanted to hug him. Trying to keep her voice steady, she said, "Hello, I'm looking for Mr Brogan. Your grandfather, I think. Could you tell him Madame Du Pre would very much like to speak with him?" She repeated her name, and the small boy sped off on the errand, running into the house by a side door.

The man who came out to meet Ariadne was big by anyone's standards. Over six foot four inches tall, and broad – almost barrel-chested. He had a well-clipped beard, just starting to turn grey, and the most piercing blue eyes Ariadne had ever seen. She knew he was expecting her to be intimidated by his appearance. He wasn't aware that after Ben he was a mere pussycat to her. "You are Mr Brogan?"

He looked almost affronted. "Yeah, that is my name."

She smiled her most captivating smile. It usually worked, but not on this man. He was holding his grandson, almost protectively, in his arms.

"May we talk privately please?" she asked, glancing at the small boy.

To her surprise, the man started speaking in fluent French. Seeing her start, he commented, "If, as I suspect, you are Philippe's mother, you must be French."

She could not deny it. "*Oui. Je suis la grand-mere.*"

She got no further. Turning abruptly, Mr Brogan motioned her to come in. The next minute she nearly jumped out of her skin as he roared to someone called Carlotta to bring coffee for two, "...and make it snappy."

He got down to business immediately. "If you have come to take Dune away, think again, lady."

Ariadne realised she had a strong opponent in this rancher turned oilman. She could imagine his presence in a boardroom, and how his underlings would quake under his autocratic rule. "No, that is not my intention. His father merely wants to have news of him. As for myself, I would not take him away from where he is obviously happy."

"You just won't get the chance."

Pretending to hesitate, she said, "I have a house in England, two vineyards – one in France and one in England – plus a chateau in France. Please feel free to come and visit me at any time, and of course bring Dune. Oh, by the way, I have a small gift for him and one for you." She opened a holdall and brought out a carved figure. It was of a Chinese workman holding a pick.

The old rancher looked at the gift. He was touched but covered this up with a gruff acceptance.

"I hope you will let me give this to Dune." She nervously handed over a teddy bear. It was not an ordinary bear. For a start, it was dressed as a cowboy, right down to miniature spurs. The ends had been carefully rounded off so there were no sharp bits anywhere. There was a spotted kerchief around its neck, and a Stetson hat. When the boy entered the room his eyes were like saucers. Ariadne parted with the toy. A voice said, "Hello, Dune. My name is Dante. Howdy, pardner."

The child was utterly enchanted. "Is he for me?" His grandmother looked at Jake Brogan. He nodded his head and Ariadne continued, "Yes, Dear, and he says more. He says goodnight when you lay him down, and reminds you to say your prayers."

When it was realised Ariadne was not going to take Dune away, the atmosphere improved considerably. Jake asked Ariadne if she would like a ride, assuring her there were some fine horses on the ranch fit for a lady to ride. The ranch hands thought they would play a trick on this "city type" as they dubbed her, not being aware of her relationship to Dune. The horse they brought was a frisky mare which was badly in need of exercise. They watched, believing she would have difficulty handling it. She proved them wrong. Ben had been a good teacher, and she smiled to herself when she saw their crestfallen faces. It was too late to return to the local town and search for lodgings, so she was invited to spend the night. There was still the problem of telling Dune who she was. How would he take the news? He was a remarkably bright and forward child for his age.

"Let him enjoy a night with his bear, and we can break it to him in the morning. He has had more than enough excitement for one day," Ariadne said.

So it was agreed, and Ariadne, who was tired herself, wished to retire to bed as soon as possible.

Chapter Three

Young Dune

However, it was late evening before they dined. Young Dune had gone happily to bed hours before, with his new 'friend' tucked up beside him. Ariadne knew all through the meal that she was being assessed by her companion. She found the food a little too highly spiced for her taste, but with many sips of the excellent wine provided, she succeeded in almost finishing the meal. She found Jake an affable host, and he was surprisingly well informed and cultured, so she enjoyed sparring with him. Coffee was taken on a cool veranda, where they watched the Moon come up. Jake said with a smile, "I don't know when I last enjoyed a meal so much. You are welcome to stay as long as you like. Please do consider staying a little longer."

She merely inclined her head, feeling too tired to argue.

Carlotta showed her to a pleasant, spacious bedroom. She had hardly settled, when there was a light tap on her door. Thinking it was Carlotta, she called "Come in", and was surprised to see Jake. It was very clear what he was hoping for. Keeping her tone light she said, "It's a long time since a gentleman came knocking on my bedroom door."

With a question in his voice Jake said, with a slight smile, "Then I hope this one is not unwelcome?"

She didn't reply, but held out her arms to him. Jake Brogan was about ten years her senior, but time spent in the open air had given his face a leathery look. Ariadne found him a sensitive lover and much amused by the absence of hair on her body. Blushing, she tried to explain it was what her late husband had liked. They complemented each other, and Jake fell asleep in her arms, his last thought being, 'What a woman!'

Ariadne woke alone to a room full of sunshine. Carlotta came in with a well-laden breakfast tray, saying it was a lovely morning and she hoped their guest had slept well. If she knew of the night's cavorting with her boss, she gave no sign.

Jake, Ariadne and Dune rode out together. The boy was in the saddle in front of his grandfather. What had happened the night before might never have been.

Ariadne felt quite put out by Jake's attitude towards her. She started to feel she must have been mad to let him have his way with her. How had she misread the signs? He had merely nodded his head, not a glimmer of a smile on his face when he wished her good morning. Was he also regretting the night's adventure? "We won't go far, Dune – just as far as the lake."

"Oh, goody. Can I swim?"

His grandfather shook his head. "No, Dune, not today, Madame and I have something important to tell you."

The boy's face fell. He sighed. How he hated being told grown-up stuff!

The lake had little boats, canoes and yachts moored, and Ariadne had a yearning to be back on the *Sirius*.

"Well, if I can't swim, can we go on your boat?" It was clear young Dune was used to getting his own way.

"Yes, but you must promise not to run about and get tired."

There was a refrigerator on the yacht – the *Maid Marion* – and welcome iced drinks were soon prepared by the steward who, together with a deck hand, were the only crew to be seen. When they were seated Dune's grandfather and Ariadne explained, as far as it was possible to explain to a four-year-old, who Ariadne was. The boy, who was old for his years, took it in. "Have I got a dad as well?"

"Well, yes, but he is very busy so he sent me instead."

"Can I see you before you go?" Jake's voice was low, almost pleading.

"But of course."

Dune had an afternoon nap, and after his lunch of milk and fruit Ariadne said goodbye. She gave the boy a hug and promised to keep in touch. She asked if she could take some photos. "I am sure your dad is expecting me to take some." She took several of the small, laughing boy on his pony and happily holding the bear she had given him.

When the house was quiet, with everyone except Jake and herself taking their siesta, he drew her into his study and took her in his arms. "Do you have to go so soon?" He took a small packet out of his pocket. "I hope you will accept these and think of me when you wear them." The earrings he pressed into her hands were probably priceless. "I have been told unofficially they once belonged to an Egyptian princess."

Ariadne owned many equally beautiful items of jewellery. Jake wasn't to know that. She was touched. "They are beautiful. Are you sure you wish to part with them?" Made of gold with lapis lazuli, seed pearls and emeralds, they were quite exquisite.

"I bought them for my daughter, but she died before I had the chance to give them to her. Please take them. I will be honoured if you will accept them."

Ariadne kissed him. His next remark left her speechless. "You do realise I have fallen in love with you, don't you? I've heard of love at first sight but hadn't expected it to happen to me at my age." He broke off and turned away.

Later, when her hand was on her car door, an unexpected arrival stopped any further declarations of love from Jake. Pag arrived and Ariadne introduced him, saying Pag was her late husband's closest friend and aide. Seeing the seeds of jealousy on Jake's face, she hastily explained how he had become a widower and how Senator Tubbs and his wife were looking after Pag's two sons. To her relief, this explanation seemed to satisfy Jake. She hastily drove away before anything more could be said.

Chapter Four

To Europe

Ariadne didn't want to cause further embarrassment, but Jake stopped her car and thrust an envelope into her astonished hands. "Please read this, and I do mean every word."

She merely nodded her head. An amused Pag teased her. He had left his hire car to be picked up later, and sat beside her, wondering what had happened to rattle her usual calm exterior. She certainly seemed different. He knew Ben had hoped she would find another partner, and not be left on her own. He wondered if this Texan rancher turned oilman was the one. The signs appeared good. "You do like him, don't you? With oil as well as a big ranch, he must be loaded."

Blushing, she sighed, taking her time to navigate around a difficult bend. "Yes, he has quite swept me off my feet, but to live on a ranch? It's really not my style."

Under Ben's influence she had acquired expensive tastes and was very much the cultured lady, more at home in Europe. The boulevards of Paris were more to her taste. Under no circumstances could she remotely see herself living on a ranch. Pag and Ariadne travelled back to Europe individually. Pag was still a pilot with one of Italy's leading airlines, and he regretted he was unable to escort her back to England. He had to travel to Houston and relieve an Italian pilot. Ariadne assured Pag she was quite capable of taking the *Sirius* to Europe on her own, and she looked forward to a quiet period of contemplation as she wrestled with the problem of deciding what to do about Jake.

It was with some relief that Ariadne turned into the drive of Swanbrook Hall. It was good to be back home. On only a cursory inspection she was delighted to see how well run everything still was. Jean-Paul was proud of his stewardship, and determined not to let Ariadne down in any way. He was lucky to have the help of his wife. Genta was a tower of strength, and helped him considerably. She did the books for him when he was too busy with other things. However, she found some of her time taken up with caring for her babies. The twins, now three, were born a year after their marriage. They – Benjamin Paul and Rebecka Ariadne – were little bundles of mischief but a great joy to their doting parents. To everyone, they were known as Benjy and Becky. Marriage had mellowed Jean-Paul. If it hadn't been for Jean-Paul's infatuation with Ben, it would have happened much sooner. Now in his middle fifties, Jean-Paul was given a lot of rope by his wife. He made the occasional visit to town and always returned with a gift for Genta and toys for the children. Genta never asked about the visits, but Ariadne wondered what exactly he got up to. Not wishing to upset the smooth relationship they all had, she kept her thoughts to herself.

Chapter Five

A Proposal

In Swanbrook Hall, Ariadne felt close to Ben and knew it was where she wanted to be. But fate had other plans for her. Shortly after arriving back she was astonished to receive an official-looking letter. It was Ben's last gift to her, and she could now call herself Lady D'Vane. Ben had had the title 'Sir', but had not told anyone. DNA tests had proved he was indeed the grandson of Lady Clarissa, and Ariadne, as his daughter, was the next in line for the ladyship. Ben hoped that although considered 'born the other side of the blanket', Michael could inherit the title of 'Sir'. Ariadne knew he wished Michael to eventually be the new owner of the Hall, providing he wished to live in England. Meanwhile she had to go and collect Annalisa from her finishing school. The girl told her she had learnt as much as she could, and the headmistress agreed, saying she was clever and far ahead of her peers. Annalisa, lip-reading the comment, was quite in agreement, but knew her manners and thanked her teacher for all the help she had been given. Ariadne added her own thanks, and they made for home. A strange car was in the drive, and Ariadne wondered who was calling. "There is a gentleman in the library and he won't go until he has seen you."

Ariadne was totally unprepared and astonished to see Jake Brogan, looking tired and older. Was it nearly two months since their hurried farewell on the ranch? He took her hands in his big rough ones and asked, "Why did you not answer my letter?"

She went to a drawer and handed it to him, still unopened. He was shocked. Ariadne said, "I thought it was an apology for our brief liaison. I couldn't bear it if it was."

Jake said gently, "Then let me read it to you now, and, believe me, I mean every word."

She nodded, and fell into a chair, as her legs felt they were about to give way. She was still afraid, and wondered what there was to say. She closed her eyes and waited, tears not far away.

"Darling girl, I want to shout it from the rooftops, 'I love you, I love you.' It is the most exciting, wonderful thing that has happened to me in more years than I care to remember. Please, *cara mia*, let me know how you feel. I am sure it was not just sex we enjoyed. I feel as if a new world has opened up for me. I, as I suspect you also are, am lonely after losing someone close. Please let me in some small way have a little corner in your heart. I know I cannot take the place completely of your Ben. I know also you will not be content to spend the whole time on the ranch. I am prepared to spend three months of the year in Europe if you will spend three months with me on the ranch. We could arrange holidays together in the other months. There are places I am sure you would love to visit. I would love to show you my favourite places, Please, Darling. I know I can make you happy. Let me know how you feel. Jake."

The letter was folded and returned to its envelope. Jake saw Ariadne was crying. He took her in his arms again, and she melted into them. "Yes, Jake, I will marry you. I am not sure of the rights and wrongs of two grandparents marrying, but if we can get around the legal side of things, I will be your wife. If not, I'll be your mistress."

Jake hooted with laughter. "Shall we tell the family?" he said. Ariadne rang a bell and on Jean-Paul answering, said, "Bring a bottle of champagne – the best. I've some news for you all. I am certain it will surprise you."

When everyone was assembled Ariadne took Jake's hand and said simply, "Jake has asked me to marry him. If there are no legal obstacles, I have agreed."

They were congratulated, although both Jean-Paul and Genta wondered how it had all come about. The only person to object was Philippe. He had recently arrived to read a paper to an auspicious group of surgeons. It was well received, and he was subsequently offered a position at a well-respected hospital. His old professor remembered him, and wanted to know where he had been hiding over the past few years, Smiling, Philippe waved a hand of dismissal. "I assure you, Sir, I have not been leading a lazy life, and my medical horizon has broadened considerably."

The eminent man was on the verge of retiring, and would have loved to have recommended Philippe to eventually take his place. Philippe, however, loved his position on the Two Islands planet, and had no desire to relinquish it.

He arrived at Swanbrook Hall to find a celebratory party taking place. When he saw his former father-in-law and Ariadne and discovered the reason for the celebration, he was furious. Speaking in the planet's language, which he had mastered, he berated Ariadne. He called her a whore and worse. Jake had never been overfond of Philippe, and although he couldn't understand what was being said, he could see Ariadne was shaken.

She turned to Jake. "I am forbidden to marry you."

He was bewildered. "Surely not. What hold has he over you?"

Tears rained down her face. What could she say?

They were so engrossed they hadn't noticed a frail old man standing in the doorway. Ariadne turned, feeling she must leave the room. When she saw who was standing there and swaying slightly, she ran and knelt before him, kissing his hands. "Uncle Bron, is it really you? I am not dreaming?"

"No, child, you are not dreaming."

Chapter Six

Uncle Bron

Jean-Paul stood behind his grandfather, with a big grin on his face. By way of explanation Uncle Bron said, smiling himself, "I believe there is a saying: If Mohammed won't go to the mountain, then the mountain will go to Mohammed. Is that not correct?"

Laughing, Ariadne had to agree.

Turning to Philippe, he said, "Remember, Philippe Tauran, I am still head of the house of D'A-Huartan, and I can overturn any decision you make, if I choose. On this occasion I do so choose, and say Ariadne is free to liaise with whomsoever she pleases. It was Prince Benon's wish that she does not remain alone for her remaining years. Return to your ship immediately."

Philippe had turned pale at Uncle Bron's words, and he silently left the gathering. Ariadne followed him out. He pushed her against a wall, saying bitterly, "I thought better of you. Do you really hate me that much?"

In reply his mother said, "No, I do not hate you, but hate the way you behave. I ask only one thing of you. Will you take Annalisa back with you? Please look at the girl. She is quite lovely, and would be a match for you. Understand, you would not be able to intimidate her. Consider her as a potential wife. Annalisa is cultured. She speaks fluent French and English, so please do not swear at her in either language."

Philippe laughed. "Then I will swear at you. *Merde alors*, you have got it all worked out, haven't you just!"

When he reached his ship, he was met by Pag and the girl.

He had already noticed her, and was looking forward to doing battle. If she was anything like his mother's opinion of her, there would be battles ahead.

Chapter Seven

Marriages

It took no time for Uncle Bron to settle into life at the Hall. He found much to interest him. He just loved television. He said it was a pity they didn't have it on the Two Islands. Jean-Paul spent as much time as he could spare from work with his grandfather. The children were very protective of the old man. They had been told by their mother to be very careful when playing near him, and not be too boisterous. They would stand each side of him, take his hands, and gently help him down steps or lead him to the small lake, where he would sit in the sun and watch the swans. The children were very thoughtful, bringing a cushion or blanket if they thought it was required.

Ariadne and Jake were married quietly, with only Jean-Paul and Genta as witnesses. Jake was astonished when Ariadne said she would fly them to where he wished. He asked her how many more surprises she had up her sleeve for him to find out about. He was also delighted to find she was an excellent sailor. On returning to the States they chartered a small yacht, and she did her share of the work of running it – and not just in the galley preparing food. She would take the tiller, or clean the decks when that was required. When on the *Sirius*, Ben had been a stickler for everything being 'shipshape'. She tried not to mention him, but there were differences between her two husbands, which she was gradually discovering. Jake was not interested in long siestas when away from the ranch. He didn't understand computers or climate change, oceanography or the numerous other interests she had shared with Ben. Jake was by no means stupid. His interests were centred mainly on the ranch, oil and his grandson. She wondered if he had had a mistress, but nothing was said, and she was loath to ask.

The new Mrs Brogan felt it circumspect to keep certain areas of her previous life closed to her husband. She found him an absolute darling. She was aware that he too kept secrets, and was almost certain that he and Carlotta had been lovers in the past, so tactfully kept out of the Mexican woman's way as much as possible. Life on the ranch was a monotonous routine of raising healthy cattle and seeing they got to market, and a constant worry about the water supply. When Ariadne offered to try her hand at water divining Jake roared with laughter. "Honey, there ain't a square metre of my land the geologists haven't covered." He was astonished when she did find a supply in a much-needed area.

On relating this to Senator Tubbs, Ariadne's old friend, Jake was dryly told, "There is a lot about your wife you have yet to learn, old pal, if she will let you."

Jake tried to draw him out, but to no avail. Their lifestyle was odd to their friends, but it worked perfectly for them. At the end of three months on the ranch Ariadne was ready to return to Europe. Likewise Jake enjoyed his visits where their time was spent, either at Swanbrook Hall or at the Chateau le Papillon.

Ariadne had bought fresh ground near the chateau, which proved ideal for grapes. She soon had a flourishing small vineyard producing excellent wine. This was well established when Jake first visited. He was more interested in spirits, but had to admit her wine was a winner.

Chapter Eight

Philippe and Annalisa

When their ship reached their own space station, Pag bade Philippe and Annalisa goodbye. His own ship was there, and he would use it to go and collect Uncle Bron. He wondered if the old man would want to leave. He appeared to enjoy life with his freshly discovered family. Pag knew that if Uncle Bron didn't return, Philippe would assume total command, and heaven knows what he would get up to. Both he and Annalisa were too busy for anything but concentrating on the task of piloting the ship. When they landed, Philippe inspected the Space Riders and, thankfully, made his way to his own quarters. He was surprised to find Annalisa there. She had dismissed his usual attendants and, clothed in the simple shift usually worn by those assigned menial tasks, waited for his instructions. They were not slow in coming. She ran the water in the Jacuzzi. With a slight sneer, he asked her to assist him. This was not unusual, as women were expected to perform this duty. Afterwards, seeing him twisting his shoulder, she massaged it for him. She was about to withdraw, when he asked her to stay and share a meal. He had a good bottle of wine, and she was completely at ease. He found, to his amusement, that he couldn't cause her embarrassment. One request, however, did. "Take off that disgusting shift. It's just not you." She was shaken. He removed it for her. She stood in her Janet Regar panties and bra, shivering a little. "Hmm, it appears Madame Ariadne is right. You are quite lovely." He picked her up and carried her, unprotesting, to his bed. "You are willing?" Her eyes said yes.

Afterwards Philippe, completely sated, looked down at his prize. "Are you happy to do this often? Become my only partner?"

"Oh, yes please."

He laughed. "You little devil. I take it you and Madame schemed. I don't think I took you. You took me, right?"

The old prince approved of the liaison between Philippe Tauran and Annalisa. He felt it was time to retire as he was well over eighty in Earth years, and starting to feel his age. He called a meeting of the Council to announce his decision and declare Philippe the leader of the residents of the Two Islands planet. Philippe was given the title of prince, as was his right as the son of Prince Benon, the details of his birth being glossed over. Not much attention was given to whether a son was considered legitimate or not. To the race he led, a son was a son, however conceived. Philippe was relieved the old prince was no longer vetoing his every move. He had taken to Pag and relied on him for guidance, which the old pilot was happy to give.

Travel between their planet and Earth was now much quicker, and Philippe was able to attend medical conferences on Earth and present papers on subjects he wished to promote.

The old prince spent most of his time in his own quarters, and no one was surprised when he died quietly, without fuss, about six months after his retirement. He wished his heart put with the others of his family, and asked to be cremated not buried and, if possible, his ashes scattered over their previous home – now a derelict shell. Philippe fell in with his request and scattered the ashes himself from the plane piloted by Pag. From then on he was a good leader but a little on the serious side, as the old prince had noticed from the first. Pag told him a lot about his father and as a result of Pag's talks, Philippe visited the family grotto and spoke aloud of his regret that Ben and he had not been able to act like father and son. It was an apology of sorts, and he felt better for it. His skill as a surgeon kept him fully occupied, and he settled into a domestic life with Annalisa.

Chapter Nine

A Pregnancy

Work on improving medical facilities on the Two Islands was in place. When, after three months, Philippe found a listless, woebegone Annalisa, crying as if her heart would break, he demanded to know what the devil was the matter with her. "Am I mistreating you? Come now, am I?"

She cried even louder. Between sobs she managed to say, "You will be cross with me. I think I am pregnant."

He hooted with laughter. Then a thought came to him. "It is mine, I trust? Tell me honestly."

"Of course, Darling. There has never been anyone else but you."

He kissed her gently, and said she should go and see Dr Milo in the morning.

Dr Milo and Philippe had great respect for each other's ability. When Philippe was asked to go and see the older man regarding his wife's condition, Philippe was worried. He had no need. "Come and look at this screen." They both looked and the older man shook Philippe's hand. "Congratulations, old man."

They turned to an apprehensive Annalisa. "Dr Milo is congratulating us both, Darling. You are expecting twins."

She nearly shot out of bed. Twins were unheard of on the Two Islands. "No. It can't be. It is most unlucky."

The two doctors were used to meeting a lot of superstition and prejudice from the people they dealt with. Philippe couldn't understand Annalisa. She had lived a long time with

Madame and been to school, where she had been considered clever and sophisticated. The two men looked at each other. Philippe sighed. He was going to be firm with her. "Nonsense! Women have given birth to as many as five babies, so stop being silly."

She shuddered. "I feel like a rabbit."

She was made to get up, and was told that apart from lifting heavy objects or riding her pony, she could lead a normal life. When she had gone Dr Milo said, "I want to keep an eye on her, as I think her blood pressure is too high for one so young."

Chapter Ten

The Twins

Dune was six years old when Annalisa found she was pregnant, but both Ariadne and Philippe decided not to tell him about her. It would have led to a lot of questions they were unable to answer. Jake also was not told. He had never really formed a comfortable relationship with Philippe. Secretly he blamed him for Duella going off the rails.

Ariadne was determined to be involved with both the births and providing the two babies with their layettes. She was an excellent needlewoman, and set to work making exquisite baby clothes. She was sure they would be a boy and a girl. Spending as she did most of her time in Europe, she was able to make up parcels, which Pag or one of his team would take to the Two Islands. Annalisa was touched. Philippe took it as their due, and only Annalisa wrote letters of thanks. Dr Milo continued to monitor Annalisa's blood pressure. He told Philippe he was worried about her, and said, "If we can't induce the infants, we may have to consider performing a Caesarean." This was, however, only as a last resort. Annalisa surprised them by going into labour early. Dr Milo was attending an accident on the large island, so it fell to Philippe to attend to his wife. She was very brave. The women on the Two Islands were stoical and not given to showing they felt pain. After five hours in the delivery room, Philippe decided enough was enough, and was thrilled to see the head of the first baby. He was almost as exhausted as the mother. He held the infant – a little girl – up to the morning sun. Dawn was just breaking. Still unable to see, she blinked, at the same time letting out her first cry. Philippe fell in love with his daughter. What should she be called? There was only one name. He would call her Aurora.

Shortly afterwards the second child made its appearance. It was a little boy. Philippe was disappointed. It seemed his sister was very much the stronger. What to call this small scrap? He was much smaller than his sister, and appeared delicate. Philippe sighed, and was glad he had another son to rely on to succeed him. Dr Milo made it clear it would be unwise for Annalisa to bear any more children.

"What name have you chosen for our son?" Annalisa was anxious to know.

Philippe thought for a minute. "How does Fallon strike you?"

Annalisa smiled. "Yes. I quite like it." So Fallon it was.

When Aurora could toddle she followed Philippe everywhere. She was certainly Daddy's girl. When he was in the operating theatre she would sit patiently outside until he was free. She would sit there until Antika came and scooped her up for a meal or bath.

While Aurora was the apple of Philippe's eye, little Fallon was equally loved by his mother. Unfortunately Annalisa went into postnatal depression after the births, and it was several months before she was anything like her old self. Philippe was very patient with her and agreed with his colleague that it would be unwise for Annalisa to have any more children. There were several nubile young women only too anxious to satisfy Philippe, and who considered it an honour. He was a hard worker and did not indulge himself very often. Work was his life and, when he had time, he gave his love and attention to Aurora. She was his main interest, after work. Annalisa worried about the slowness of Fallon's development, and consulted Dr Milo. He examined the child, who was used to him and sat quietly on his lap while his mother was questioned. Dr Milo sighed. "Have you heard of the condition known as autism?

I think Fallon may have it, and unfortunately it is the reason for his slow development."

Ariadne and Jake were together nearly fifteen years, and they were extremely happy. Jake suffered his first heart attack whilst out riding and was warned by his doctors to take things easy, which wasn't his way. "I won't lead the life of an invalid," he grumbled to Dune, and lived life to the full. He didn't tell Ariadne, as she was in Europe at the time. Dune broke the news to her and she rushed to Jake's side, imploring him to slow down. He had two further attacks, then a final, fatal one. He was just seventy years old and died as he would have wished – "with his boots on" – out on the range. His horse brought him home slumped in the saddle. He had been dead for hours. Ariadne was heartbroken. She had loved him – not the way she had loved Ben, but with a quieter, placid love with no histrionics. Attorneys came and went until she was nearly at screaming pitch. She told them she wasn't interested in his money, and had more than enough of her own to live on. She knew the jewels Ben had given her – now in a bank vault – were worth a small fortune. Philippe came to see her to support her. He was happy with Annalisa, and Ariadne was always pleased to have news of his family.

Ariadne finally agreed to a foundation being set up in Jake's name, to help clever but underprivileged children in his state.

When the funeral was over, Jake was laid to rest next to his first wife. Ariadne had insisted on this, feeling it was the correct thing to do. Many people were surprised to hear she and Jake had been married. Many of their neighbours thought she had been just Jake's mistress. Senator Tubbs was the exception. He had not enlightened anyone, at their request. It was fun, Jake said, to keep people guessing. Dune became an air cadet, and his greatest wish was to fly in space. He was unaware that flying was in his blood, and was never happier than when in the air. He promised Ariadne to visit her should he be transferred to Europe.

Philippe was dismayed when Milo told him of his son's condition. He felt guilty as he had not given any attention to this child, lavishing all his love on his beautiful daughter Aurora. He said he would endeavour to find out about autism and what could be done to help his son's chances of becoming as near normal an adult as possible.

Aurora was still his main concern. She naturally spoke the Usaurian language, and her father taught her to speak French and English. He taught her much more besides, but realised her active and quick brain needed extending. Reluctantly he asked Ariadne to take the girl under her wing. She was delighted, and agreed to do this for her granddaughter. Ariadne had seen little of the family as all her time had been spent either in Texas or Europe. She now had two vineyards to oversee, and her time was fully occupied, but she was lonely following Jake's recent death. Caring for Aurora was just what she needed. Aurora was barely in her teens when they met. Her grandmother found the girl needed a lot of coaching before she could be sent to the exclusive finishing school in Switzerland Ariadne had picked out for her. She spoke excellent French but her English was spoken with the soft Highland lilt her father had picked up from Nurse McGee. There were many English girls she would meet, and she might feel an outsider.

Chapter Eleven

A Meeting

Aurora enjoyed mixing with girls of her own age, and was popular. She was good at sport, and her teachers approved of the bright, clever girl. She soon made friends, who were always made welcome when they visited Swanbrook Hall. When still only fifteen her air of sophistication made her appear much older, and everyone loved her, especially her grandmother. She was very like Ariadne. Her hair was not the same wonderful shade of red, but a soft brown with hints of red in it. They often rode out together, and gradually Aurora acquired a string of admirers from among the local youth. She was a bit of a daredevil on a horse, and this brought her to the attention of many would-be suitors. One afternoon during the summer holiday she was sitting on the swing that Jean-Paul had installed for the twins, singing softly to herself, when she became aware of being watched. A pleasant voice with an American accent said, "Hi there, little lady."

Aurora wasn't easily put out, and remained cool as she looked the stranger up and down, rather liking what she saw but not going to give anything away. She cocked her head on one side and coquettishly fluttered her eyelids at him. He was vastly amused, and wondered how old she was. About eighteen, he supposed.

"Let me see," Aurora said. "You must be about six years older than me, I guess." He was actually seven years her senior. A little taller than Aurora, with fair hair and eyes an incredible bluish grey.

"Are you a Canadian?" she queried.

"No. I am from Texas, so I guess that makes me an American." He went on to explain he had been considered too tall to fly American fighter planes but the RAF were delighted to accept such a skilled pilot. He was hoping he could eventually get accepted by the Americans, as pilots with his skill were expensive to train, and eagerly sought. He could never understand why he had been turned down originally, and thought it was something to do with quotas.

Aurora jumped off the swing. She looked the stranger up and down. "Who are you?"

He saluted. "Flight Lieutenant Dune Du Pre at your service, Miss."

She tossed her head and looked at him, smiling. "Well, you must be here for a reason. By the way, I am Aurora Villiers, and I am staying here with my grandmother Madame Ariadne."

He smiled down at her. "Well, if this isn't just dandy. She is my grandmother also. We must be cousins."

Delighted with the stranger, who somehow seemed familiar to her, Aurora said, "Race you to the treehouse." He wasn't slow to follow her. She was up the tree in a flash. He caught her ankle, and she kicked out, laughing all the while. He fell, also laughing, on top of her. Their faces were close together, and he bent and kissed her. He felt she was just so drop-dead gorgeous he couldn't resist her. She put her hands up and, drawing his face down to hers, kissed him in return. "Wow" was all she said.

Dune said, "We ought to go and find grandmother."

When Ariadne saw them together, she was relieved. "I am so glad you two have introduced yourselves. I always felt it should have happened long ago." Ariadne was getting a little short-sighted, so she didn't notice the flush on Aurora's cheeks. Dune said there was a dance at his base, and asked to take Aurora. Their grandmother gladly gave her consent, pleased they had bonded so well. Aurora was a vision in her dress of red silk. It was a little old for her, but with her hair dressed in imitation of a style she had seen Ariadne wear, she looked quite sophisticated. When Dune introduced his cousin to his chief, he was most impressed. Dune realised before long that he was in love with the girl he thought was his cousin.

Chapter Twelve

In Love

It didn't take Aurora long to realise Dune loved her. It thrilled her, and soon she was as besotted as he was. Like lovers the world over, they made plans. "I know my father and grandmother are going to say we are too young. At least I am. Dada is very protective of me. He is a wonderful person. I am sure you would get on well."

Dune telephoned her one day to say he wanted to see her urgently.

He would not disclose anything over the telephone, but looked worried when they met. "I am being posted to Germany."

Aurora burst into tears. "Oh, no!"

He tried to console her. "There will be leaves, and you can come and visit me there."

Dune was aware that plans were already in place to offer him the position as a brevet captain and aide to Colonel Colburgh – an old friend of his late grandfather. The colonel was anxious to have Dune on his staff, especially as he was a fellow Texan and an accomplished linguist. Dune had inherited the family ability with languages, speaking French and Italian fluently. He had majored in law and languages at university, and was in the process of mastering German, which was just as well as his posting would be first to Westphalia, and then to Frankfurt. The colonel was also keen to have a fully trained pilot at his disposal. The American forces were fully stretched, and a new interchange system had recently been put into action, with excellent results. In time Dune could expect to achieve his full rank as captain. He was delighted to accept as it had long been his ambition to join an American unit. He didn't tell Aurora any of his proposed plans as he wasn't sure how she would take it. Badly, he feared, and was proved right. One person who was pleased was Mrs Colburgh, who went out of her way to mother him, much to his embarrassment. She had no children of her own and was a bit of a joke to her husband's staff, but they knew she meant well and had proved a useful ally on many occasions. Dune had arrived at Swanbrook Hall with the express purpose of telling Madame Ariadne about his posting but his meetings with Aurora, which, unknown to Madame, were fairly frequent, had upset things. He wondered whether he should tell the colonel he couldn't accept the position, but felt that after all the trouble and string pulling, he couldn't let his chief down. He told himself he was a coward, but he wanted a smooth transfer, and the opportunity was too good to miss.

When he had gone Aurora moped about the house, and started looking off-colour. Ariadne did not link Dune's leaving with her granddaughter's moodiness. One morning Aurora was violently sick on rising. She had seen pregnant women being sick on the Two Islands and, going to a chemist where she was not likely to be known, bought a testing kit. Yes, it was positive. She was pregnant. She told herself not to panic, and asked Ariadne if she could go to France for a holiday "with a group of friends". She made for the base in Westphalia, where she knew Dune was stationed. He was delighted to see her.

"How soon can you get permission to marry me?" she asked.

The questioned stunned him. "It is not as easy as you think, Honey. Why the rush? I thought we agreed to wait a while."

He was dismayed to discover she was pregnant. He asked to see the colonel's wife. Mrs Colburgh was extremely fond of Dune and, knowing he was an orphan, had taken him under her wing. "Why, Dune, what a lovely surprise! What can I do for you?"

She listened in silence as he poured out his worry at his

dilemma. "We are in love, Ma'am. I know there are all sorts of tests she has to have under military law, but we were intending to wait until she is eighteen, and do it in style."

Mrs Colburgh loved romance. There was nothing she liked more than arranging marriages, and she had engineered quite a few in her time. "Will you bring your girl to see me? Let's say tomorrow morning at eleven o'clock, in time for coffee."

When Aurora was introduced Mrs Colburgh was charmed by the girl's obvious breeding. Aurora dropped a small curtsey and spoke English with a faint accent, not at first recognised by the elder woman. She commented on it and a smiling but nervous Aurora explained that although French was her first language, her father had taught her English, and he had learnt it from his nurse, who stayed with him until he was nearly four, and she was Scottish. She was even more impressed to learn Aurora had just finished her first term at a most elite Swiss finishing school. "Your family have money then?"

Aurora laughed. "Yes. I think, too much, sometimes."

Mrs Colburgh was relieved to know Aurora was not interested in Dune merely because of his money. She knew he was a very wealthy young man. She told the two lovers, "I am willing to help you, although I know the colonel would not approve."

Arrangements were made for them to fly to Berlin. A pastor familiar with 'shotgun' weddings was found and he officiated, after which a large sum of money changed hands. It was just the newlyweds' bad luck that Captain Anion had flown into Berlin and by sheer chance saw them leaving the small church. When he heard an American lady congratulating them he was horrified. What was going on? They were so engrossed he wasn't noticed. He followed them to their hotel and gave a note to a bell-boy for Aurora. It told her that 'Uncle' Pag had brought her father to Berlin for a medical conference. She looked up and, seeing him, told the group she was going to the ladies' room.

"Why, Uncle Pag! Fancy seeing you here! Come and be introduced."

He glared at her and said, "What have you done, girl?"

She gave a little laugh and patted her stomach. "We intended to wait a while, but a little stranger has made it necessary to bring our wedding forward."

He closed his eyes and swayed a bit. It was worse than he had thought. What Philippe would say, he just could not imagine.

"Will you break it to Dada?"

He heard her name being called and said simply, "Be at the Hilton before ten in the morning. He will want to talk this over with you. I take it this is only a short stop-off?"

She nodded. "Dune has to be on duty early tomorrow, so I can follow him. I know this is going to upset things, but we are in love, so if he doesn't like it, then too bad." With that final remark, she turned and made her way back to Dune and their small group.

Philippe had enjoyed the seminar he had been attending, and was looking forward to a quiet evening. He was surprised when Pag asked to see him urgently. "Won't it wait until the morning?"

Pag knew he and Philippe were both tired, but felt he owed it to Aurora's parent to acquaint him with what he had discovered about Aurora and Dune. On entering the suite – one of the Hilton's best – he went to the drinks bar and poured out a stiff Scotch for himself, and one for Philippe. "When you hear what I have to tell you, this will be the first of many, I guess. Aurora is in Berlin. Only by chance did I see her. She is fine." He went on to relate what he had uncovered. "It is clear they have no idea they are so closely related. I assume she thinks they are cousins. She is pregnant."

Philippe was silent. Pag saw tears pouring down on the younger man's face. "It is all my fault," Philippe lamented. "I kept the two of them apart. I felt Aurora was too young, and might have given away things about us that we both know would have caused immense problems."

After bidding Dune a tearful goodbye in the morning after a

sleepless night – Dune had left for his base at six in the morning – Aurora went to face the 'fireworks' and was waiting to meet her father long before the expected time. Pag saw her sitting, looking lost and forlorn. He took pity on her. "Have you had any breakfast?"

She shook her head. She drank a small cup of coffee and ate a small piece of toast, hardly aware of what she was doing.

She found her father dressed in his Space Riders commandant's uniform. He looked very stern and formidable. "Sit down, girl."

She was trembling. Surely it wasn't meant to be like this. He began, and Aurora was completely shattered. She couldn't believe her father, who she was sure loved her, could be so harsh. He gave her a choice: either return to the Two Islands with him and have her child there; or, should she decide to stay on Earth posing as Dune's wife, she would be stripped of everything she had been given. Her mother had died a year before and her mother's jewels, which she had inherited, would be taken from her, and the sizeable bank account and store cards closed. She would not be allowed to live in any of the property owned by the family. She would be disowned by him, and ostracised by the family.

It was more than she could bear. "Why? What have we done?"

Her father's face did not soften. "Don't you know?"

She shook her head.

"I have a tale to tell you. Listen and understand."

It was a few minutes before Aurora realised Dune was her half-brother. She listened while her father described Dune's mother, how he had been ordered off the ranch by Jake and forbidden to have any contact with his son Dune, and how his father-in-law had blamed him for Duella's death. Her father would not accept that she was a thoroughly bad lot, with no love for him or their child.

Aurora started to weep.

"Remember, girl, I can make things very difficult for Dune, should I choose. You consider yourself very grown up but if your years are measured by the calendar used here you are under-age for sex by nearly two years. Dune could go to prison. Come back with me now, and nothing will harm him."

She said meekly, "Can I see him before I go?"

Her father shook his head. "Go and get ready. We will leave before dawn."

The next one to see was Dune. Philippe wasn't exactly relishing the meeting. He left a message for Dune at his base, requesting he meet him at his hotel. He was told, "Ask for room 16. That is where I am."

Father and son looked at one another. Philippe felt love for the young man so intense he could hardly find words to begin. He knew he was going to shock and dismay the young man who he knew was a brave flyer. He must have had to steel himself to meet Aurora's father. "So we meet at last," Philippe said.

Philippe had not bothered to change out of his uniform. He could see Dune trying to place his rank and country. "I am not going to enlighten you, Dune, except to say I hold a military rank, so stop trying to place me. You have no idea who I am and how I should be addressed. There is one title I have waited so long to hear you use, but more of that later." There was a tap on the door and a waiter brought in a tray with coffee and toast. Philippe said, "I am sure you were too anxious to have any breakfast." He then offered coffee and toast to a bemused Dune. When Dune had drunk a little and nibbled at the toast, Philippe said, "Now you have had a taste of my hospitality, let's get down to business." He made it clear to the young man he could not consider himself married to Aurora. "I will arrange for a quiet annulment."

Dune lost his temper. "Hasn't Aurora a say in what we do?"

"No. She will do as she is told. So will you, Dune. You both will."

Philippe didn't mince his words. "You will obey me for two reasons. The first is that sex with an under-age girl is against the law. Aurora was barely fifteen when you started your affair. Secondly, you had sex with a close relative – also forbidden." He held his hand up as Dune started to protest. "Hear me out. Aurora is your sister, well, half-sister to be exact. Yes, I am your father, Dune. The old man threw me out. The start of Madame Ariadne's liaison with your grandfather began because they met when I asked her to go and find out about you. The rest is history."

Dune was too dumbfounded to speak. His father poured out a glass of brandy. "A bit of a shock, eh? Get this down. It will help." His tone was rough but as a doctor he was used to handling difficult situations. He was pleased to see his son was man enough to accept the facts without questioning them further or breaking down. He couldn't have stood tears.

Dune managed to gasp, "I thought Aurora was eighteen. She certainly acts it and looks it."

Philippe agreed. Her mother had died a year before, and since then, Philippe had to admit, the little madam had got her own way. He knew he had spoilt her. She had always been able to wrap him around her little finger and get her own way. Philippe said, "Why don't you resign your commission and return to the life you were meant for. Marry a local girl and forget Aurora."

Dune asked, "Where are you taking her? Can I say goodbye?"

Philippe was about to say no when the door flew open. She was there, wearing a similar grey uniform to her father. Philippe said, "I'll give you five minutes, and then we must go, as time is running out."

The two lovers embraced. Aurora said tearfully, "I'll never forget you. I will love you always." Dune tried to get her to say where she was going but she brushed this aside. "Don't ask me. I am not allowed to tell you."

They were destined to meet again many years later. Dune,

his wife and daughter were in London, and he was waiting outside Harrods for them to come out.

The one person to blame in the whole sorry saga of Dune and Aurora was Philippe himself. Ariadne wasn't slow in telling him, "If you had not insisted on keeping them apart and giving them different surnames, they would not have assumed they were cousins."

To his credit Philippe had to agree she was right, but had no intention of letting her know his feelings on the matter. He was extremely proud of Dune's achievements in the Air Corps but, realising there was every chance of Dune being killed, urged him yet again to return to the ranch. The colonel was reluctant to let him go, and Dune had to finish his tour of duty in Germany. Mrs Colburgh was also sorry. She couldn't understand why Aurora had disappeared from the scene, but was given to understand that her family were having problems, which kept her away from Dune's side.

Dune had no news of Aurora but was surprised when a letter came from Madame Ariadne asking him to see her as soon as possible. "Congratulations, Dune. You are a father. Aurora gave birth to a fine boy six weeks ago. We didn't tell you before because it was a difficult birth and it's a wonder either of them survived. Her father never left her side for the first five days. He is, as you probably know, a wonderful doctor."

Dune was stunned. He had put Aurora out of his life and not given a thought to her pregnancy. "Why was I not told?" He asked Ariadne what name the child had been given.

"Aurora wanted to call him Dune, after you, but he will have his great-grandfather's name Benon, and Franklin as a typical American name to follow." Dune liked the choice, and had to be content with the scant information given him.

Over the years Aurora kept Dune informed of Benon's progress. The boy had a fine sense of fun and was always in some sort of scrape. His sunny disposition and air of innocence led him to get away with things other children never could.

Chapter Thirteen

Prince Benon

Aurora married Georgio not long after the birth of Benon. It was a marriage of convenience. Georgio was so much older but she needed a partner, and he wanted a wife who would understand the reasons for his long absences. He had marvelled how tolerant his mother had been to Pag's frequent departures. His mother-in-law told him that Dorita Maria had often wondered if Pag had someone else, and if this was the reason for his being absent so often. The old easy relationship that Aurora had enjoyed with her father had gone for good, and she decided to live in Italy with Georgio's Italian family. She quickly learnt to speak Italian, and got on well with everybody. It was a gift she had, and she was soon accepted. It was thought that Benon was Georgio's child, and nothing was done to deny this. Aurora and Georgio had one child – a girl they named Marissa. Although he loved his daughter and they became very close, Georgio would have loved to have had a son of his own.

Aurora made frequent trips to see her grandmother Madame Ariadne, and Benon often accompanied her. Benon was soon a favourite with Madame, and a little spoilt. Aurora and Dune were both in London when they came face to face again, and it was clear the old fascination was still there. They were both shopping in Knightsbridge – still the Mecca for people with money wanting the best and willing to pay for it. The family were going to meet up with Sandy, who had remained in America and was on a flying visit to London. He worked for

Dune on the oil production side of his business. He and Dune were good friends and as he had attended the funeral of Pag and Philippe who had been killed in tragic circumstances, was combining business and a family meeting. Dune was now also a rancher, but still interested in oil. He found Sandy a very able assistant.

Dune knew Aurora and her family were having a brief stopover in London, following a harrowing double funeral. Philippe and Pag were killed in a flying accident. They had decided not to fly themselves but took the journey with a firm they had used before. They had always found it safe and reliable. However, the small plane met a severe squall, and it ditched in the English Channel. Philippe tried to keep Pag afloat but it was wintertime, and the water was very cold. He was begged by the old ex-pilot to save himself, but he would not leave his friend. They died of hypothermia before the rescue launch could reach them. Their pilot managed to survive, and he told Aurora there was nothing he could have done to help them. He was not unscathed, as he lost several toes due to exposure. The coroner said their deaths were caused by extreme conditions in the English Channel. Even if the rescue launch had reached them it would have been unlikely they could have survived. They both hated the cold, and were conditioned to the heat of the Two Islands. Their bodies were not accustomed to extreme cold. Aurora was not given the opportunity to remove their hearts for transportation to their own land. It was decided to cremate both of them instead. Aurora's family returned from Dorset, when it was decided to stop over in the flat in Chelsea for a few days. Aurora and Georgio's young daughter, eleven-year-old Marissa, had begged to be allowed to visit London Zoo. She had been so well behaved during the joint funeral service that her parents had willingly agreed, and as a further treat there was a visit to Harrods, where she enjoyed a knickerbocker glory ice cream. She told her mother, "There was a girl with fair hair wearing a super blue dress sitting near me. She kept looking at me and pulling faces. A bit childish, don't you think?" Marissa would never know, like herself the girl was Benon's half-sister.

Dune recognised Aurora immediately. She was even more lovely than he remembered. He knew the boy next to her looking seriously at him was their son. Her greeting was cool – the greeting one would expect from a casual acquaintance. "Hello. Fancy meeting you. This is my son Benon. A very old friend of mine I haven't seen for years – Mr Brogan."

The boy shook hands with his father. He was very perceptive and could not fail to see the way they looked at each other. An American woman of about thirty years of age accompanied by a girl a little younger than himself came out of the shop's entrance with a pile of boxes. Amid the flurry of loading their taxi, the two groups split up.

Benon knew Georgio was not his father. He had never got his mother to talk about what he knew was a sensitive subject. He had noticed the stranger had a cleft chin, not unlike his own. There was only one person he knew whom he could ask. That was his darling great-grandmother. He would contact her before arrangements were made to go on to France. The family visited the chateau whenever they could, and he loved it. Once back in the flat he telephoned Ariadne and asked if he could pay her a flying visit. The excuse he gave to the family was he was tired of shopping, and wanted a few days away from 'women'. His sister threw a cushion at him. "You mean a few days away from me, you pig."

Georgio thought it was a good idea. He had business to conduct, and Benon would otherwise be left to moon about in the flat while the 'girls' shopped.

Chapter Fourteen

A New Beginning

Benon, having obtained his stepfather's permission to visit Madame, then asked his mother if he could call on Madame again. "I expect she is still feeling upset after the double funeral, and will be glad of some company."

His mother, knowing he was a little restless and moody, gladly gave her consent. Georgio had arranged to take Marissa to the ballet, and Aurora could spend a peaceful time on her own. Benon found Ariadne sitting in her favourite spot in the garden of Swanbrook Hall. The garden was a delight, and the cherry trees were in full bloom. It was her favourite time of the year. "Your phone call was a lovely surprise."

Smiling down at her, he said, "I think we had better get you out of this cool breeze otherwise you might catch a chill, and we mustn't risk that." He was very fond of her, and he a great favourite of hers.

When they were sitting in front of a blazing log fire, before which he started to toast crumpets, Madame, placing a hand on his shoulder, said simply, "Now, dear boy, I can see you are here for a reason. Tell me what the problem is. I can see something is worrying you."

Taking hold of her hands, Benon said gently, "Tell me, Madame: is Dune Brogan Du Pre my father?"

Ariadne was silent. Then sighing, she replied, "Yes he is. Your grandfather once said there must be a curse on our family. We have always got our relationships in a mess. Your mother was only fifteen when she and Dune met. They fell madly in love and thought they were cousins, as I was their *grand-mere* and their surnames were different. They married, but the liaison was very brief. Their love turned to ashes. The marriage was annulled, and they were not allowed to meet again. You, as a result, have never been able to know your real father."

Benon told of the London meeting and how they had looked at each other. Benon looked at his great-grandmother. The next question made her laugh. "Are you very old, Grand-mere?"

She stroked his hair. "You, Benon, are my favourite great-grandson, and yes, I am very old."

He hugged her. "You don't look it." The smell of burning crumpets made them come down to earth. He enjoyed that visit. He asked if she could give him Dune's address. She did this gladly. Benon wasn't to know that this happy little episode was the last time he would see her.

Benon stood outside the ranch house for a few minutes, and wondered what kind of reception he would get from the father he had seen only briefly in London. He didn't have long to wait. Dune looked at his son. "So you have found me. Come in; come in." There was so much to say and so much to see.

"Where is the family? Are they on vacation?" asked Benon.

His father's face hardened. "I am thinking of divorce. I've had enough. All my wife wants to do is socialise in expensive clubs and spend my money as if there is no tomorrow. She is bringing my daughter up to be just like herself." He made it clear he did not wish to pursue the subject. "How about a beer, or are you considered too young?"

Benon laughed. "Just watch me."

Dune and his son bonded well. When the suggestion was made to ride and see the ranch, Dune was delighted to see how well Benon handled his horse.

It was what some English poets describe as the 'sweet of the year'. Ariadne was sitting in her favourite spot, reading a slim book she had recently discovered in the library. The room had been Ben's sanctum. He had made it his own. It was where he had worked, smoked his fragrant cigars, interviewed people, occasionally 'blown his top' when things hadn't gone his way, and at times shut himself off from everyone when he wanted a little peace and quiet. Ariadne, browsing through rows of volumes – many still unread – came across a book written in what appeared to be Old English. It was a translation from a Latin manuscript, author unknown, probably originally from a monastery. Intrigued, Ariadne decided to take it into the garden to read quietly on her own.

The book detailed the musings of a holy man – one who had been anything but holy previously. As she read, Ariadne became aware of everything around her changing. Birds were singing louder, and a cheeky robin came and dug a worm out, inches away from her seat. The sun seemed more intense, and a breeze ruffled her hair. She read: "There is no sex in heaven, no carnal desire – just the joy of overwhelming love." The book fell from her hands and she suddenly felt very tired. A voice called, "Ariadne, Ariadne." It was a voice she recognised from long ago. Ben was standing before her, holding out a hand. She rose to meet him, and was not surprised to see her body still remained on the seat. "What kept you?" came a typical Ben remark, and she, laughing, replied, "Looking after your difficult family."

His reply was gentle. "I know, and what a lot of problems I left you! They are on their own now. Come; there are many wishing to meet you."

She smiled at Ben – he who had been the love of her life. Happily, hand in hand, they went together into another dimension, content and at peace.

Benon was his father's son. As well as loving horses, both loved flying. When they had been riding for some time, Dune was surprised when the boy said quite casually, "My plane is over there, and someone is there I know who is longing to meet you again," and Dune was overjoyed to see Aurora. Benon climbed into his cockpit, saying he would return in two days' time.

"Does he mean what I think he means?" Dune asked.

She smiled gently. "He is giving us this time together. It will be our last, but he is very wise for his age. If we ignore morality, he hopes we will take up from where we left off."

They still loved one another, and spent two blissful days together. They made love frequently, and clung close when they heard the plane returning to collect Aurora. Dune said. "I can't bear to let you go."

She touched his cheek. "I am afraid we must part, Darling. Never forget me. I won't forget you."

Benon came and also embraced his father. "Goodbye, Dad."

Dune didn't see the plane take off. He was blinded by tears.

Mother and son did not speak much until the plane landed, when, with eyes also wet with tears, she said, "Thank you, Darling. It was generous of you to give us so much time together."

He said dryly, "I trust you made good use of your time."

Her blush confirmed they certainly had.

Before they returned to the Two Islands they decided to call once again on Madame Ariadne. They arrived to find the place in uproar. Genta and the twins were in tears, and poor Jean-Paul looked devastated. "Madame is dead," he said.

Aurora also burst into tears. It took all Benon's skill to restore order, but soon he had the house calmer, and proceeded to take charge of the necessary arrangements.

It was a sad little party that boarded *Sirius IV*. Benon reverently carried the casket containing Ariadne's heart on board himself. The ship was a new one. Its three predecessors were now on display at open air space museums. Georgio hung back, as did Marissa. "Are you not coming with us?" Benon queried. His mother was at his side. She looked at Georgio enquiringly.

"May I speak with you privately?" Georgio asked.

She nodded.

Georgio continued, "And if you agree, Marissa will remain here with me. I know you have met Dune again. I have met a very beautiful Italian contessa. We have formed a liaison. Marissa is also quite fond of her. There is an excellent school she can attend close to Sophia's villa outside Venice. I have been offered a job as pilot in my late father's company. I will be working between Earth, the Moon, and Mars. You know of colonies on the Moon. We are hoping to start one soon on Mars. It will be very interesting work and an opportunity I do not wish to miss."

There were tears in Aurora's eyes as she agreed. They all embraced and, with a final wave, they bade each other goodbye.

Benon noticed Aurora spent the first two months of the journey in a very depressed state. As the third month started she seemed to change her attitude completely. If asked to describe her, he would have said she appeared to glow. Curiosity got the better of him. "Tell me why you have suddenly changed from being miserable to such a state of euphoria?"

Aurora took a deep breath. "You were kind enough to leave Dune and me alone for two days. How do you think we spent that time?" He waited. "He has given me, no, us, the most wonderful gift. I am pregnant with his child. You will have a brother or sister very soon."

Benon took his mother in his arms and hugged and kissed her. "As long as people don't think it is mine."

Chapter Fifteen

Epilogue

Although still considered a little on the young side, Benon soon showed he was the only one the people of the Two Islands could possibly consider as their future leader. His mother stood in for him when required, as he was spending two years on Earth at university. He was truly a chip off his great-grandfather's block. No one could have been more like Ben, but there was no one of that generation left to tell him. At Ariadne's funeral only the family had been present. Not only were Pag and Philippe now dead but Lucien Gervaise also: he had died six months earlier. He had never married, having loved Ariadne from their first meeting. When Benon eventually was declared leader he showed true statesmanship. Earth was feeling the effects of global warming. It seems after Ben's death little notice was taken of the 'prophets of doom', as they were called, who warned Earth's days were numbered. Benon sent delegates to Earth with an offer to help repair the ozone layer and show the people of Earth how to process Helium 3. Fossil fuel supplies were almost used up, and strictly rationed. He told the United Nations that help would only be given if there was peace on the planet. "We manage to live without wars. Why can't you?"

Aurora was seen by doctors at the Two Islands hospital – a brand new one built while she was on Earth. She was totally unprepared to learn she was expecting twins. "Well, well, don't be so surprised. You were a twin, and they do tend to run in families. Tests show there will be a boy and a girl, and everything is going fine."

Dr Milo came to see her. He had retired but still was interested in what happened to the family. His expertise was often called upon, and much appreciated by the new members of his profession. He told her how he missed Ariadne, Pag and Philippe. "When one gets old it is hard seeing all your friends vanishing. One is left wondering how soon it will be your turn."

Aurora's twins were born not many months after she returned to the Two Islands. They were beautiful babies. The boy was named Darren Drake and the girl Ducilla Amanda.

On Benon's instructions a message was sent with news of their births to their father. Aurora had a photograph taken of her and the babies. It was enclosed with the message. In time, she promised Dune, she would bring the children to see him.

The third island was growing, and it was soon clear the planet would need a new name, but what? Aurora had the answer. "Let us stop the wrangling over a name. Why not call it Terra Nova?"

This suggestion was accepted, and the name formally adopted. The planet's new name coincided with an influx of people from Earth. It was agreed not everyone would be accepted. Those who came had to contribute to life on Terra Nova. Teachers, doctors, artisans, artists – they all had to accept the strict regime. Life had never been easy, and there was no room for hangers-on. Several millionaires and starlets of various sorts tried, but they were turned down. One whom they did accept was Annalisa's son Fallon. He had been studying music in Paris. Everyone was amazed to find he had married. His wife was a rather plain girl, but one with a loving disposition. She was soon a favourite with everyone. She was very protective of Fallon. His autism had almost disappeared, and he was soon able to join in the life of Terra Nova. It wasn't all work. Everyone enjoyed the concerts he was able to give. He was a skilled musician, as was Alicia, his wife. So with the passing of Ariadne, our story is nearly over. Earth's days were numbered. One dawn, towards the end of the twenty-second century, a bright light was seen in the sky. It might have come from Earth. Did it? Well, that is another story.

About the Author

Patricia Connor Williams was born in Derbyshire, near Chatsworth, to an Irish father and a English mother. She had one sister who died in her teens from meningitis. Her father's job took the family to Portsmouth where she received convent school education.

After school, Patricia joined the ATS and later the TA. She joined the Control Commission for Germany and lived abroad for some time. Returning to the UK, worked for many years in London as a secretary and joined the Civil Service. She has one son and two grandchildren.

She divorced her husband and later married a Cornishman, but they both worked in Cheshire, living in an extraordinary house purported once to be the home of Charles Kingsley, author of "The Water Babies". The Victorian PM William Gladstone is believed to have been a frequent visitor.

Upon retirement, Patricia and her second husband moved to Shropshire and did voluntary work for the Citizens' Advice Bureau. Returning to Cheshire she did secretarial work for the W.R.V.S.

After her husband's death from cancer, she moved to Lancashire to be near her family